Calusa Spirits

Pirate of Panther Bay Series
Volume III

SR Staley

Published by:
Southern Yellow Pine (SYP) Publishing, LLC
4351 Natural Bridge Rd.
Tallahassee, FL 32305

www.syppublishing.com

This is a work of fiction. Names, characters, places, and events that occur either are the products of the author's imagination or are used fictitiously. Any resemblance to actual persons, places, or events is purely co-incidental.

The contents and opinions expressed in this book do not necessarily reflect the views and opinions of Southern Yellow Pine Publishing, nor does the mention of brands or trade names constitute endorsement.

ISBN-10: 1-59616-078-0
ISBN-13: 978-1-59616-078-1
ISBN-13: EPUB 978-1-59616-079-8
ISBN-13: Adobe PDF eBook 978-1-59616-080-4
Library of Congress: 2018956092

Cover Design: Fay Lane

Printed in the United States of America
First Edition August 2018
Reprinted with new cover April 2026

Dedication

To Colette R. Willins

Fiction by SR Staley

Pirate of Panther Bay Series
Calusa Spirits (Volume III)
Tortuga Bay (Volume II)
The Pirate of Panther Bay (Volume I)

St. Nic, Inc.
Renegade
A Warrior's Soul

West Cuba, Circa 1787

Florida's West Coast, Circa 1781

1

Juan Carlos clutched his head, pushing his palms against his temples in a desperate attempt to stop the ringing that drummed through his brain. Pain overwhelmed his senses, erasing the image of the blue cloud spitting from his pistol's muzzle and the face of the Spanish soldier climbing into his cabin through a shattered window.

His knees thumped the hardwood deck as he rolled off a cot, shooting streaks of pain into his thighs and his hips. Peering into a thinning haze, the acrid smell of spent gunpowder taunted his nostrils as he struggled to train his eyes on the now empty window frame. Another Spaniard would appear at any moment, although the lifeless body of the marine collapsed against the cabin wall was proof enough that his aim was true. How long could he hold them off?

Muffled noises from more men outside the window told him a boarding party had latched onto the *La Marée Rouge's* stern. A spent pistol clattered to the floor as he lifted a hand to peel away an infection-soaked bandage strapped around his shoulder and chest, the wound stubbornly resistant from healing in the tepid Caribbean Sea. Weeks of Doc's attention would not help much if he died now.

Juan Carlos summoned as much strength as he could muster into his arms and hands. He scrambled to one knee, leaning toward the bed as he grasped for the hilt of a sword he knew—prayed—was still nearby. Fingertips tapped the wood until they glanced off the cold steel of a grip guard. He curled a finger through the curved brass to pull the sword into his hand, lifting the blade to his chest, and securing it with the other arm as he rolled into another crouch facing the window.

Deep oranges and yellows, unloosed by the sun rising behind Cuba's southern hills were fast fading into pale blues. The smell of salt wafted into the room and into his nose. Shards of glass from the window littered the oak deck, a painful welcome for another intruder…, if he let them get that far.

Juan Carlos steadied his blade, its grip comfortable in his battle-tested palm despite the pain from his shoulder, and poised to spring forward at the first sign of another enemy. Boots thumped against wood under the open portal, foreshadowing the emergence of two hands gripping the window sash and the plume from another marine's hat. Juan Carlos directed his blade in an arcing cut, slicing through the invader's fingers. Another scream, and the soldier fell back through the window into what was now a clear pale abyss. A splash told him his enemy fell into the sea, ten feet below.

Muskets cracked from outside and wood splintered as lead balls lodged themselves into the beams overhead. Juan Carlos blinked, raising his forearm to shield his eyes, as frayed pine chips fell around him. He had to stay focused on the bigger threat—more soldiers climbing up the ropes. He crouched, saber ready, knowing the musket balls couldn't breach the wooden hull.

Just minutes earlier, lead balls had broken through glass, stirring his senses awake, and the sharp knocking of boots against the hull had jerked him from slumber. Now, the clamor of another battle seeped from the ceiling. He immediately recognized telltale signs of the *La Marée Rouge* in the thick of battle: screams from wounded men, muffled pops from pistols, the frenzied thudding soles of leather boots.

A pistol preceded another face adorned with a thick moustache at the window. The gun flashed as soon as the muzzle penetrated an invisible plane separating the sea from the cabin. Juan Carlos fell back toward the cabin door as a ball whizzed past an ear, cracking the wood behind him. He thrust the tip of his blade into the exposed forehead of his attacker, pushing the head from the cloistered space, unphased by the inevitable wretches bursting from the man's throat as he fell out of sight.

Juan Carlos lunged for the mattress. The sponge-like cushion, created by the Spanish moss fill, slipped through his fingers before he

2

tamed its movement. Just hours earlier it had served as a seductress, lulling him into much needed rest. Now he had to transform it into a ship-saving barrier.

He pulled the bedding toward the window, lodging his knees onto the wood for balance and leverage. Another shot pierced the exposed room, sending more metal into a beam. He turned the mattress, using his full body to push it up so that it covered the window, cloaking the cabin in gray. He nodded, unconsciously, calculating the extra minutes he had created, looking at the cabin door just a few yards away as his back leaned into the soft barrier. Another bullet thudded into the canvas but failed to find its way through the moss. He needed to warn the crew that the fight was also on the lower deck, not just the main gun deck above him.

"Ahhh!" he groaned, his ribs protesting the pull of the mattress and triggering a quick pivot toward the cabin door and an escape. Juan Carlos leaned forward, dropping the tip of his sword to drive it into the wooden deck and anchor his body as he pulled himself from his knees to his feet. Two steps later, he fell against the wood door standing in the way of an easy exit, pressing his ear to listen for any noise that might betray combat on the other side.

Hearing nothing but the sounds of the fight above, he pulled the iron latch, releasing the door. He peered into what now appeared to be a cavernous tunnel. Sunlight beamed from an open hatch to the upper deck, illuminating steps that led to the gun deck. The feverish sounds of boots, blades, and pistols told him the battle was engaged too late for cannon to be of much use. A nighttime ambush? Enemy sabers were likely already engaged by the time the last tar made it from their hammocks to the fighting deck.

A soft yellow glow bobbed to his right. Juan Carlos turned to see figures around a table, urgent voices instructing and directing.

"Louis!" one voice ordered. "Staunch that wound in his side. We've got to keep the blood under control."

"Yessir," said a small, tentative voice, his French accent so thick Juan Carlos almost could not recognize the words. "*Comme ça?* Like this?"

"Aye, just right," the older man responded, urgency tempered by the boy's action. "Keep it there, lad. Good, good. I've got to figure out how to close this up. It's a bad one."

The boy, not more than twelve years old, reached with the tips of his toes from the top of a wooden box to press a blood-soaked cloth against the body of a man stretched out on the table. *"Oui, monsieur docteur. Comme cela."*

The moans of the wounded now invaded his consciousness as Juan Carlos stepped toward the table. He peered at the shapes, trying to identify the members of Isabella's pirate crew, some huddled on deck and others slung on hammocks. One tar, propped up against the wood partition separating the captain's quarters from the officer's staterooms, turned his head to watch Juan Carlos as he stumbled forward.

"Do we have any able-bodied crew on this deck?" Juan Carlos asked, his voice directed toward Doc. Louis and another pirate on a makeshift crutch leaned over the wounded man, their hands and bodies pressing him to the table. Doc didn't look up as he focused on tying two flaps of skin together over a gapping cut. "Got no idea; I'm jus' trying to keep as many alive as I can. There, Louis. Hold that skin together until my needle pulls the thread all the way through."

Juan Carlos weaved and dropped his blade to the deck, lodging its tip in the hardwood to steady him. "We have a boarding party coming through the aft windows. I stopped two, but more are climbing up into the cabin."

"Damn dagos," the sailor propped against the wall said as he pushed himself into an upright position. He drew a long knife into the open and looked at Juan Carlos. "Present company excepted, Señor Santa Ana. I know they're your brothers, but I'll be damned if I'll let them take this ship and what's mine."

"Curious words for a pirate, Patrick," Juan Carlos said. "We're all damned in the eyes of King Charles III. Any blood we held in common drained into the streets and alleys of Port-au-Prince weeks ago. My former brothers would like nothing more than to see me strung up on a yardarm with you, Isabella, Jean-Michel, and anyone else from *La Marée*

4

Rouge. They'll get their wish if we don't find some way to keep them off this deck."

"Come on boys," Patrick yelled, his voice stronger than his body acted. "We've got work to do if we're going to live through this one."

Patrick's rally stirred other bodies nearby. Dark upright masses begin to limp their way toward the captain's quarters, shadows cast from the morning light, charting a path to more battle and probably death.

Juan Carlos turned to look at his makeshift barricade. The small space was an advantage—only so many able-bodied marines could climb through the window at one time. But crawling wounded were not an effective defense. He scanned the walls of the lower deck, his vision clearer and the images sharper as he ducked to keep his head from hitting the beams overhead. His eyes caught a hint of long rods stacked against the hull. Pikes. The long poles with pointed ends were useful weapons when they boarded a merchant ship, fierce enough to intimidate their target's imaginations into surrendering before they were speared. Now, they could serve another purpose.

Juan Carlos dropped his blade outside the door and stepped over to the lances. He started pulling them from the stack.

He thrust one of the pikes toward a pirate just about ready to pass into the cabin. "Put the tip up against the mattress. Lock the base into the deck with your foot. That way, the Spaniards will be in for a surprise when they try to push the bedding away from the window."

His initial shots must have forced the invading marines to regroup, buying minutes rather than seconds for Juan Carlos to organize the wounded pirates with their spears. Now, the rattle of boots banging against the hull signaled the ascendance of more attackers clambering up the rope ladder. They hadn't a second more to spare. Pirates braced four pikes against the mattress, their tips already cutting into the fabric.

Another pirate stepped into the cabin, brandishing a hammer and nails scrounged from the storage area. He started to drive the nails into the mattress, wood floor, and hull, converting their temporary defense into a more permanent one.

The mattress began to bubble inward as the hopeful invaders pushed against it from the outside. One pike's tip finally bolted through the fabric, picking up speed as it ripped through the tangled moss. A muffled shriek forced Juan Carlos to blink, as the image of the tip piercing a soldier's body flashed through his brain. He signaled for his men to quicken their pace, nailing the remaining lances into place, as another tip speared through mattress. This time, no cry of agony could be heard; the attackers had figured out their defense. But it was too late; each pike was firm and steadfast. The mattress was fortified, its repurposed role as a barricade strengthened with each tip forced into the moss, an impenetrable briar patch for weapons or the hands of a mortal boarding party.

"Bueno!" Juan Carlos cried, as he rushed the crew from the cabin. He clapped Patrick on the shoulder. "Quickly, Patrick, check Jean-Michel's cabin. That's the only other room with windows large enough for a soldier to squeeze through. Use the pikes and one of the mattresses to create the same defense."

Juan Carlos felt the strength in his legs and arms, his body fully awake and energized by his work on the lower deck. He retrieved his sword from the pine planks. He turned to inspect the nearby space. Bodies seemed to materialize and surround him. Doc continued to work at a hectic, if expert, pace.

He looked toward the ladder leading to the main deck, his sword tight in his grip, ready to deploy.

The crack from the musket sparked a dodge from Isabella. Her body flew from the bullet's path as if yanked by a protective ghost. She rolled, her blade extended, using the force of her twirling body to bring her back onto her feet and close to her target. Battle-hardened instincts thrust the tip of her sword into the ribs of a Spanish soldier, his dark blue half-coat now marred by an expanding, deep red oval. Her target gasped, the pain combining with the force of her thrust to slow, then halt his attack. Isabella pulled the blade from his chest and turned the edge to execute an upper cut through his shoulder. The man fell, minutes if not seconds away from death, unable to grip a weapon or defend himself.

She turned toward sounds of battle, knowing any hesitation could lead to her own death. The military fashion of the Spanish marines and navy did her a great service as she scoped the deck for more attackers, registering men in the last throes of life as well as those already introduced to death's ghost.

She and her pirate crew would be given no quarter. The viceroy for New Spain had put too high a price on her head, a pirate of the worst kind—an escaped slave and a woman—to make thoughts of keeping her alive more than momentary fantasies. Juan Carlos would be spared from an immediate death in favor of a long, slow, tortured one for his treasonous behavior against His Most Catholic Majesty King Charles III of Spain and the Spanish Indies. Each royal sailor and marine fighting on her vessel today would be happy to see her head on a pike when they returned to San Juan harbor under the watchful defense of El Morro castle.

Isabella's eyes and ears focused, sensing someone too near for her to be safe. She began to turn, but an arm clasped around her neck, forcing her torso to arch backward as her feet lifted from the deck. The marine's arm braced her neck, a thick rod of blue fabric and muscle pulling against her windpipe as she gasped for air. Letting her sword drop freed her fingers to lock onto her attacker's forearm and to lift her legs, bringing her knees to her chest. The sudden shift in weight surprised the Spaniard, and he stepped back to regain leverage. Isabella shot both feet forward as she forced the top of her head into the face of the marine. The outward force of the kick unbalanced him again. His movement reversed, and he began to fall forward. She relaxed, holding his arm as she let the weight of her body pull her into a crouch as the soldier tumbled over her shoulder and landed flat on his back.

The marine spread his arms to steady himself, twisting onto his side. Isabella stepped forward to drive her boot into his head, but the man dodged the kick, trapping her leg in the crook of his arm and sending Isabella sprawling to the deck.

7

Ahhhh! she screamed to herself, realizing his weight alone would be enough to finish her if he gained further advantage. She twirled her body in midair to land on her back, but the marine was already turning her knee as he rose from the deck. She launched her free foot into a kick at his wrist, forcing a flinch and instinctive relaxation of his grip on her leg. She used her grip to pull herself closer, to give her body more leverage, and fired a second kick at the soldier's knee. The marine cried out and his leg buckled. Isabella discharged another flurry of kicks at his wrist and arms, freeing her from his grasp.

She launched herself into a backward roll, using its momentum to vault her into a standing position away from the Spaniard. She stepped back until she felt the girth of the main mast at her back, giving her a chance to survey the deck. Her sword lay more than a dozen feet away. The wounded marine was clawing his way toward her despite his useless leg.

Isabella grabbed at ropes secured to the mast, knowing they led to a belaying pin somewhere that could become a club. Her fingers found and wrapped themselves around the rounded head of a loose pin, and she pulled. Isabella charged the marine unleashing sweeping swings onto his head. The marine crumbled, unconscious, allowing her to jump over his body and retrieve her sword. The blade shielded her as she backed toward the gunwale, heaving to pull air into her lungs.

The noise of battle faded as she regained the strength she needed to survey the deck. Bodies with blue coats and bloodied white breeches lay strewn across the deck, intermingled with others outfitted with the slapdash uniforms cribbed together by pirates. Two pirates stood across from her, their cutlasses brandished but with no one to cut, testing the bodies of fallen Spaniards and pirate tars for signs of life.

By Isabella's count, the crew of *La Marée Rouge* fared better than the professionals the Captain-General of the West Indies had sent to capture them. More than a score of pirates remained on deck, cutlasses, pikes, and other weapons at the ready, but barely a standing Spaniard, sailor or marine, could be seen.

She lifted her head to scan the full sweep of the gun deck, the haze of spent flint and gunpowder now barely noticeable, swallowed up by a gentle but steady sea breeze. Her cannon sat useless on the carriages even though they stood watch loaded with powder and shot.

Isabella shook her head—they were of little use during a nighttime ambush. The Spaniards must have used small boats to row up close, right under the noses of the *La Marée Rouge's* cannon and the night watch. Isabella's legacy as the Caribbean's most notorious pirate, the Pirate of Panther Bay, had grown even longer by dodging yet another determined attack from the Spanish pirate hunters.

An angry heat began to build in her chest. Incompetence or treachery? she wondered. She would have words with Jean-Michel as soon as they cleaned up this mess and were underway.

Isabella leaned over her pirate brig's railings to cast a glance toward the southern coast of Cuba. They had hauled up for the night about three miles off the coast. This part of the island was practically uninhabited. The plantations were to the west, in the savannas, and the larger fishing towns were much farther east.

She searched the horizon behind her and then toward the west. Two rowing cutters were pulling away from *La Marée Rouge* with barely enough men to man the oars. Two men in Spanish navy clothing were hauling up a sail to tack on a northeasterly route. The other men, marines by their uniforms, sat or stood, their listless bodies pointing muskets toward the pirate vessel in a dispirited attempt to ward off a riposte. But Isabella could tell by the meanderings of her able-bodied crew, they had little appetite for more fight. And the cutters had pulled too far to make a sniper's shot useful. Several of her deckhands stood ready, holding loaded muskets.

"Let them go," she called out. They turned toward the sound of her commands and lowered their weapons. "We have no need to waste powder and shot. We've given them a message they won't want to report to their officers or Captain Muñoz."

Isabella took in a deep breath and expelled the air as she melted back against the railing. The clanging of the ship's bell had woken her in the dark of the night, but shots from muskets and pistols rallied her from her bed. By the time she was on deck, the melee was in full swing. Now, her arms and legs ached. She lifted her arm to sweep the sweat from her brow and eyes, the scarlet bandana wrapping her head soaked through and no longer able to dam the flow down her face. All she wanted to do now was return to her cabin, climb into her bed, and bury her head in Juan Carlos's chest.

She closed her eyes, letting her chin dip. "Please God, protect him," she whispered. "Keep him safe until I figure out how to do it myself."

2

The clacking of approaching boots snapped Isabella's mind back to the deck.

Her chest tightened as she turned toward the swarthy pirate approaching her, his taut face smudged from spent gunpowder and the sweat of the firefight. His gait was strong and sure, his grip on a cutlass firm. His breeches and wool shirt bore the blood of more than one vanquished enemy, but his clothing and skin didn't hold the stains of the smoke and fire from duels of cannon. The lighter dust from flared pistols did little to obscure the gray streaks channeling through his beard or the hair pulled back in a ponytail, the only signs her quartermaster had more than a decade of age over his captain. As he approached, Isabella could see softened eyes, relieved to see her alive.

"Tu va bien, mon cher?"

Isabella nodded, not even registering Jean-Michel's slip into his native French. "The crew?"

Jean-Michel shook his head. "We lost too many. Doc's busy. He's got three men working with him, including Louis."

"What the hell happened? How did they get on board so quickly?"

"I do not know. I heard the bell when you did. Sarhaan was on deck watch."

Isabella looked at Jean-Michel, her eyebrows raised.

"I do not know what happened," he insisted. "We will get to the bottom of it soon."

Isabella nodded. "We should watch Louis. The blood and splintered limbs are an awful lot for a ten-year old boy to take in. Just three weeks ago he was driving a carriage for the Governor-General of Saint

Domingue on the streets of Port-au-Prince. He has barely had time to adjust to the loss of his mother, let alone understand the workings of a warship."

"Oui," Jean-Michel said, a concerned look clear in his expression. "I was worried. But Doc has kept him busy. He seems to be very interested in the surgeon's work, and he hasn't had much time to be afraid."

"I think he was safe below deck." Isabella cast a glance toward the hatch leading to the lower deck. "The attack was limited to the gun deck." She turned her attention back to the scenes of her battles. "Have you seen Gabrielle?"

A smile spread across Jean-Michel's face. "She is quite a fighter!"

Isabella chuckled. "She learned more than a trick or two working as a barkeep in *Le Coq Fontôme* in Port-au-Prince!"

Jean-Michel's smile broadened. "Ha! I think the sight of an African French woman attacking them with swords and pistols, sending… colorful… words their way took them by surprise!"

Isabella cast a playful look toward her quartermaster. "I think your interests are not just military."

"You should have seen her fight," he said, ignoring the pirate captain as a sparkle lit up his eyes. "She disabled two dago marines before she even got started. Her cutlass sent three into the sea before they could even step foot on the deck."

Isabella smiled and nodded. Then the smile faded. "Did Spaniards board from both sides?"

He nodded. "As best I can tell, two cutters approached from the port side, three from the starboard side, and one from the aft, aiming for the captain's quarters."

Isabella's shoulders squared as her back straightened, her eyes widened as she looked back toward the hatch leading to Doc's makeshift hospital.

Jean-Michel leaned toward Isabella, lifting his hand to her shoulder. "He is fine. Juan Carlos was in the thick of the fight on the gun deck."

She turned back to Jean-Michel. "He should have stayed below. He's not healed."

"He's a trained soldier. An officer of noble heritage. He can't stay away from a fight. His honor would force him to be in the thick of the battle."

"But he's wounded—"

"He's a soldier, tested in the battlefields of middle Spain. You saved his life in *Le Coq Fantôme* and on the streets of Port-au-Prince. He is devoted to you. He will do what he can to protect you."

"But sacrifice his life—"

"He has already done that for you. Off Privateer Pointe one year ago. In the dungeons of El Morro. In the offices of Captain-General Rodriguez in Puerto Rico."

"And he survived," Isabella said, lifting her hand to her head, letting her fingers stream through her hair.

"And he survived," Jean-Michel confirmed.

She looked down the deck, checking the bodies of those who had fallen and the faces of those who still stood or walked about.

"He is resting midship," Jean-Michel said, waving his hand toward the bow of the boat.

Isabella started toward the front, stepping over bodies, careful to avoid tripping over bayonetted muskets, dislodged boots, or snagging clothing. Despite no signs of life among these fallen figures, their contorted limbs seemed staged, too complete and detailed.

"A very tidy battle," she mumbled. "Silent cannon disguises the human toll. We will still have a time washing the blood from the decks. Bodies bleed just as much when sliced open by a blade as when limbs are torn apart by shot from a warship's cannon."

Passing midship, Isabella's heart quickened as her eyes darted from form to form, dead and living. She remembered the feel of Jean-Michel's hand falling on her shoulder, a reminder that he had seen Juan Carlos alive.

One more step brought her over another body and close enough to the foremast to see beyond a cluster of pirates and into the bow. She sighed as she recognized the slim physique and well-defined Latin features of Juan Carlos. His shirt and breeches bore the soiled blend of wounds too stubborn to heal, and the fresh sweat and dirt of the melee.

13

The bandage around his chest was missing, revealing a large darkened splotch around his wounds. The arm attached to his wounded shoulder lacked life. But he seemed intact from this distance.

Juan Carlos caught a glimpse of her striding toward him. Before he could rise from the deck, Isabella leaned down, brought her hand to his cheek, and pulled him into a kiss.

"I am happy you are alright," Juan Carlos said as he lifted a hand to let his fingers run through her hair.

Isabella unlocked her lips and tipped her forehead to touch his. "I was afraid."

Juan Carlos chuckled. "Of what? A few Spanish marines trying to bring us in to San Juan with our heads on a pike? I've learned that will not happen. Besides, you were the one at the center of the battle."

"Humph," Jean-Michel growled behind Isabella. "We've got work to do."

Isabella straightened up, keeping one hand on Juan Carlos's shoulder. "Relax, Jean-Michel. I doubt any of our crew are surprised by my worry. After all, we risked our lives to escape from Port-au-Prince with the fearless Spanish army officer, Capitán Santa Ana."

Jean-Michel pointed to a cluster of Spanish marines and sailors held at bayonet point just a few yards away. "It's not our crew we have to worry about."

3

The Spaniards sat on the deck, pirate bayonets inches from their heads. The cluster included four marines and nine sailors, gauging by their attire. All directed their eyes toward the deck and away from their captors.

Isabella secured a scarlet sash around her waist and tightened her wool shirt, its color darkened by the soot of sparked flint and powder. She checked the bandana on her head. She held her sword by the hilt, its scabbard likely still resting on the floor of her cabin, dropped when the ship's bell summoned her and the rest of her crew to the main deck.

She looked at a pirate nearby.

"Herrera. Organize details to clear and scrub the deck," she said, keeping her eyes trained on the prisoners. "Who's checking on Doc and our wounded and dead?"

"I sent Sarhaan below deck to check on Doc," Jean-Michel said as he grouped the remaining crew and tasked them with stripping the dead of useful clothing and arms before casting their bodies overboard. "We should have a count soon."

Isabella waved an arm at the prisoners. "Why aren't they back on Muñoz's ships?"

An older pirate with unkempt hair and a full beard walked over. "Looks like they didn't have much of a chance. Suddenly the dagos were pulling out as fast as they could, and we had this group cornered. I reckon they thought their chances were better with us pirates than with the sharks."

Isabella cursed under her breath and glanced over to Jean-Michel. She couldn't see him roll his eyes, but she knew what he was thinking.

Jean-Michel didn't let her speak. "*Pas de problème*. We will land them on a beach as soon as we know Rodriguez does not have another gunboat on our tail."

Isabella gave a quick nod, affirming the plan. She stepped closer to the marines, inspecting their uniforms. "None of you carry the braids or epaulettes of a commander." She tipped her blade toward one of the marines. "What is your rank?"

The prisoner looked up at his captor, his eyes weary. "Corporal."

"On what ship were you stationed?"

The prisoner kept his eyes trained on the deck, as if embarrassed by his leg coverings and blood-spattered boots. Isabella directed her blade to the prisoner's mouth and hooked it under his chin, prompting him to turn his face up even as his eyes trained on the hardwood oak deck. "*Santa Mónica*," he said through clenched teeth.

Isabella glanced over to Jean-Michel, and then to Juan Carlos. "Muñoz hasn't given up."

"Did you really think he would?" Jean-Michel asked through tight lips. "Our escape from Port-au-Prince embarrassed him. And Juan Carlos's betrayal? Lost to The Pirate of Panther Bay, no less?" The quartermaster shook his head. "Muñoz can't go back to the Captain-General empty-handed, especially after losing his trusted military advisor and attaché from His Most Catholic Majesty's Royal Court. His failure to control piracy in the West Indies led to his demotion from Viceroy. Capitán Juan Carlos Maria Lopez de Santa Ana may be more hated than you right now!"

Isabella nodded, choosing to ignore Jean-Michel's sarcasm. "We'll run eastward tonight, double back, and drop these prisoners off on the island. That should give us time to get back under sail as the winds pick up."

"Aye, mon cher."

In another hour, Isabella surmised, the dead bodies would be cleaned from her decks, and *La Marée Rouge* will be under full sail. The crew would swab the decks of debris and blood. Then, tonight, she would call a meeting of the crew to discuss their course for action.

A sudden weariness swept into her shoulders and thighs. How much longer could she keep this pace up? Rodriguez wouldn't stop until she was swinging from the gallows of San Juan. Now her love, Juan Carlos, was destined for the same fate. Where could they go? She only knew the Caribbean, the world of pirating, and the memories of a plantation slave. And the overseer's post where she was flogged.

Isabella started to turn away from the prisoners and back to her crew, but an unsettled feeling pulled her back to the cluster of vanquished attackers. She sent a curious look toward each of the men, noticing a smaller sailor, his face obscured by the forward fall of a red, baglike barretina hat. The chapeau didn't seem to fit the man or the place. The other sailors' hats were nowhere to be seen, and the bicorn hats worn by the marines also seemed lost to the battle. How did this one manage to keep his? The man's stature was smaller, and he sat with his legs crossed and his hands on his knees. She pursed her lips as she noted the odd posture.

Isabella looked closer at his arms, exposed to the sun by wrapped sleeves from his shirt. His skin was an unusual color, too dark for a European but not dark enough to be African. The hue was like a light-colored olive, not that much different from her own. His black hair fell straight to his shoulders. Creole perhaps?

She nudged him with her blade. "You," she said in Spanish. *"Quién eres tú?"*

The man looked up, his calm eyes peering straight into hers.

Isabella suppressed a gasp. His rounded face and narrow eyes reminded her of native peoples she had met on the islands and the mainland of Mexico, but she had never seen a man such as this. He was not European or African, or, she thought, a mix of any of them.

"My name Omena."

"You… you speak English?" Isabella stammered, struggling to recognize the accent.

"Yes," he said without expression or movement.

She felt the presence of Jean-Michel by her side. *"Ceci est très intéressant,"* he said with a studied tone. *"Chinois.* A Chinaman."

Isabella raised her eyebrows. "Chinaman?"

17

"From the Far East. The Orient. I met some while in service to King Louis IV on a trade mission."

Isabella cast a sideways glance toward her quartermaster.

Jean-Michel nodded. "Before I was a pirate. We were trading in porcelain. Chinoiserie is quite popular in Paris."

His words didn't tamp down Isabella's skeptical look toward her ship's second in command.

Jean-Michel chuckled. "Chinese culture is very prominent in France. Even Voltaire, may he rest in peace, loved the Chinese. He said they knew everything we know now four thousand years ago." Jean-Michel hesitated. "I think he even wrote a book on the subject, *Art de la Chine*."

"Jean-Michel is an odd duck for a pirate," clucked a gruff voice on Isabella's other side.

Isabella smiled. "Si, Señor Herrera, Jean-Michel is an odd duck. His noble upbringing apparently served a purpose."

She dropped her sword to the side, bringing her other hand to her waist. "This is a first. We've captured a Chinese."

Omena eyes seemed to harden. "No Chinese."

Isabella looked at Jean-Michel, then back to the prisoner. "Then where are you from?"

Omena's eyes slid to Jean-Michel. "Nippon."

Isabella thought she heard Jean-Michel catch his breath.

"Nippon," Herrera repeated. "What's a Nippon?"

"Nippon," Jean-Michel said, the reverence in his voice catching Isabella's ear. "The Land of the Rising Sun. Japan. No Frenchman's set foot in Nippon for over one hundred years. No one official that is. I've never met a Japanese before."

He leaned down toward Omena, narrowing his eyes to sharpen his look. Omena turned his head, as if warning Jean-Michel not to come closer.

Herrera stepped forward, raising a pistol to Omena's head. The Japanese kept his eyes on Jean-Michel, challenging him, ignoring the gun. The pirate pulled the hammer back on his pistol. "Watch how you treat our quartermaster, Chinaman."

18

Isabella put her hand on Herrera's shoulder. "Let it go. He can't hurt anyone right now." She gently squeezed his shoulder, and Herrera let the muzzle fall away from Omena's head.

"Now, Mr. Omena," Isabella said, letting herself fall into a crouch as she trained a determined look into his eyes. "How did you end up on a Spanish gunship chasing down the Pirate of Panther Bay in the middle of the Caribbean Sea?"

4

Isabella waited, continuing to look at Omena, even though she was sure he wouldn't respond. "How did you end up on the *Santa Mónica*?"

Omena shifted his eyes to the deck.

"You won't get anything out of him," a prisoner said.

Isabella turned to the Spanish marine, letting her raised eyebrows ask the question.

"Omena doesn't speak much. Keeps to himself."

"Then how did he end up on a cutter with a detachment of Spanish marines ambushing my ship?"

"No one much cared for him on the *Santa Mónica*. Officers couldn't talk to him."

Isabella huffed in frustration. "How did he end up on the *Santa Mónica*?"

"Came on board in Puerto Rico, from another ship that sailed from Cadiz. A merchant ship by my guess. I guess we were taking anyone willing to run the rigging as we started our chase. We didn't care what he did as long as he pulled at the oars and ran the yards."

Isabella shook her head, unconvinced.

"Portugal," said Juan Carlos.

Isabella stood, keeping her eyes trained on the Japanese sailor. "What do the Portuguese have to do with Japan?"

"They opened up trade with Japan and sent missionaries. Other than the English, they have been about the only Europeans to have a presence in the country for hundreds of years. He probably signed on or stowed away on a ship from the Dutch East India Company, unloading shipments in Lisbon. Given that he made it to San Juan, my guess is he signed onto a merchantman in Cadiz."

Isabella nodded, putting the pieces of the puzzle together. "These Japanese know how to sail, then."

Juan Carlos and Jean-Michel couldn't contain a quick guffaw.

"I forget that your world is still very small, mon cher," Jean-Michel said. "Japan is an island. I suspect this man learned to fish very young. He earned his sea legs as a boy. He is small and thin, which would help him in the rigging. I would sign him as a tar, with a bet he would become a good sailor on square-rigged ships very fast."

Isabella turned to the Spanish marine corporal. "How was this man as a sailor?"

"I'm trained to fire weapons, climb ropes, and board an enemy ship," the Spaniard said, staring forward without looking at Isabella. "I'm not a sailor."

Juan Carlos walked to the other side of the Japanese, as if a new angle would give him a clearer understanding of his role on the *Santa Mónica*. "The fact he is on *La Marée Rouge* right now is a good sign he does well on the masts and yards."

The Spanish prisoner turned his head away from the pirates. Juan Carlos smiled and nodded at Isabella and Jean-Michel.

Herrera turned toward Isabella. "What are we going to do with them?"

"Let's get *La Marée Rouge* under way first. How long before we're under full sail?"

Herrera looked at the rigging, inventorying sails, yards, stays, and ropes, and then logged the progress on the gun deck. "The attack was at night. And by water. Our cannon and rigging are intact. We should have the bodies disposed of soon. I'll check with Smoothy about the guns and stores, but I think we can be underway by late morning."

Isabella nodded. "Let's take advantage of these winds. We'll sail east but stay clear of the Archipiélago de los Jardinas de la Reina. We'll turn south but north of the Cayman Islands. Once we clear Isla de la Juventud, we'll tack northwest into the Golfo de Batabano and drop off our prisoners. We can take advantage of the night and sail back into the Yucatan Channel and stay clear of Muñoz and his gunships."

Jean-Michel shook his head. "That is a lot for one day's sail."

"I know, but we need to get out of these waters, and it's safer than trying to drop them off further east. They should be able to walk the lowland plains due north to Havana within a day. They won't have to navigate hills; just plantations and savanna."

Herrera waved his pistol at the prisoners. "We could just take care of them right now."

Isabella scowled.

The pirate released the hammer on the pistol, letting it rest against the flint without a spark. "*Supongo que no.* That's unfortunate for me."

Isabella laughed. "I am sorry to disappoint you Señor Herrera. I am sure Rodriguez and Muñoz will give you another opportunity before we leave these wretched seas."

She pivoted to look directly at Herrera. "Secure them. I'm going to check on Doc." And Louis. But where was Gabrielle?

Isabella seemed to descend into a stove lit by long-burning hardwood as her boots hit the steps to the lower deck. Her lungs struggled to inhale the thick air as the morning sun on the gundeck kept her eyes from adjusting to the darkness. She exhaled, letting her chest compress and calm her as she entered an all too familiar hell. How much longer could she survive this life?

A chorus of full-throated moans foreshadowed the depth of the horror. *The living dead,* she thought. She could smell their blood, unleashed by the cuts and gashes created by hand-to-hand combat, but absent the nauseating hint of burned flesh from the fires spawned by broadsides. She opened her mouth to avoid digesting the stench through her nose.

The hammocks remained strung from the beams, hardly touched since her crew rolled from slumber into the flash of a fight for their lives.

Isabella barely remembered the spark that pulled her into the fray, as if she were transported in an instant from a deep sleep next to Juan Carlos into an unfolding carnage amid muskets flashing at enemies cloaked by smoke. But she must have run down this deck, slapping the hammocks with the broad side of her sword to rouse her crew as she rushed and reached for the ladder to the gun deck. She wasn't a ghost, or an apparition, that melted through walls and ceilings and hulls unnoticed.

She turned toward the aft, a bright glow bobbing over a table surrounded by dark figures, providing glimpses of the doors to her cabin and Jean-Michel's stateroom. Her eyes began to recognize the outlines of men laying on the deck, and she noticed the bulges of bodies filling in hammocks closer to the surgeon's table.

She felt the soft press of a comforting hand on her shoulder. "The price of freedom," Juan Carlos whispered in her ear.

Isabella closed her eyes and let her cheek rest on his fingers. "Si mi amor."

Another squeeze of his hand seemed to acknowledge a sadness in her tone. "*¿Estás bien?*"

His chest pressed into her back, and she felt the light touch of his lips on her neck. Isabella drew in a deep breath and let her chin drop in a small nod.

Then, the pirate captain stepped toward Doc and a huddle of assistants working on a fallen sailor, letting her movement lead Juan Carlos as if he were the tether for those following him.

"How are they," Isabella asked, watching the steady tap of Doc's hands as he threaded a wound.

"Monsieur Docteur thinks he will live," said a small voice—Louis, his French accent heavy—drawing out the last word as if it were pronounced "leev." Louis kept his focus on the wounded sailor, his eyes flicking up toward Doc, as if waiting for a signal. His small hands, hardened by weeks of working the sails and ropes of a warship, held a damp cloth, prompting Isabella to wonder how many wounds were necessary to capture enough blood to bequeath its burgundy color.

A pirate leaned over the wound as Doc finished his last suture. He balanced his weight between a makeshift crutch and the table as he wiped blood away from a slice across the pirate's abdomen.

"Pete's lost a lot of blood," he said as he raised his hand and pointed to the body.

A tar, his arm in a blood-soaked sling, tipped an oil lamp hanging from a bulwark over the center of the table. Isabella now saw that Doc's sutures had closed just one of more than a dozen wounds now disfiguring Pete's chest and waist.

Doc started to wring his hands with a towel. "Damn grape shot," he muttered. He started to inspect the unconscious body beginning at the head and moving methodically toward the toes as Pete's chest rose and fell with heavy, struggling breaths.

Isabella felt tears gather behind her eyes. "Pete's been with me since the start. Since Jacob. He helped us take back this brig from that mutinous Stiles off Privateer Pointe."

Doc looked up at Isabella, allowing her to see his rounded face; several days of stubble discolored his chin and upper lip. He shook his head. "I tried to get it all out, but I think some of that lead is there to stay."

Juan Carlos's hand slipped off her shoulder to her lower back. "I would not be alive today if Pete and Jean-Michel hadn't searched Port-au-Prince for you."

Doc turned back to the battered pirate. He lifted the unconscious sailor's eyelids, holding them open for several seconds as he peered into the pupils. "Good news is the pain knocked him out about half way through the surgery."

Louis pointed to an empty tin on the table. "He had much demon water. Monsieur Docteur said it would help the pain."

A small smile cracked Isabella's lips. "I am sure the doctor is right. Any wounded pirate on my ship can have as much rum as he wants."

Louis smiled.

She let her hand fall to the top of Louis's head. "Until he's ready to get back into the yards and topsails to keep us free!"

"Monsieur Docteur worries about infection," Louis said, his smile fading as he lifted a stained towel to blot perspiration from Pete's cheeks and forehead.

"He's the last for now," said Doc, putting a knife and a saw in a wooden box next to the table. "We'll clean up the tools and get the table back in order, Captain."

"*Gracias*, Doc," Juan Carlos said over Isabella's shoulder. "*Desgraciadamente*, we don't have much time. Muñoz isn't going to let us regroup, not if it means that he's going back to Puerto Rico empty handed. He doesn't want his head to be hanging from the gallows of El Morro any more than we do."

Doc nodded, and then turned to Isabella, a glint in his eye. "Aye, but cleaning up my table is going to be a hell of a lot easier than putting your quarters back in order!"

Isabella's eyebrow turned up, as if asking him to explain.

Louis turned his head up to Isabella, his face brightened by gleaming teeth against mahogany skin. "Monsieur Santa Ana was very smart. *Très intelligent.*"

Doc flipped a casual finger toward Juan Carlos, a smile breaching his dour look. "You can let your dago lover explain."

Isabella cocked her head toward the door of her stateroom, the door ajar. "Why is it so dark? It's well into mid-morning. What's blocking the light?"

Doc turned toward his instruments, using a cloth to clean blood as he put them back in their rightful place.

"*Allons y, mademoiselle,*" Louis said, smiling as he pulled at Isabella hand. "I will show you. *Très intelligent.*"

Juan Carlos's hand slipped off her shoulder as the boy pulled Isabella forward.

The forms strewn across the floor took on more hardened shapes as she stepped away from the table. She could make out the slipshod clothing of her crew, usually bare feet showing under the shredded legs of wool pants or leather breeches, with a tunic or darker shirt covering

25

the torso. The darker forms intrigued her more. She could see the double-breasted half coat from Spanish marines, some of whom, she was sure were cut down by the aim of her pistols or the slash of her sword. Or Jean-Michel's.

Louis dropped her hand and grabbed at the door to her stateroom, pushing first with his hands and then with his body.

"Louis," commanded Juan Carlos in a stern voice. He stepped forward and put his hand on the boy's arm to hold him back.

"It's stuck!" Louis said, the desperation in his voice racing toward the edge of panic.

"Wait," Juan Carlos said, his tone more forceful. "Look." Juan Carlos pointed to the planks and Louis stopped.

Isabella followed Juan Carlos's voice. An unmoving head and arm lay sprawled on her cabin floor, the edge of the door now appearing like an upended table top for a decapitated body. Juan Carlos must have killed a Spanish marine, and his fallen body was now blocking the door.

Louis's hand reached for his head. "What I am going to do?"

Juan Carlos chuckled. "We're going to have to move the body."

"I am not going to touch a dead man. It bad luck for me."

"What is a dead Spanish marine doing in my stateroom?"

Juan Carlos turned toward Isabella, his eyebrows creased. "He wasn't coming for breakfast."

Isabella glared at Juan Carlos. "They've never tried to board us from the stern before."

Juan Carlos turned back to the door and body. "They got smart." He pulled one of the pikes from its place on the wall and signaled for Louis to help him as he lodged it against the lifeless body.

"What about Jean-Michel's quarters?"

"I don't know. These marines could barely make it through the windows in your cabin." Juan Carlos turned to Isabella, his look transformed into an inquisitive squint. "You have larger windows." His tone made it a statement rather than a question.

"In Panther Bay," Isabella said, recognition relaxing the muscles in her cheeks, "before we sank the *Ana Maria*—and captured you the first time—I had the ship's carpenter add more light. The cabin was dark, and after Jacob's death…."

"Si, I understand, *te entiendo.*" Juan Carlos nudged Louis to take hold of the pike as he placed it against the torso of the dead marine. "When I count to three, push very hard." He paused. "Unfortunately, the added light gave the Spanish a way to attack us from below. Uno… dos… trés."

The boy and man threw their weight against the pole, grunts channeling their will and effort down through the stick and into the body at the end, pushing it away from the door. Another combined grunt, and the door was cleared enough to see the rest of the stateroom.

Isabella slipped her arm around Juan Carlos and rested her head on his shoulder. "I thought you would be safe."

"It is good that you left me in bed," Juan Carlos chortled. "Next time leave me with more pistols and powder."

"Tools for a true warrior," she said, a smile breaking through her lips. She stepped forward.

Juan Carlos and Louis pushed against the door, pushing the body even further, revealing the defense that may have saved the ship.

"Very clever," Isabella said. "You were right Louis. *Très intelligent.*"

"Be careful." Juan Carlos stepped over the corpse and started to pull at one of the pikes. He tugged at another pole. "The tips on these pikes have gone all the way through. We'll have to pull the whole mattress out."

Louis tugged at Juan Carlos's shirt sleeve. "Do you think there are dead bodies on the other side?"

Juan Carlos looked at Isabella and back to Louis. "Perhaps you should go back to Doc and see if one of the other sailors can give us a hand. I don't think you are big enough to pull those pikes back."

"Oui, Monsieur Santa Ana." Louis dodged Isabella as he darted out of the cabin.

Isabella shook her head. "We'll have to find something else for our bedding."

27

She stepped over the dead body and toward the wooden frame of the cot. She slipped her hand across the small of Juan Carlos's back and surveyed the damage. "We should just throw the mattress out the back and into the sea. We'll board up the windows for now."

She felt blood course through her veins and into her chest. "Damn those Spaniards! Why don't they quit?"

Juan Carlos pushed one of the pikes further into the mattress and then pulled back, letting the full weight of his body attempt to jerk the pole back into the room. "We might have to cut it out."

"The pikes are worth saving; the mattress is not. Let it fall into the water and let the sharks have it for dinner."

Isabella sat down on the side of the cot, letting her face fall into the palms of her hands. She drew in a deep breath, pulling her fingers across her cheeks, as her shoulders slumped further forward.

Juan Carlos stepped over and let his hand lay gently on her head. "I'll have one of the sailors make a new bed for the cot and you can sleep for a few hours."

Isabella shook her head. "I don't need sleep. We've got too much work to do."

"You have to sleep, Isabella. Now is the time. Muñoz will be back, but he will need a few more hours to count his losses and come up with a new plan."

Isabella looked at the speared mattress and the body on her cabin floor. "I don't want to do this anymore."

"It's too late for that," Juan Carlos said, his voice even. "Rodriguez has a price on your head. Muñoz wants your head regardless of the price."

Isabella looked up at Juan Carlos. "I think Muñoz wants your head more than mine right now." She drew in a deep breath and let it out. "I want more than a life running from King Charles, his army, and his navy."

"You want to abandon your fight for freedom?"

"No, of course not. But we're up against the entire Spanish fleet. I don't have an army that can seize territory and defend it. France sees my victories as an opportunity against Spain. Spain sees my victories for

28

what they are—a threat, a revolution in the making. But I don't have enough men… or women… to make good on that threat."

"So you want to quit the revolution?" Gabrielle's voice seemed to grab Isabella's head and pull her chin up from the cot.

Her thick French creole tones reminded Isabella of the voodoo priestess that prophesied her rise to lead a revolution in the mountains of Saint Domingue over a month ago. She thought the prophecy meant she would lead a revolt of slaves and *gens de coulour* against the French in Port-au-Prince. But that couldn't be. D'Poussant was a ruthless leader of the rebels. He would have been as terrible leading a free Saint Domingue as the French planters or the Spanish on the eastern side of the island. If she wasn't destined to free Hispaniola, what did the prophecy mean? A life playing cat-and-mouse at sea?

La Marée Rouge had a nearly full hold of silver, fine clothing, and furniture seized from Spanish and French merchantmen. Her crew would be happy when they sold it at auction. But who would buy it? Planters? The cycle would continue.

Isabella stiffened. "How many men have we lost today?"

"Sacrifices are necessary if we are going to destroy Spain… and France."

Gabrielle's thin frame couldn't deflect the fierce determination surging from her glare. Growing up in her father's inn, *Le Coq Fantôme*, did little to soften her understanding of the world. Standing in the threshold of the cabin, a bloodied dagger still firm in her grip, she left little doubt about her resolve.

"You know I detest the Spaniards," Isabella said, her stare hardened. "But your King Louis is no better. The peasants are rising against him in France. But they are not rising for our freedom. They are happy to drink their coffee with the sugar reaped off our backs, just as the Spanish and English sleep soundly at night without thinking of the scars that mark us as beasts of burden. We are no more human to the French, Spanish, or English."

Juan Carlos lowered himself to the cot, positioning himself next to Isabella.

Gabrielle's eyes darted to Juan Carlos. "I killed five of them this morning. I can kill scores more!"

"You know Juan Carlos is not one of them."

Juan Carlos winced as he touched Isabella's knee with his arm, the stiffness returning to his shoulder without the constant movement of the fight. He opened his mouth as if to say something but stopped when Isabella lifted a hand to his cheek.

Isabella nodded. "We know, Gabrielle. You are fierce in battle, and I would not... Juan Carlos would not be here today if it weren't for your bravery in *Le Coq Fantôme*. D'Poussant would have happily traded our lives for his revolution. But what would we have gained?"

"Our freedom!" Gabrielle said.

"What freedom?" Isabella stood up from the cot, squaring herself opposite Gabrielle. "You were *gens de couleur*. Your people were not slaves. You are the free blacks of Saint Domingue. What did you have to gain?"

Gabrielle lifted her dagger with a deliberateness suggesting more emphasis than threat. "Equality. I didn't work the fields, but I never pretended I would be invited to a nobleman's table to eat from the same plates or drink from the same goblets."

Isabella looked directly into Gabriella's eyes. "No one sits at their table except other noblemen." She lifted her hand to Gabriella's wrist and gently pressed the dagger to her side. "None of us is their equal."

"You never will be their equal." Juan Carlos's voice was weary. "I will never be their equal. They want us all dead. Charles will never give us a reprieve as long as he reigns over Spain. Rodriguez will not let us rest until our ships are at the bottom of the sea, and our heads are displayed on pikes on the walls of El Morro."

Gabrielle threw her head back and looked up the ceiling. "So we just give up?" Her head dropped to look at Juan Carlos and then Isabella.

"Gabrielle," Isabella said, "I've been fighting Rodriguez for six years on sea, my entire life on land."

Gabrielle shook her head, turning her eyes to the deck. "Port-au-Prince burns for nothing!"

"We need a fleet," Juan Carlos said. "We won't be able to defeat Rodriguez without a fleet. We can strangle him with a fleet."

"We can barely manage two ships," Isabella huffed. "We don't have the crew to manage a fleet. The last time we captured a ship, we ended up being chased into Port-au-Prince Bay and blockaded by Muñoz."

Juan Carlos raised his eyebrows in silent agreement. "We escaped—

"Chased out, more like it, *mes amis.*"

The group turned to see Jean-Michel in the cabin doorway, Louis just in front of him. "We would come in, but it looks a little tight. Three is a crowd; five is a mutiny."

Isabella stood, her hands on her hips. She turned to one of the pikes burrowed in the upended mattress, grabbed it with both hands, lodged her boot against the cotton fabric, and pulled. "Arrrrgh," she yelled as she heaved. The mattress relinquished several inches of the pole's buried sheath. She pulled again, finally dislodging it with a jerk that tore the canvas as the blade released. She threw the pike outside her cabin.

She turned back to another pike and pulled. Several more tugs produced another blade and another pike on the deck next to the makeshift floating hospital. Gabrielle stepped up, grabbed another pole, and pulled. They handed another freed pike to Jean-Michel, who transferred it to Louis, who began stacking them against the hull. By the time the last pike had been pulled, a blanket of tangled strings and clumps of Spanish moss carpeted her cabin.

Isabella retreated to the cot's frame, lifting her sleeve to her head to soak up the sweat that once again streamed down her face. She turned to look at the ropes strung between the bed posts and rails. "We'll take some spare canvas and layer it into the ropes for a bed."

Jean-Michel touched Louis on the shoulder. "Louis, why don't you take a look at all this moss. Anything with blood on it, throw out the window into the sea. Anything that looks clean, wrap it in a hammock. That might help Captain Isabella sleep a little better tonight."

"Oui, Monsieur Jean-Michel." Louis started sorting through the mattress filling at his feet. Without looking up, he tossed a few globs of dried green moss to the side, throwing discolored pieces toward the

31

window. A pile of stained moss began to build a foot away from the windows.

Isabella smiled as Jean-Michel rolled his eyes.

"Louis," he said. "Where does the bad moss go?"

Louis looked up, he's face contorted with irritation. "Out the window!"

Jean-Michel pointed toward the pile of morbidly splotched moss.

"Ohhhh!" Louis walked to the pile, picked it up and threw it out the window. Then he strode over to his original spot, sorting the rest the same way.

Gabrielle giggled. Isabella raised her hand to her forehead as her smile broadened. Jean-Michel heaved a sigh.

"Louis."

Louis looked up, sending a scowl toward Gabrielle and Isabella. "Yes, Señor Santa Ana?"

"Why don't you start at the window, and work toward the door?"

"Why?"

"That way you don't have to walk as far to toss the bad moss out the window."

Louis nodded. He walked over to the window as he sorted through a labyrinth of snarled mattress bedding and dropped the bad moss into the ocean.

Isabella leaned over into Juan Carlos's ear. "Very clever, my captain."

Juan Carlos smiled. "I have trained many warriors."

Isabella laughed. "You seem to have a knack for the little ones."

"You question my professional abilities?" Juan Carlos looked at Isabella, his eyes wide and playful with a turn of his mouth showing a small smile.

"Hah," Jean-Michel huffed. "Training a ten-year old is a harder task than working with the tars pressed into service for the King's Navy."

Gabrielle shook her head.

"You are making short work of that bedding, Louis," Isabella said as he cleared a space big enough to see the oak planks below the windows.

"Merci, capitán!" Louis started to pick through the moss at a faster pace.

"New Orleans."

Isabella turned to Jean-Michel, her head cocked as if asking a question.

"*La Nouvelle Orléans?*" he repeated.

Juan Carlos looked up at him. "*Nueva Orleans?* It's a backwater. Spain has to bribe Germans to settle in that god-forsaken swamp."

"A backwater can hide much," Jean-Michel said. "France used it to establish our trading routes along the Mississippi River. The bayous are fertile hiding places for pirates."

Juan Carlos nodded. "Spain controls the city and territory of Louisiana now. Bernardo de Gálvez is the governor."

"And doing much to help the Americans in their fight against the British. He has already achieved victories in Pensacola, seizing Western Florida for your King."

Juan Carlos eyebrows ticked up in recognition. "His reputation was great in Madrid. The dispatches were very colorful. But Spain controls New Orleans. How does that help us?"

"They take their orders from Havana, Cuba. The Viceroy of New Spain has no interest in this backwater."

Isabella shook her head. "But Rodriguez—"

"Works under the Viceroy of New Spain," said Juan Carlos, a small sparkle in his eyes. "The Captain-General of Puerto Rico cannot operate outside his jurisdiction."

Jean-Michel leaned against the wall of the stateroom. "We are going to return our prisoners to Havana. They will testify with their own experience that they have been treated well. The authorities will have no taste for sending a squadron to chase down pirates in New Orleans, especially with the distractions of the American rebellion and the loss of La Florida to the British."

Isabella let her eyes drift to the deck, her hands rubbing against her thighs. "How far is New Orleans?"

Jean-Michel straightened his back and shifted to the threshold of the door. "About five hundred and eighty nautical miles. I think we can push

33

La Marée Rouge to average twelve or more knots in the open sea, even with a hull full of treasure. We could be in New Orleans within a week if we take a straight shot and the weather is fair. If we follow the coast of La Florida, we can sell some of our booty in the coastal ports: Pensacola, Mobile are probably big enough to turn a pretty penny. We can unload the rest in New Orleans." Jean-Michel paused and glanced at Isabella. "A better strategy might be to lure Muñoz back to Puerto Rico by sailing eastward and up through the Straights of Jamaica."

Gabrielle turned her head in a sharp rebuke. "Back toward Rodriguez?"

Jean-Michel stepped over to Gabrielle and put his hand on her shoulder. "A ploy. Muñoz knows we are short on provisions. He will think we will go west, toward the open sea and Jamaica, to flee."

Isabella shook her head. "It's risky. Muñoz knows the French and their governor in Saint Domingue have no interest in chasing us."

Juan Carlos looked up at Jean-Michel. "Do we know where Muñoz is now?"

"We think he is west of us, chasing us toward the east."

Gabrielle's eyes widened. "So we sail right into his sights?"

Isabella looked at Jean-Michel. "It's a narrow strait, but it still covers a lot of water."

"Oui," Jean-Michel nodded. "He will think we are sailing east, to return to Panther Bay or Charlotte Amalie. But we will turn south and sail west to release the prisoners to Havana. Then we slip past Isla del la Juventud—"

"Those shoals—"

"We've navigated worse." Jean-Michel put a finger on the wall of the cabin, tracing the long, narrow arc of Cuba. "Havana is here," he said, his finger resting on the northern shore at the peak of the curve before it turned down. "Juventud Island is here." His finger traveled south and drew a circle below the southern coast. "Even if Muñoz thinks we are not returning to Panther Bay, he will naturally think we are heading south, perhaps to the Cayman Islands, but more likely Jamaica. The British have no love for the French or the Spanish since they are helping the American revolutionaries."

"Revolution?" Louis's eyes grew large as he stepped up to Gabrielle's leg and looked for her hand. "*La révolution* killed *ma mére.*"

Gabrielle brought her hand over the top of Louis's head and let it rest, pulling him closer. "D'Poussant killed your mother, Louis. Not the revolution."

"Don't worry, *mon petit*," Jean-Michel said with a soft voice. "*Ne t'inquiéte pas.* We will stay far from the revolution."

"But how will we stay ahead of Muñoz?" Juan Carlos's voice was still full with doubt.

"We will do what he does not expect. We will sail north, toward La Florida and then New Orleans."

Juan Carlos threw his head back, letting out a clipped sigh. "Another Spanish colony!"

"Isabella's hatred toward Spain is legendary," said Jean-Michel. "Rodriguez and Muñoz will think we are heading back to St. John and Panther Bay."

Juan Carlos shook his head as he stared at the wall. "The Golfo de Mexico is as big as an ocean. No one has completely charted it."

Jean-Michel bellowed a guffaw. "You are sounding like the land lubber all army men are in their hearts!"

Juan Carlos cast a scowl toward Jean-Michel. Isabella turned toward the door, rolling her lips to tamp down a chortle. Gabrielle lifted her hand to her mouth in a half successful attempt to hide a smile.

Jean-Michel lifted his hands. "Do you have a better plan?"

Juan Carlos shook his head. "But we are very low on provisions. What is between Cuba and New Orleans along the western coast of La Florida? This journey could take weeks if we take an eastern route. Sailing to New Orleans without repairs and re-provisioning puts too much at risk."

Isabella stood up and paced the cabin, picking up her foot to avoid Louis who had turned back to working on the last few feet of fouled moss. She looked out at the water and could see no signs of the debris he had shoveled into the sea. A breeze broke through the open window, and she felt the tilt of the floor below her as the main sails caught the wind above them. "We've run out of time to make a decision."

She turned to Juan Carlos. "I would like to sail clear of this hell as soon as possible." She sighed. "But I think Juan Carlos may be right. We have too much sea to cover with meat, hard tack, and fresh water as low as they are. Without replenishing our supply of lemons, Doc will be treating the men for scurvy before too long. We don't just have to worry about the Spanish. And the French fleet has been dispatched to Virginia to join the Americans and fight the British. But other pirates roam these waters. Those rogues are more dangerous than a well-trained colonial navy."

Juan Carlos looked at Isabella. "You were almost caught by Muñoz a month ago. You were saved by the storm that blew us into Port-au-Prince."

"Muñoz was sailing south through the Straits then," Jean-Michel said. "This time, he is to our south, tacking north against the prevailing winds just as we are. That gives us the advantage. We're faster."

"*La Marée Rouge* is a nimble ship," Isabella said, her tone calculating as her decision gave her confidence. "She can outmaneuver the *Santa Mónica*. The smaller sloops don't have enough sail to match our speed. They are worthless without Muñoz's guns anyway."

Jean-Michel lifted his hands to his face, letting the fingers slip down his bearded cheeks. "I hope you are right, Isabella. Now is not the time to under-estimate Muñoz."

36

5

Juan Carlos gripped the railing as he looked toward the narrow opening into the Golfo de Batabanó from the deck of *La Marée Rouge*. The breeze coming from the east was strong enough to give their vessel enough headway to maneuver, if needed, but how long would they last once the sun set over the island's western mountains of Pinar Del Rio?

"Relax. Muñoz did not follow us into the bay."

Juan Carlos didn't turn to face Jean-Michel and continued to look out toward a dark slit that was Caya Largo on the western horizon of the bay. "Muñoz will not let us go."

"Oui, I hope not. I am counting on it."

"You are putting too much faith in how well you play the game, mi amigo."

"Ahhh, how much choice do we have? The games are played; *les jeux sont joués…*, whether we like it or not."

Juan Carlos straightened his shoulders, shifting his feet. "I wish I had your confidence."

Jean-Michel nodded. "I don't know these waters well. But I have sailed enough merchants and warships… and pirate ships… to put my coin on this crew and her captain."

He waved his hand toward the back of the boat where several deckhands were making adjustments to a cutter, readying it to launch over the side. "Would you rather play out our hand on land? We're about to put the prisoners in the water and land them on the southern coast of Cuba. They'll be on the sand in twenty minutes. In Havana in a day, two at the most."

Juan Carlos shook his head. "I have traveled too far on this ship for land to give me comfort or confidence."

Jean-Michel cocked his head, stepping closer to the rail to see Juan Carlos's eyes. "Where is your loyalty?"

Juan Carlos closed his eyes. "I love Isabella. You know that."

"She risked everything for you."

Juan Carlos sent a sharp look toward Jean-Michel. "I know that, too, Jean-Michel."

"You would be dead without her sacrifice."

"Si. But I have sacrificed as well. The blood of my comrades glistens on the streets and alleys of Port-au-Prince. Because of me."

"You did a fine job of bottling us up in Port-au-Prince harbor. Muñoz should be happy enough."

"I have nothing to return to. I have no family. No King."

"None of your landing party survived that night. The city was in flames. D'Poussant covered your tracks as well as his own."

"I fled with Isabella. I fled with you."

Jean-Michel turned toward the bay, bringing his fingers through his hair to rest on the back of his neck. "I don't understand your doubt."

"I don't doubt my love for Isabella." Juan Carlos raised his hand, and then brought it down with a thump onto the railing. He turned back to Jean-Michel. "Do you understand what I have given up?"

Jean-Michel rolled his eyes, crossing his arms as he leaned back against the rail. "I am the third son of a French nobleman. I was given nothing to lose."

"I had a royal commission!"

"You were born into your status," Jean-Michel retorted with a huff.

"I had to earn my captaincy."

"Juan," Jean-Michel said, the crispness in his tone sharpening his glare. "You were sent to the West Indies to serve under the corpulent mass of an incompetent!"

"And another step back to His Majesty's Court and my King's good graces."

Muffled voices swirled in their direction. Bodies began emerging from the deck below as Spanish marines and sailors lined up against the cutter, sharpened pikes keeping them at a distance from the pirates. Jean-Michel arced his arm and pointed a finger at the group. "Then join them!"

Juan Carlos chuckled. "To go where? To Havana? To Puerto Rico? I have failed in my task and in my service to King Charles. I would be executed. If I were lucky."

A plucky tar seemed to skip up to Jean-Michel, a full beard revealing his identity as he closed in on the pair. "Got'm ready. All accounted for."

Jean-Michel nodded, ignoring Juan Carlos for the moment. "Got room for one more, Smoothy?"

Smoothy's eyebrows raised as he pulled himself to stop. "One more? Someone want to join our merry band to oversee my work? Don't worry, I'll slice any of 'm up if they try anything."

"Any of our crew ready to try land for a while?" Jean-Michel asked without breaking his sight on Juan Carlos.

Smoothy sent an awkward look to Jean-Michel before his eyes darted to the former Spanish captain. "Uhh, no sir, can't say's I've heard anyone say so."

Jean-Michel leaned back against the rail with his arms crossed. "What about the Japanese…, Omena?"

Smoothy paused. "He's staying on board. Says he don't want to be with the dagos." Smoothy looked over to Juan Carlos. "Must think he's better off among pirates than His Most Catholic Majesty's crew."

Jean-Michel lifted his hand, flicking two fingers toward the Spanish prisoners. "Then off with them. Make sure they are guarded all the way to shore. Keep blades close. We do not want them turning those boats around on us and finishing the job they started."

"Aye, sir."

Juan Carlos stepped away from the rail. "Where is Isabella?"

Smoothy smiled. "Below decks with Louis and Gabrielle. They been talkn' to Doc. Got a couple of Spaniards and our boys that need attendin'."

"And the Japanese?"

Smoothy turned back to Jean-Michel. "Sittin' quiet like back with some of the crew. Seems to be thinkin' about something deep. Didn't see no need to disturb him."

"Be careful with the Spanish," said Jean-Michel. "They may not appreciate our generosity. It's not very pirate-like."

Smoothy let loose a cackling laugh. "Aye, Jean-Michel, but it's very Isabella-like!"

"Isabella's surely a different breed of pirate," the French quarter master said, as Smoothy made his way back to the prisoners and the long-boat that would row them away from a rogue's life as a pirate and into the safety of colonial military. Or so they hoped.

"Si, she is very special." Juan Carlos turned to Jean-Michel. "Do you remember El Morro's dungeons?"

Jean-Michel felt his mood darken. "Oui, how could I forget? She accused me of disloyalty."

Juan Carlos put his hand on Jean-Michel's shoulder. "She was weak. After she was tortured, I brought her back to life. Her will... her strength..., I had never seen that in a woman."

Jean-Michel's eyes turned hard. "Growing up under the lashes of an overseer's whip will harden anyone."

Juan Carlos turned toward the deck. "The whip hardens all those who survive. But Isabella...." He shook his head before casting his gaze toward the boat rowing to the south coast of Cuba and freedom... for some. "But Isabella was not defeated by the whip. She held onto life. How?"

"Jacob." Jean-Michel paused. "He loved her and showed her she could rise above the fires burning on the plantation. Rise above the violence that destroyed her family and her love."

"She says very little about him."

"I sailed with Jacob for five years before he discovered Isabella. She was barely alive, her body and mind wracked by too little water and food. He saw life in her, knew she would rise up." Jean-Michel's voice trailed into a whisper as his chin sank into his chest.

"He saw her rise again," Juan Carlos said in a quiet voice. "A Phoenix."

"He saw her recover. Get stronger. Learn how to use a sword. But she was never healed."

Jean-Michel looked across the deck toward the shores of Cuba. Steady puffs of air cooled his cheeks and shifted the valleys in his shirt as it hung loosely over his breeches. "Looks like Smoothy's on the way back."

"What happened to Jacob?"

Jean-Michel stepped away from the rail, positioning himself for a clearer view of the cutter. "Half hour and we'll be on our way."

Juan Carlos opened his mouth, but shut it, and leaned over the rail. "Isabella is an amazing woman."

Jean-Michel turned back to Juan Carlos, a glisten in his eyes. "Be true to her."

Juan Carlos lifted his hand to Jean-Michel's arm. "She has all of my heart. I have nothing to return to."

Jean-Michel looked around the deck of *La Marée Rouge*, his eyes engaged in a steady search. He moved closer to the nearest cannon, a ten pounder, resting his hands on the barrel as his fingers drummed the rounded iron. "Something is not right." He brought his hands to his chin, looked around the deck again as he rubbed his cheeks.

He looked up into the rigging of the main mast, onto the quiet platforms scores of feet above the deck. "Get Herrera and the crew on board quickly. Secure the cutter. Tell Herrera to set full sail and head out of this bay and into open water."

Jean-Michel started toward the hatch leading to the staterooms below. "I need to find Isabella."

Isabella stood at the threshold of her cabin, but her brain couldn't resist the clatter of boots clambering down from the gun deck above.

Louis and another tar in her cabin stopped driving nails into a board they had stretched across broken window panes. "What's wrong?"

"How long have the fighting tops been empty?"

Isabella watched the familiar bulk of Jean-Michel make its way toward her, batting hammocks from his path. "A watch should be posted."

Jean-Michel shook his head. "We need someone up in the tops, now." He turned toward the swinging canvas beds, eyes watching him from heads bobbing in the air.

Jean-Michel seemed to leap at the closest hammock. "You," he barked, tapping its head. "Grab the glass. Get to the top of the mainmast. Tell us what's entering the bay from the East." He looked at the next hammock, recognized a darkened bandage across his chest, and stepped to the next makeshift bed. "You! Follow James up the mast. I want double confirmation of friend or foe." The second tar swung out of his bed, scrambling after the first and up the ladder onto the main deck.

"Where is Herrera?"

"About ten minutes before the cutter can be back on deck."

Isabella stepped outside the cabin, searching the lower deck and shadows for more crew capable of standing or walking. "Sarhaan! Send a rigging crew up into the yards. We need to make way—now!"

The lean frame of the brig's helmsman lept toward the steps, his shape almost invisible in the deep gray untouched by lamps, his voice summoning tar after tar to life. More forms scrambled through the darkness, following him as his commands pulled them up into the light.

Jean-Michel looked over toward another form leaning over a dark clump against a wall. "How are the wounded, Doc?"

"We'll lose a couple more before the night's over, but the rest should live. The first twenty-four hours usually give us the answers we need. We've got twenty-five crew who won't be able to lift a pistol or blade of any sort any time soon."

Isabella mumbled some numbers before blurting, "That puts us at about one hundred and twenty able bodies."

Jean-Michel cursed.

Isabella started a short pace, hands on her hips. "Did you see a sail?"

"*Je ne suis pas certain*," Jean-Michel said, his raised eyebrows projecting his uncertainty. "We need to set sail. We cannot risk sitting in this bay any longer. With winds from the East, we are sitting ducks for Muñoz's frigate and two sloops."

"How many Spanish decided to stay?"

Jean-Michel lifted his hand, bending his fingers as he counted. "Seven total. Plus the Japanese."

Isabella gave Jean-Michel a sharp look at the reference to Omena. "What do we know of him?"

Jean-Michel's shrugged. "He knows enough English to take orders."

"Captain!"

Isabella stepped toward the hatch leading to the main deck. "Aye, Sarhaan!"

"You better get up here!"

Isabella turned toward the surgeon as Doc stepped into the light conjured up by a lantern. "I'll get my tools ready." His movements opening up his tool box were as fluid as his fingers guiding a knife through a patient's arteries.

Louis appeared as an apparition next to the doctor, preparing for the worst.

Doc didn't look up from his storage box as he started to check his tools. "Garçon, I will need your services again."

"Oui, Monsieur Doc."

"We need to clean off these tools," Doc's words were as bland as they were unnecessary as Louis set to his tasks. The boy, already matured by too many battles on land and sea, pulled a saw from the box and grabbed a linen rag laying at the end of the table. He inspected the blade and started to rub it.

Isabella watched Louis work, wondering for a moment how she could shield him from the carnage of another battle. She sighed. It was too late. That time was in Port-au-Prince. He had grown past any protection she could provide.

She turned back to Jean-Michel. "Now, we'll see what these Spaniard marines are really made of. Bring them up to the main deck."

Jean-Michel set toward the bow and the makeshift prison now housing seven Spaniards and a Japanese.

Isabella swung her feet onto the first steps of the ladder, skipping every other step to get to the deck with no seconds to lose.

Isabella didn't have to open her mouth before she saw Sarhaan's lean fingers pointing behind *La Marée Rouge*. "I not know how long," he said, his native West African Ibo tones accented even more by the stress, "but the lookouts spotted sails before their climb up the ratlines was finished."

Isabella looked up into the yards, watching the canvas fall as pirates unleashed them. She turned back to look across the deck and saw Herrera yanking a tar over the railing. "Señor Herrera—"

"Si, captain! Saw the men in the yards and tops. Figured we had company. Put our backs heavy into the oars to get us on deck as fast as we could."

"Smoothy—"

"Guns'r still primed. Ready to fire at your command, Cap'n."

Isabella felt the crusty old seaman sidle up to her.

"She's too far away to do much now, not even w' the long-guns."

"Agreed, Mr. Smoothy. But she's running with the evening wind and we are dead in the bay. We won't be fully underway for at least a half hour."

A bell clanged, drawing Isabella's gaze toward the ship's tiller as pirates spilled onto the deck from below. Sarhaan had already looped two ropes around the wooden arm to keep her course steady. *La Marée Rouge* creaked, its deck pitching forward with a gust pulling at its one hundred-twenty-foot tall oak main mast. Yards clutched at the canvas pulling the pirate vessel westward.

Isabella turned back toward the eastern horizon off their stern. The identifiable characteristics of a large sailing vessel were now visible:

stacked white sails on a dark speck of a hull pulling in front of the islands and reefs she had sailed through not three hours earlier.

"Muñoz?"

Isabella kept her focus on the boat but angled toward Gabrielle's voice. "I don't know for certain. But if I had to wager our next prize on the outcome, I would bet yes."

"What about the other boats? The sloops?"

"I can't be sure until I have the glass." Isabella turned toward the bow. "They should be nearby... if it's Muñoz."

Steady gusts now pressed against Isabella's cheeks as *La Marée Rouge* gained speed. She turned toward the hands manning the tops. "What see you?" she called.

"Just one vessel," a pirate called down. "On the eastern horizon. She's definitely cleared Cayo Largo. She's still a bit away, Cap'n. Seven, eight miles by my reckoning."

Isabella inspected the streaming sails. A weathered red pennant flapped from the main royal sail. "By the looks of the wind, we might have an hour if we wait for her. We'll have a bit more time if we get on." She turned toward Sarhaan. "Stay with the wind, Sarhaan. Let's take advantage of this late afternoon luck and run with it. Our way out is between the shoals to the right of Isla de la Juvenatud."

A cluster of loud grunts mingled with the mounting rush of bow waves as the brig picked up speed. "Cutter's not clear of the water yet!"

"Aye, Señor Herrera! We don't have time to wait. Grab a few more hands and land her on deck. Fasten her down, and we'll worry about stowing her once we're clear of any danger."

Isabella looked over the rail, stepping up on a cannon carriage for a clear view. "Calm waters. The islands and reefs do a nice job of keeping her protected. We should be up to seven or eight knots soon enough."

"Should we start clearing the decks and prepping the small arms?"

"Gabrielle," sounded a throaty response, "any gun on a pirate ship that is not loaded doesn't have any business being on a pirate ship."

Isabella breathed easy at the sound of Jean-Michel's voice and even allowed a smile. "I learned that soon enough while sailing with Jacob."

Jean-Michel leaned into the rail next to Isabella and looked toward the growing dot on the horizon. "Can't see much from here."

"How do you rate the prisoners?"

Jean-Michel lifted a hand to his beard, stroking it twice. "We will only know when they are tested. They had a chance to prove their loyalty to Spain and go ashore with the others. They chose to stay."

Gabrielle huffed. "Spies perhaps?"

"Always a risk," Isabella responded.

"Oui." Jean-Michel began to tap the railing. "I have worked pirate crews for fifteen years. From before Jacob. I've worked the decks of French Merchants. I can usually pick out the spies. They are the calm ones."

"Pirates are excited for a new life?" asked Gabrielle.

Jean-Michel laughed as Isabella allowed a knowing smile to cross her face. She turned to her friend. "They are the desperate ones, where the prospect for some wealth is preferred to the torture of serving a king."

"All people want freedom from serving a master."

Jean-Michel nodded. "*Trés vrai*, Gabrielle. At least I believe you speak a truth."

"We all fight for that truth. Whether we want to or not. We are the damned. The only alternative is death." Isabella's expression turned sober and hard. "On the sea, on this vessel, we can choose how we die. We can die with our blade in our hands or our fingers on the trigger of our guns. Or we can die by the plantation's whip or hanging from a governor's gallows."

Isabella lifted her palm to Gabrielle's cheek and stroked it with her thumb. "You made your choice when you helped me save Juan Carlos and Louis. We are bonded by our trials in *Le Coq Fantôme*. You and your father sacrificed much."

Gabrielle turned away at the mention of her father.

Isabella let her hand slip to Gabrielle's shoulder. "We will find out your father's fate. But now, we have Louis. We need to keep him alive. We need to give him a new life; a future."

A deep grunt swept across the deck followed by the sound of a thousand wooden casks tumbling over. They all turned to find that long-boat resting on its side, surrounding by more than a dozen tars brimming with sweat, some heaving for air, and others sitting to gather themselves. Herrera turned to the cluster of pirate commanders not more than thirty feet away. "Cutter on board!"

Jean-Michel stepped forward, a pace closer to the tars. "Send the men to water. We need them rested if cannon balls and musket shot come our way. Report as soon as you can, Señor Herrera."

Isabella took in a deep breath. "We're down to just one hundred and twenty able-bodied crew and thirty wounded below. We'll need some luck, or the grace of God, if that ship is Muñoz."

Jean-Michel scanned the deck as Smoothy made his way to each of the cannon and other deckhands readied their weapons. "This time we're ready for him. If he couldn't take us at night by ambush, he won't take us at dusk when we've been warned."

La Marée Rouge plowed forward as her sails filled. The creaks from the oak poles receded into a steady hum as the wind seemed to push the vessel's bow through the bay. Isabella nodded, recognizing the even plane of the deck was a sign Sarhaan's compass was true to the wind and course. If the winds shifted left or the right, she would feel the tilt of the deck as the wind pulled *La Marée Rouge*'s hull to one side. "Well done, Sarhaan. Stay the course."

"Sails! Off the bow!"

The call from the rigging high above brought all heads forward. Isabella darted toward the bowsprit, letting her hands glide off the railing as she scanned the horizon.

"Just to the starboard of the Isla de la Juventud," the voice instructed.

"How many?" Jean-Michel called up.

"Two vessels!" the tar barked after a few seconds. More seconds passed. "Lateen rigged."

The crew looked into the western horizon to try and spot the tell-tale triangular sails of the single-masted schooners.

Isabella shook her head.

Jean-Michel brought his fist down on the rail. "Muñoz!"

"How do you know?" Gabrielle asked. "They are so far away. I can barely see them."

"Two sloops and a larger vessel in the same area? My bet is on Muñoz." Jean-Michel shook his head. "He guessed right."

"I agree, Jean-Michel," Isabella said is a low steady voice. "Muñoz is clever. Somehow he calculated we would come into the bay. He sent the sloops south of the island to head us off while he followed us to take advantage of the prevailing winds and keep up his speed."

"Surely he knew we could take the sloops," Gabrielle said. "They are small. Even if they are filled with marines they won't get close enough to board us."

Isabella chuckled. "Muñoz knew I would come in here. He knew I would let these Spanish prisoners return by way of Havana. He also knew that either evading or engaging would slow us down, giving him time to catch up with us and bring his heavy guns to bear."

Jean-Michel nodded. "If we chase the sloops, they will evade us. That will still slow us down, perhaps enough for his frigate to catch up."

"Then let's not do either one."

Jean-Michel and Gabrielle both shot startled looks toward Isabella

"Let's not evade them. But let's not engage them. At least not directly. Let's let the sloops choose whether to engage us." Isabella looked up, inspecting the fill of the sails again. They were full, and she could feel the forward tilt of the deck as the wind continued to drive their bow against the water.

She pivoted to her quartermaster. "How long do we have before those sloops are in range of our bow chasers?"

Jean-Michel pondered the horizon and then the sloops. "If we hold this speed, twenty-five minutes. More if we lose what little wind we have."

"Steady course toward that opening to the west. Instruct Sarhaan to tie the tiller to that course. Even if he is shot, or killed by shot, that tiller needs to keep *La Marée Rouge* headed out of this bay and away from Muñoz."

6

The quiet reminded Juan Carlos of the afternoon of his twentieth birthday. The sun, high above, unleashed a deadly heat that had felled two of his men before a shot had been fired. Barely enough time had passed for his field promotion to be recorded, let alone sent, to the court, and he was about to lead a company of men across the craggy rocks of western Spain to ensure His Most Catholic Majesty King Charles III remained the undisputed ruler of all the Iberian Peninsula. God. King. Country. Like the day before, he would charge forward, leading his men to destroy the insurgency. Death in the fight for the Glory of God and King was a noble end, even at twenty years old.

Now, as the Caribbean sun uttered its last gasps, he was with another band of men. These were the godless men. These men had been rejected by his king, his country. And they were led by the most powerful woman he had ever met, more fierce than any insurgent he faced on the continent, more noble than anyone tied to the Royal Court, more passionate than any soldier in the Kingdom of God. And she was a black. A slave. Not even ranked among the free persons of color. And he was in love with her.

The wind held steady as *La Marée Rouge* cut through the ripples of the bay; a favor Mother Nature was unlikely to extend once the last remnants of the yellow sphere dipped behind the western mountains of Cuba. Unless they cleared Isla de la Juventud, they would be caught in a deadly nighttime fire fight with Muñoz's frigate and sloops.

Juan Carlos turned to gauge the distance of the frigate as it bore down from the east. Isabella's plan needed to work. If the wind died, or the sloops slowed their momentum, Muñoz would catch them and the odds of survival would be low. The question for Juan Carlos was how he would die, and whether he would give Muñoz the choice. He had seen the cages hung from tree limbs where criminals and runaway slaves were pinned, letting the birds pick at their flesh for days before the victims finally died. Or perhaps dismemberment would be preferred. A quick death—a shot to the head or run through by a blade—was too civil. Juan Carlos understood why these pirates, more than a third escaped slaves, would fight to the end.

Isabella would fight. She would fight to win. She would fight to save her crew. She had endured too much to be afraid of death. He had seen her endure the torture of El Morro's dungeons. And he had helped her escape. His first capital act against his king, but an act of love to God.

He would fight with these men and women. For Jean-Michel. For Louis. For Gabrielle. For Herrera, Smoothy, Sarhaan, and the others. But most of all for Isabella, the woman who made him see his humanity and the true meaning of the Kingdom.

Juan Carlos closed his eyes, letting the salt air fill his lungs, listening to the steady heave of *La Marée Rouge* as she ran for her life before the wind, feeling the anticipation of a crew once again facing life or annihilation. Another gust of the evening air and his back straightened, his left hand falling to a pistol tucked in his sash, the other brushing against a battle-worn saber.

The thud of the distant cannon could only be heard because of the silent anticipation of death on the decks of *La Marée Rouge*. The whistle of the ball was easy to note as its harsh sound gained power hurtling toward its target. The scream of the tar shredded by splinters as the ball crashed through the gunwale left no doubt his fate was at hand.

Smoothy's order came two minutes after the first Spanish cannon ball tore through *La Marée Rouge* and two pirates, a lucky shot that happened to find a weakened point of the gunwale. The pirate gunner's mate's carefully aimed shot from the nine pounder now provided a response. The battle was enjoined.

Smoothy had ordered two nine pounders mounted in the bow, one on each side. On a good piratical day, they were enough of a warning for a merchantman to haul up and let them board rather than suffer the fate of an angry, murderous crew. But these guns were more than a warning. In the right hands, in Smoothy's hands, they could take out an enemy before they had a chance to close in.

As soon as the shot cleared the cannon's muzzle, Smoothy jumped to the second gun. The two sloops were attacking from both sides. Muñoz had gambled that Isabella and Jean-Michel didn't have the crew to fully man batteries on both sides of their brig. Even though the sloops were smaller, a pirate crew ravaged by battle probably couldn't keep up the pace. Isabella would have to maneuver to bring more guns to bear on one gunboat while the other sloop sailed to the vulnerable side, slowing the brig. The frigate could then gain on them faster and overtake them. *La Marée Rouge* would be vulnerable, surrounded, and struggling with a crew weakened by fatigue as they tried to defend themselves from three sides.

But they hadn't counted on Isabella's boldness.

Smoothy's cannon barked, sending a ball toward the second gun boat.

The Spanish warships returned fire, but Isabella's choice to attack by running between the two sloops gave her attackers a slim line. The Spanish shots sailed down the sides of *La Marée Rouge*, splashing into the water one hundred yards off her stern.

"Haha," cackled Smoothy. "That'll teach you to put the young'uns on the small boats!"

Juan Carlos tried to hold back a laugh. The Spaniards fired too soon and would soon pay the price of impatience and inexperience. Isabella's crew held their fire, waiting for Smoothy's orders, knowing a shot fired at the wrong time could spell disaster. They were disciplined, more disciplined than the Spanish, a benefit of seasoning in battle and the battle-tested leadership of their captain.

Time seemed to speed up as the gunboats closed in on each other. Juan Carlos eyed the sails. He was getting better at reading the wind, its push on the hull, and the drag on the brig's ability to maneuver. Setting their sails square to the wind, he now understood, would give them speed and power, but limit their ability to steer away or toward targets. If the captains of the sloops did what Isabella hoped, *La Marée Rouge* would run between them, allowing cannon on both sides of her brig to fire shots at the Spanish gunboats as they passed, pecking at their rigging and hulls. Each of the cannon had one shot, and one shot only, to do their damage. They had to disable the sloops and the guns. Otherwise, *La Marée Rouge* would line up in the sights of the Spanish chasers as they raked their stern, sending shot through the deck from stern to bow. Muñoz would close in on them, joining the fight with his frigate, making the engagement a fight to the death—for the pirates.

How well did Muñoz really know, Isabella? Juan Carlos asked himself. Not well enough.

Isabella surveyed the length of the deck just paces from Sarhaan and the two additional men assigned to keep their vessel's course steady. They wrapped themselves around the tiller, committed to the westward course, confident the winds would take them through the shoals and out of the bay. Two ropes tethered to the rudder's wooden arm served as back-up in the event one, two, or all three men were shot away from their task.

Another cannon ball whistled overhead, its arc descending toward Isabella. She fell to her knees as the nine-pound ball of iron cleared the stern railing and dropped into the sea. Her eyes darted to the men at the helm. They remained steady against the tiller, no sign of adjustment or movement.

A thump and cloud of smoke rose from one of the front chasers and disappeared at midships. A whoop from Smoothy and his gun crew signaled success, although how much was invisible to Isabella. Smoothy scampered to the other gun, loaded and ready for the gun master's expert aim.

"Bring her a point to port," Jean-Michel said from a perch in the main sail rigging. "Make them think we've targeted one of their sloops."

The tiller shifted, and the brig angled toward the Spanish gunboat on the left. Just as the course adjustment moved the bow, another shot rushed from one of the gunboats, finding its mark by fraying the edge of the main sail's canvas.

Isabella held her breath, glancing up to Jean-Michel.

"We'll be okay with those, captain."

Isabella didn't respond, knowing two more shots in that sail would take several knots off their speed, perhaps just enough to give Muñoz the advantage he needed.

"Gunboat on the port is coming about!" Jean-Michel yelled.

Isabella jumped up on the gunwale, grasping at a rope to steady her view.

Juan Carlos peered over the gunwale just below her. "Muy loco!"

Isabella looked over to Jean-Michel as he focused on the sudden change of course.

"Look smart, men! The dagos' are bringing their other guns to bear."

Idiots! Isabella swore under her breath.

"Guns Eleven and Twelve!" Jean-Michel shouted. "Step over to help Guns Four and Five. Turn that shot around quick. *Vite, vite!* We have two of those Spaniards on our starboard side rather than one."

Isabella shook her head. "Send the sharpshooters to the bow. The Spaniards will be close enough to make our muskets count."

The Spanish boat captains are clever, she said to herself. There were only so many muskets they could bring to bear from the bow. Their aim would be unsteady as they shot from on top of the rounded barrels of the chasers.

Juan Carlos looked up to Isabella. "Stack the guns!"

Isabella caught her breath, her uncertainty transparent in her hesitation.

"Aye, brilliant!" Jean-Michel responded. "Herrera! Line the men up so the best shots are shooting from the bow. Then stack the men two deep behind each shooter. Pass the spent guns back to be reloaded and brought back to the bow. Don't give the dagos time to blink!"

Herrera ran up the deck, tapping the shoulders of tars who waited with their heads down and guns low to bring them forward.

"Captain Santa Ana," Jean-Michel called. "Do you want to join the men at the bow?"

Juan Carlos raised a hand to acknowledge Jean-Michel and sprinted toward the front of the brig.

Isabella nodded a small smile toward Jean-Michel. He lifted a hand in a salute to Isabella.

"We cannot have a trained army officer laying around a pirate ship with nothing to do," he said. "Idle hands are the devil's work!"

Another boom and smoke on the starboard side signaled the discharge from the second cannon aimed at one of the attacking sloops.

The first gunboat finished its turn, on course to cross the bow of *La Marée Rouge*. The completed turn triggered another boom and puff of smoke from one of its cannon. A ball crashed through the pirate vessel's gunwale, barely missing three of its crew as the spent ball deflected off the main mast to rest on deck. Another boom and the second gun from the sloop jettisoned another round of iron, this time glancing off the leeward gunwale, shattering more wood, but failing to damage armament or people.

Another deep blast came from the bow of the front of *La Marée Rouge* as Smoothy sent another ball from the chaser into the tacking sloop. The ball hit its mark, its triangular sail fluttering as the ball forced the boom into an odd-shaped angle. Without the canvas full and held fast, the boat slowed to a groggy pace.

"She's not going to make it across our bow," Isabella yelled. She turned to Sarhaan at the tiller: "We're going to ram the gunboat. Hold fast."

The cracks of muskets began as pirates started pouring shot into the sailors and marines in the gunboat. *La Marée Rouge* seemed to pick-up speed, charging forward as the sloop sputtered, unable to regain its momentum.

Isabella looked behind her. The frigate was still out of range for its chasers. But Muñoz's ship had gained on them. "Another point to port" she yelled to Sarhaan.

"The shoals," Jean-Michel called from across the deck. "We'll have to turn to regain the wind and sail between those reefs or go aground!"

"We can't afford to lose speed by ramming that gunboat," Isabella retorted. "Our sharpshooters can still send plenty of lead onto their deck if they clear us to the starboard."

Isabella looked forward. The sloop's bow had crossed theirs. Another few seconds and their mast will have crossed fully over to the starboard.

"Arghh!" Isabella yelled. "We're going to cut them on their aft deck!"

She felt the *La Marée Rouge* nudge to the left, providing a few more precious feet for the sloop.

"Not enough!" Isabella yelled. "Captain Santa Ana, keep those long guns raking the sloop's deck. Smoothy! Keep those cannon firing."

"Guns Thirteen, Fourteen, Fifteen, and Sixteen, shore up the crews on the starboard side. Keep those guns on that other sloop."

The tars stood to shift their positions just as *La Marée Rouge* shuddered with the groan and tear of crushing wood. The brig slowed, sending most of the men rolling to the deck as the crew remaining at the guns clutched at anything to hold their balance.

Isabella cursed. "Move on, men, move on!"

The tars scampered to their feet.

Two booms from the second sloop sent a ball crashing into the gunwale, driving shards of wood into the chest and arms of two pirates. The second ball sailed over the railing and hit the back of a carriage on the far side of the deck, splitting the wood and releasing the full wait of the iron cannon to crash onto the deck, its barrel pointed stupidly toward the sky.

Isabella jumped from the railing and ran toward the bow. "Keep those cannon firing at that boat! We're broad side to her, so make every shot count!"

Isabella felt the aft deck of *La Marée Rouge* heave upward, angling the bow closer to the water, as the force of the collision worked against the brig's forward momentum. The masts creaked from the wind pushing against sails that seemed unrepentant in their efforts to keep the brig crawling forward through the water. The sloop caught the brig's hull as the stern of *La Marée Rouge* began to swing the boat to the side, a tack that would pull them straight onto the Cuban beaches and away from their passage to safety.

Both vessels locked together, *La Marée Rouge* pushing forward, while pulling the Spanish gunboat with it.

Yells directed Isabella's eyes to a flurry of arms, legs, and bodies struggling near the cannon lining the starboard deck. The flashes of white breeches, black leather shoes, and blue waist coats stunned her for a moment—how did Spanish marines get on deck? The crack and flash of flint sent a pirate to the deck, grasping at his shoulder, a blade clattering to the deck. A blue and white clad body fell to the deck, a thick maroon streak crossing his torso from his neck to his waist.

"Herrera!" Isabella yelled, calling his attention to the boarding attack at midship.

Isabella pulled her sword and advanced into the melee. Her gun crews used their stanchions and rams to ward off cuts from sabers and daggers. Another pop from a pistol sent another pirate to the deck. A Spanish marine crested the railing, a pistol and dagger in his hand. Before he had time to jump onto deck, Isabella's blade cut into the back of his calf, sending him reeling over the railing. Another marine clambered into battle, but Isabella threw an elbow into the side of his face and pushed her blade into his throat as he tried to pull himself onto the deck.

A sudden weight pulled at her shoulder, forcing her to stumble backward until she fell. A marine lifted a pistol to her head as a shadow seemed to lift him from the deck, forcing the pistol to discharge into the air, as the body spun from her sight. Isabella scrambled to her feet, but the attacking marine had disappeared. Dozens of pirates now threw themselves into the fray. The Spanish marines fell back, leaving a half dozen of their comrades lifeless on the deck of the pirate ship.

Herrera and Juan Carlos kept the muskets firing from the bow, a steady supply of newly loaded guns enabling each sharpshooter to send a round into the Spanish sailors and marines on the disabled sloop's deck every fifteen seconds. The crash had thrown equipment and men into an upended jigsaw puzzle. Their officers yelled orders in vain attempts to rally the troops. Just as a Spaniard raised his gun to fire, a hail of bullets from the pirates withered his body. Dozens of men littered the deck of the Spanish sloop, the planks taking on the character of a morgue.

La Marée Rouge groaned against the ensnared sloop, pushing its bow like the hand of a clock. The brig's bowsprit became snarled, mixed up with the Spanish gunboat's main sail, unable to free itself.

Isabella scanned the deck for Smoothy. She spotted him directing his crews to train their cannon on the second vessel, which was about to fire another round into the brig.

"Train that starboard chaser on the sloop's mast," Isabella yelled. She noticed a tar bringing up chain shot to load into the gun. "Our target isn't the crew. Load the cannon with ball. Target the base of the mast."

A second pirate brought the ball to the cannon. A third hand rammed it down the barrel to seat it in the charge at the base.

The deck shuddered as the cannon boomed, sending its iron sphere into a cloud of gray smoke and the acrid smell of burnt powder into the faces and lungs of the pirate crew. The crew swabbed the barrel and removed the burned paper from the charge. They swabbed it again, dowsing any stray sparks hiding in the barrel. Another pirate loaded a charge, while another rammed it down to the base, followed by another ball. The gun captain lit the charge, and another shot crashed into the deck of their target. Isabella saw the mast on the Spanish sloop shudder, and she knew her crew had hit their mark.

The brig pushed forward through the web of friendly and attacking canvas, wrenching the Spaniard's sail around its mast. The pole resisted, then snapped backward, leaving empty sky over the gunboat as the falling rigging tethered the sloop in place with the weight of a waterlogged sail. The sloop's bow ground into the hull of *La Marée Rouge*, forcing it to pivot, yielding to the surging pirate ship.

"Keep firing!" Juan Carlos ordered. "Don't let them lift their heads. If anything moves, shoot it!"

Three more blasts created a gray mist over the deck of *La Marée Rouge*, obscuring the effects of their marksmanship.

Isabella raced down the deck, lifting her head to see how much ground Muñoz had gained. Two small puffs of cotton from the front of the frigate sent Isabella's head below the railing. With no whistle in the air to alert her to incoming shot, she figured the shot must have fallen short. She turned to look at their position. The crash had more than compensated for her two-point turn to the port. They were now tacking northwest.

"Bring her back onto course," she ordered.

The sounds of cannon fire filled the air around her. She leaped toward the starboard railing.

Isabella looked down on the hell her pirates had created. The sloop listed badly; the fallen mast was bringing the boat to the point of capsizing from the weight of its useless sail. The few marines and sailors still able staggered to different stations and attended to the wounded. Isabella closed her eyes, trying to blot away the carnage that likely meant half of the Spanish crew would never see land again.

"She's not going anywhere soon," Jean-Michel said.

The second sloop hauled up, keeping its distance, but still training its guns on *La Marée Rouge*.

"The boat's got just one working cannon," he said. "Smoothy did quick work on their guns and rigging. She can't run with us now."

Isabella nodded. "They may be done, but Muñoz isn't through with us."

Jean-Michel, secure above the gun deck in the rigging, turned toward the last of their pursuers. "We might be able to outrun him."

Isabella's feet seemed to move out from underneath her as *La Marée Rouge* jerked backward, then heaved forward again.

Jean-Michel cursed. "Bring her back to port two points!"

The ship jerked again, this time turning slightly.

Isabella swore and looked into the sea. Reefs and coral looked like they were just about to crest the surface of the water, an illusion, she hoped, created by the bay's clarity and the magnifying effects of the water. They had drifted too far toward the reef.

"Herrera," she yelled. "Get two men in the bow. Start taking measures to check our depth."

"They must still be a good fifteen feet below us," Jean-Michel surmised. "We must be scrapping the tops of some coral with our keel."

Isabella peered into the sea, checked the sails and the angle of the deck. "We need more speed. But if we hit more of those ridges, we won't have much of a keel left. Muñoz won't have to shoot us. We'll drown!"

She looked back toward the frigate. It was gaining, taking full advantage of its ability to run with the wind. She turned to the sky. Another hour and the night would cloak their escape.

A thud announced a cannon ball tipping over the aft railing.

"He's wasting a lot of shot," Jean-Michel chuckled.

"The next ones won't be so kind unless we get off these reefs and pick up speed."

The soundings confirmed Jean-Michel's suspicions. Sixteen feet, fifteen feet, fourteen feet, fifteen feet, thirteen feet. The depths were uneven, but they were no longer heading into the shallows. A few more soundings, and they seemed to be clear. The wind held, and a few adjustments to the sails captured another knot of speed.

Jean-Michel descended from the rigging, taking a spot next to Isabella as they watched the frigate continue its pursuit. The lack of puffs of smoke was a strong sign *La Marée Rouge* was at least holding its distance.

"Looks like we bought a few minutes to take stock and tend to our wounds," Isabella said.

"Oui. I saw a couple of men go down, but I don't know how serious their wounds are."

"I'll check with Doc," Isabella said, her tone weary.

"Did you see the Japanese?"

Isabella turned to Jean-Michel, her eyes unfocused.

"I've never seen fighting like it," Jean-Michel said. "When the Spaniards boarded, they just seemed to disappear when he faced them. I didn't see him fire a weapon, but they just fell over the side."

Isabella shook her head.

Jean-Michel's confusion seemed real. "I don't understand it. It's almost like he used magic."

Isabella smiled. "Battles are intense. Our mind plays tricks on us."

Isabella closed her eyes and took in a breath. Madame Rêve-Cœur had foretold her future high in the mountains of Saint Domingue. What magic did she use when she conjured up those visions? Isabella's memories melded into the carnage of D'Poussant's failed revolt on the streets in Port-au-Prince. Did she really see the priestess rise above the table in a trance? How did she know her mother had given her the African name Binta? How did Rêve-Cœur know her mother's prophecy? Was that the power of voodoo magic? Do the Japanese use voodoo?

"I am just telling you what I saw," Jean-Michel insisted.

"Well, we'll just have to ask him about that magic."

7

Isabella heart fell with each step into the abyss, the stench from wounded flesh washing over her senses and into a dull churn in her stomach for the second time in two days. She lifted her hand, clutched the bandana securing her hair, pulled it over her nose, and ducked into the void. The shadows of bodies and their battle-worn accessories were barely visible, the fading light of the evening on deck was gone once she was submerged below the gun deck.

Isabella slapped her hand against a beam. "Strikes for those lanterns!" The cloth wrapping her face did little to squelch the bark of her command. "Make these minutes smart. The dagos are off the stern, still in pursuit!"

Yellow flickers grew into bobbing bulbs as flames chased away the black. Isabella picked up her pace in the new-found light and made her way to the surgeon's station. Louis was already putting knives, clamps, and saws into Doc's tool chest. The table was clear, if not quite rubbed clean. The wounded had vacated the surgeon's work area. The corner of Isabella's eye caught two large motionless hulks against the wall leading to Jean-Michel's stateroom.

"Lucked out this time," Doc said, wiping his hands with a rag before dipping his nose in his sleeve to wipe his brow. "Two dead. Seven wounded. Four have a better than average chance of seeing land again."

Isabella looked at the table, letting her fingertips fall to its surface.

"The fight was not so terrible, Ms. Isabella," came a familiar, small voice below the table.

She looked down at the boy, his hands now visible grasping the table as he lifted himself upright. "Aye, Louis. We lost fewer men. But their loss still weighs heavily."

Isabella took stock of the room, mentally scoring the tars filling out the slings and hammocks. She inhaled the scent of damp cotton and drying blood. Her nose felt the trigger that took her back to a cold cell, deep in San Juan's El Morro fortress almost two years earlier. Her muscles tightened as she remembered the betrayal, and the empty accusations that justified the lashes against her back. Jean-Michel would never have betrayed her. Her heart knew it, but she had allowed the anguish of her capture to beat down the truth. Isabella reached to the back of her neck, letting her fingers touch the leathered ridges that lined her shoulders and back; scars that bore testimony to her childhood under the whip of an overseer and the cruelty of Rodriguez and his henchmen.

She imagined how her body looked as she was laid on the cold stone floor, her Creole blood dripping from the gashes opened by the leather whip. Her senses registered the screams from her body as if she were reliving the time a vanquished sailor sought his revenge on her back in El Morro. Crimson streaks of open flesh raced up from her waist and across her shoulders, the pain searing up through her neck and into her skull as each lash pushed her further against the dungeon's wall. She felt as if the pain would blast the scalp from her head as her skull exploded. Instead, she passed out.

Doc and the others in the room faded as blood surged through Isabella's veins. She straightened her chest and shoulders with a deep drag of air into her lungs. The sounds of the room evaporated, following the shadows of her crew, as her eyes rolled into the back of her head and then shut. Isabella fell forward, her torso landing on the table, her face turned at a slight angle to the side, her arms outstretched and her palms up. Isabella tried to lift herself, but to no effect; her body would not respond. It didn't matter how loud she seemed to scream her thoughts. The damp warmth of the officers' table top leached into her cheeks.

Isabella's throat tightened, staunching any human sounds from leaving her mouth. Her eyes opened to stare into a fog. Everything around her was obscure, hidden. Her arms and legs lightened, as if they had disappeared, disembodied. Her head began a slow spin, making the difference between up and down little more than a desperate guess. She struggled to take in air, the weight of her body against the table keeping her lungs from expanding.

"Mademoiselle! Mademoiselle!"

Louis's muffled, distant calls seemed to travel hours to find their way into her brain, only to be blocked by an invisible wall. Her body lightened. She felt it lift above the pine tabletop, rising inches, maybe a foot or more. She no longer needed hands, arms, legs, or feet. She felt her shoulders pull up, bringing her head up off the table to her body, her face lifting toward the ceiling. Fresh air filled her lungs.

She gasped for air, letting her chest become full as her shoulders and arms lay limp, her feet dangling without purpose.

Binta, a voice hissed in her ear. *You are With God. Binta. The One! They will follow The One, for you are With God.*

Isabella felt the air clutch at her throat as she gasped for more. She was so light, her body not even feeling the weight of a corpse.

Binta, she repeated to herself. *I am With God.* Where do I go?

Search for the truth; Voyage vers la vérité.

How do I travel to the Truth?

Vous savez la vérité!

How can I know the Truth?

Vous savez la vérité.

How will I know the Truth? Isabella felt her chest tighten, a deep well of tears rushing into her head, swirling behind her eyes, and then wrapping around her in blues and greens. "Madame Rêve-Cœur, guide me. Guide me! *Guide moi!*"

Vous savez la vérité. Voyage vers la vérité.

I need your help! *J'ai besoin de votre aide!*

Isabella gasped as her body regained its lost weight and collapsed, dropping back to the surgeon's table.

"Mademoiselle!"

Isabella's eyes opened with a start, triggered by a deep heave of her lungs. She could feel every inch of her body and where each point touched the hard surface of a plane as she lay staring at the beams above her.

"Isabella," a soft voice whispered as a hand touched her forehead.

"Mi amor." Isabella lifted her hand to cover the hand on her head. She used a gentle tug to pull his palm to her lips. "Mi amor."

Her lips touched the cup of his palm, and she remembered the tender feel of hands cleaning her wounds at death's door in El Morro. She closed her eyes, trying to remember whose hands, whose voices, had guided the healing of her body. She brought the hand to her chest, pulling it until it covered her heart. "It was you."

Juan Carlos cocked his head, opening his mouth but failing to utter any words.

Isabella smiled. "I am not crazy."

Juan Carlos nodded. "You didn't see what we just saw."

Isabella sighed. "I heard her voice."

Juan Carlos raised his eyebrows as he pulled a damp cloth from a bucket next to her cot.

"Madame Rêve-Cœur," she prodded.

"Ahhh, you said her name." Juan Carlos put the wet rag on Isabella's forehead. "Who is Madame Rêve-Cœur?"

Isabella chuckled. "Didn't Jean-Michel tell you?"

"He wasn't here when you went into your... umm... spell."

"I am not sure what I just went through, but I am feeling better."

"*Bueno*," Juan Carlos nodded. "Doc was very worried about you. So, was Louis."

He looked into Isabella's eyes. "They were not the only ones worried. *Mí también.*" He leaned down, and their lips touched.

A thin smile crossed her face. "I am fine."

"I am sure the heat of battle finally got to you. We had more than two dozen men collapse once we were clear of Muñoz 's guns. Fear can keep even the toughest fighters going for just so long."

Isabella felt her muscles tense. "I was fine after the battle."

64

"Isabella," Juan Carlos said, his tone leveled to convey a sternness more suited to a commander. "Heat sickness is expected. *La Marée Rouge* has barely had time to rest. Everyone is exhausted."

Isabella propped herself up on her elbows. She turned her head to see the wash basin against the wall and the makeshift boards covering an opening in her room. She was in her cabin.

"I am fine," she said, pulling a leg up and beginning a swing toward the edge of the bed. Juan Carlos brought his hand down to her knee and pushed it back as if swatting a mosquito in slow motion.

"Rest," he ordered. "*La Marée Rouge* is keeping its distance from Muñoz's frigate. In fact, we are gaining distance. Muñoz cannot keep up. We will lose sight of him by morning even if he guesses we are tacking north after rounding the western edge of Cuba."

Isabella lifted her hand to Juan Carlos's chest, and cupped his jaw with her palm. "Juan Carlos, mi amor, listen to me. I am fine. Madame Rêve-Cœur spoke to me."

Juan Carlos curled his eyebrow and shook his head. "The only people around that surgeon's table were Doc, Louis, me, and two deck hands. No other women, not even Gabrielle, was near."

Isabella shook her head. "Madame Rêve-Cœur is a priestess. She lives in the mountains above Port-au-Prince."

Juan Carlos's eyes widened. "Isabella! I know sailors are superstitious, but a priestess? Since the Church does not allow women to preach, you must mean a voodoo priestess. Do not listen to pagan mystics."

Isabella sent a piercing look into Juan Carlos's eyes, triggering a quick blink. "Catholics don't listen to mystics?"

"Of course not!"

"You have never known a priest or brother to confess a vision?"

Juan Carlos turned his eyes toward a bucket resting near the bed. He bent over the rim and started to soak and then wring out water from the cloth. "Their visions are different."

Isabella laughed. "Where did Moses get the commandments?"

"The prophets spoke directly with God."

"What prophets? Christ Jesus? Didn't he speak with God? Along with how many others? Did anyone see them speak to God?"

"Not all prophets spoke with the true God."

"How do you determine which ones are real and which ones are not?"

Juan Carlos paused. "Our priests and bishops..., the Church scholars..., they have argued and discussed the Truth of the Holy Bible for ages. The Bible is the word of God."

Isabella's body seemed to revive with a renewed sparkle in her eyes.

Juan Carlos turned back to look at Isabella. "It's our faith."

"Si mi amor. And I have my faith, too. My faith is very close to yours. But my life, my history, is also part of my faith."

Juan Carlos reached down to hold both Isabella's hands. "Get some rest. We can talk about this later."

Isabella cast a smirk toward Juan Carlos. "Do you know what Madame Rêve-Cœur said to me?"

Juan Carlos began to open his mouth, as if to say something, but stayed silent. "You were asking her for guidance to somewhere when you were in your... spell."

Isabella paused, as if reminded of an event long ago. "Madame Rêve-Cœur called me by the name my mother gave me. My African name. Binta." She paused as if to emphasize the name. "The name means With God."

She waited another moment as Juan Carlos's face lost its visible expression. He turned his eyes down to look at his hands as they clasped together. He rubbed his laced fingers against his lips, deep in thought. Isabella turned to lift her hand to his face, letting the light touch of her thumb rub his cheek.

"My mother named me Binta when I was born. The plantation overseer gave me the name Isabella. My mother told me I was to fulfill a prophecy, and Madame Rêve-Cœur knew that prophecy. That's what I discovered in the mountains of Saint Domingue. D'Poussant's treachery in *Le Coq Fantôme*, Gabrielle's family home and business, revealed the truth behind the prophecy, but not the direction I should take."

Juan Carlos drew in a deep breath. He shook his head. "Isabella, you were a slave. You now captain a pirate ship—a very successful one I might add. But you were born a slave, not a free man. You stumbled into this captaincy. What prophecy could you possibly fulfill?"

Isabella let her hand drop to the side of the bed. "You doubt my purpose?"

"Of course not! But leading a pirate ship is not the same as a revolution."

Isabella pushed her legs across the bed, forcing Juan Carlos to stand before being knocked onto the floor as she pulled herself erect. "My captaincy on *La Marée Rouge* is not an accident, or a privilege of wealth or the admiralty. This crew binds itself to Articles. They have elected me captain at every opportunity since we retook her from the mutinous Stiles off Privateer Pointe. No one is forced to stay on this ship. I lead because my crew has faith in me!"

"I... I... Isabella, I know, that's not what I meant. *¡Eso no es lo que quise decir!*"

She steeled her look. "My reputation around these islands, in this sea, ensures every merchant ship under the flag of Spain, France, or Britain posts a watch to increase the odds they will make their next port of call. My captaincy has put a price of more than two-hundred pounds on my head. Rodriguez has loosed an entire squadron into the Caribbean for the sole purpose of capturing me!"

"Rodriguez is a madman."

"Rodriguez runs the colonial captaincy of the West Indies for His Most Catholic Royal Majesty King Charles III of Spain. He has the authority to use whatever means and resources are necessary to capture me. I am his biggest prize, his ticket back to the halls of his King. Your King's authority rises and falls with my success or failure."

"You may have forgotten that Charles is no longer my King. I gave up any claim to his Kingdom, my family, on the streets of Port-au-Prince." Juan Carlos looked into Isabella's eyes. "You are not God."

Isabella cocked her head. "I don't have to be God. I just have to free my people. Or die trying."

Juan Carlos lifted himself from the bed and stepped toward the shattered remains of the stern windows. "How are you going to do that? By raiding one merchant ship at a time?"

Isabella leaned back on her boots, crossing her arms. "I will use Spain's own wealth to destroy her power."

"By seizing the cargo of merchant ships?"

Isabella pivoted toward Juan Carlos, her eyes steady and clear. She nodded as if coming to a final, determined, resolution. "We will use the treasure we seize to give slaves and freed men, *gens de couleur,* what they need to break those chains."

Juan Carlos lifted his hands. "Seizing merchant ships barely satisfies the lust of your crew. How can it fund a revolution?"

Isabella's face calmed. "It can't. Not by itself. I thought it would when I started on this journey with Jacob. But the last two years have shown me it's not enough. My fleet will never be big enough."

She walked toward the boarded-up windows of her cabin, peering out through a slit between two wooden planks. "Perhaps the Prophecy is not about Hispaniola or even this sea. Perhaps it's something much bigger than islands and an ocean."

She turned toward Juan Carlos, and stepped over to him. She picked up his hands as she peered into his eyes. "*La Maree Rouge*... this pirating life... cannot give me the base I need for a real revolution. We are a floating business with shadow customers that fade and take shape with the winds and seasons. The treasure serves the purpose of its buyers in port or an exchange house. They all support the plantations, the kings, and princes. I need to build wealth. I need to build it with stealth and deliberation, somewhere no one has heard about the Pirate of Panther Bay. Somewhere my fortune can save thousands, or topple princes. But not here, not among these islands. Establishing a business in the West Indies simply provides a steady target for Rodriguez to send Muñoz and others to shoot." A smile broadened across her face. "We have to find a new world with a new beginning. We have to sail to New Orleans."

8

"Have you seen the Japanese?"

Doc nodded his head as he threw darkened rags in a pail and tossed others into the water. "I am glad to see you up, Captain Isabella. But, perhaps you should rest more."

Doc shifted his head, hoping for a better view into Isabella's cabin. Juan Carlos was standing by the aft window, looking out over the stern into the dark night sky.

Louis stepped over to Isabella from the shadows. He pointed toward the bow, lifting his jaw as if it alone indicated Omena's location.

Isabella looked into the sea of slung hammocks, bodies filling out their bulk as her crew grasped for a few hours of sleep. She disguised a deep sigh. Some of those makeshift beds included tars that would never see land again. She looked over at the two lifeless bodies lodged against the stateroom wall, still holding ghostly vigil over Doc's work station.

She lifted her hand to the boy's shoulder, letting her fingers cup his neck and pull him closer. She leaned over, letting her lips touch the top of his head. "I am sorry, Louis."

Louis looked up at her, his eyes and face void of any expression.

She smiled. "I know you don't understand all of it." Her smile faded. "Alas, you will understand sooner than anyone your age should. I will get you out of this life."

"Who will take care of me?"

A tear welled up in Isabella's eye. She pulled him into a firm hug. "You have a ship's crew to take care of you. I will not abandon you."

She heard a sniff from Louis's buried face. "*Je manque ma mère,*" he said, snaking his arms around her waist. "I miss my mother so much."

Isabella crouched on her knees so she could look into his eyes. "I will not abandon you." Louis diverted his gaze to the planks on the floor still marked by spilled blood. "*Je ne t'abandonnerai pas.* Nor will Jean-Michel. Or Juan Carlos."

Louis' sniffs were unable to hold back his tears. "Mademoiselle Gabrielle?"

"We will not abandon you." Isabella lifted her hands to his face, using her fingers to wipe away his tears. She then turned her fingers toward her face and spread them under her eyes as if painting her cheeks with them. She felt the lines made by the tears dry. "See? You are part of me now. You can never leave me, and I can never leave you, because you are part of my blood and flesh."

Louis collapsed into Isabella's arms and held tight.

"Okay," she said after a few minutes, kissing the top of Louis's head. She straightened herself up. "You need to help Doc. He is doing very important work, and I can see he depends on you to help our sailors get better."

As she turned toward the bow, she caught a glimpse of Doc looking at her as if saying, "Don't make promises you can't keep." Isabella redirected her eyes forward. *I will keep this promise*, she told herself.

Isabella walked to the ladder leading up to the gun deck. She needed to check the watch. She needed to check in with Smoothy and Herrera. She needed to check their course with Jean-Michel. Most of all, she longed for Gabrielle.

She wondered if her tears would dry before she reached the gun deck, but she refused to wipe them away.

"I will not abandon him. He cannot be abandoned again."

9

Juan Carlos sprung from the lower deck, his boots landing with a loud clack as the sun's rays transformed the last remnants of night into the bright tan of pine planks.

Jean-Michel let loose a howl that drew curious looks from deck hands tending to ropes, fallen rigging, and misaligned cannon. Three sailors paused to identify the source of the clatter, taking advantage of the unusual sound to suspend efforts to scrub the maroon-stained sawdust from the deck.

The quartermaster grabbed a rope and let his weight swing as he leaned toward Juan Carlos. "Señor Santa Ana! I think you have just come from a very pleasant conversation with the captain of *La Marée Rouge.*"

"She is impossible!"

"Of course she is! How else could she get two-hundred, water-logged rogues to follow her into certain death in front of guns sited by the Devil himself?"

Juan Carlos shook his head and began pacing the quarter deck. "How can she think she can bring down King Charles!"

Jean-Michel shifted his weight so he leaned against the gunwale, resting a foot on the carriage of an eighteen-pound cannon and draping one arm over the muzzle. "I don't think she does."

"She thinks she can rescue her entire race!"

"Well, that's a different matter. That goal seems much more focused."

Juan Carlos shot a glare toward the Frenchman who was now stroking a beard that he was sure hid an amused smile. "Plantations keep the sugar and tobacco flowing to the continent. King Charles knows slaves make that possible."

Jean-Michel raised his eyebrows as he gave the iron cannon a strong pat. "The American colonists say the same about cotton and tobacco."

Juan Carlos lifted his head and hands in vindication. "*Gracias!*"

"That does not make it right, mon amie."

"She is one person." Juan Carlos swept the deck with his hand. "With a handful of rogues and criminals."

"Oui, but she is not one person. Thirty-five of these rogues and criminals—at least those that are left and able-bodied—are Africans or Creole."

"They sail for money, for greed."

Jean-Michel laughed. "King Charles does not hold his colonies close for greed?"

"He serves his people. His power comes from God himself."

"Is that what His Holiness Pope Pius VI believes?"

"The power of God reunited Spain and purged Iberia of the Moors."

Jean-Michel pushed himself up from the cannon and cast a serious look toward the Spanish army captain. "The Jesuits protected the natives in these lands from slavery, but the Catholic Church purged them as heretics."

"A mistake, I agree." Juan Carlos looked out over the sea as the *La Marée Rouge* rolled over gentle waves, carving a course north. "The Holy See is rumored to be ready to restore the Jesuit order."

Skepticism softened Jean-Michel's expression. "Even the Jesuits didn't defend the Africans when they came to this world in chains."

Juan Carlos looked at the weathered, bearded face of the pirate. "I am surprised by your compassion, Jean-Michel. Compassion does not serve a pirate well."

The Frenchman leaned away from the gunwale and stepped over to Juan-Carlos. "I have learned that life is more than booty and conquest."

Juan Carlos looked past him and into the sea. "I am learning that life is more than service to King and country."

"A lifetime of commitment and loyalty is difficult to cast off."

Juan Carlos sighed, turned toward Jean-Michel and clapped his shoulder. "So I am finding out, mi amigo."

Jean-Michel smiled. "Isabella is not a normal pirate."

Juan Carlos chuckled, shaking his head as he gripped the railing. His eyes fell into froth of *La Marée Rouge*'s bow waves as it chased azure blue water out to the horizon.

"She has been called," Jean-Michel said.

Juan Carlos nodded. He lifted his hand to his shoulder, the ache tempered by the memory of Isabella's gentle but direct probing as she directed him to safety when revolutionary fires consumed Port-au-Prince. He lay in the bow of a tender, he recalled, as it pulled away from a wharf under fire from D'Poussant's doomed legion of *gens de couleur*. She and her pirate crew were taking him to safety, to be mended by a surgeon, on this pirate ship. He remembered the pops of the muskets as she leaned down to his ears to confess. She understood the prophecy, she had whispered to him. "She has been called to New Orleans?"

"Ha!" Jean-Michel lifted his hand to clap Juan Carlos's shoulder. "Joan D'Arc."

Juan Carlos cast a sideways glance toward the quartermaster.

"The Maid of Orleans," Jean-Michel said. "She ended the siege of Orleans after just nine days, leading the way to France's victory over the English."

"Wasn't she burned at the stake?"

"By the English at nineteen years old. Isabella has survived revolution, mutiny, betrayal, and torture at the hands of slavers, pirates, and your precious former viceroy and now Captain-General in Puerto Rico. She has already outlived a martyr. My bet is still on Isabella."

Juan Carlos sighed. "I hope your bet is more than a gamble." He turned his eyes back to the horizon. "New Orleans. New Spain. Why do I think we are sailing to our own funerals?"

"*C'est vrai.* Spain controls New Orleans, but with its army not its soul. The port is a gateway to the interior of the Americas, but the city is a backwater, a swamp. Spain cannot even bribe its own citizens to colonize that place. The Duke of Orleans needed the dubious activities of its finance minister to lure Germans into the bayous but to no avail!

Spain has given up on taming New Orleans as long as they ship their furs to Europe. The king's attention is now focused on reclaiming the lost colony of La Florida and helping the Americans against the British. He has little time for pirates along the American coasts. They are an annoyance, but not a real threat, unlike our illustrious captain who is targeting their coveted plantations.

Jean-Michel cast a concerned look toward Juan Carlos. "Personally, I am more concerned about surviving this trip. We are too low on necessary provisions to feed and clothe our crew. Powder, guns—that we have plenty of. We even have salt to preserve our meat if we can find it. We cannot eat gold or jewels, and salt is of no use without meat or fish to preserve it. I have reduced daily provisions to three quarters for the men. We will need to make port somewhere along the coast of La Florida."

"I know little more than legends about La Florida. Nothing seems to take hold."

Jean-Michel lifted a hand to his chin, his elbow resting on the other arm as it crossed his chest. "Legends of ancient monsters with scales, long teeth, and tails. They crawl on their bellies but strike swiftly from under the water. I have heard many men disappear if they wander into the swamps."

"Then we stay out of the swamps."

Jean-Michel smiled. "Where we will make land, everything is a swamp. At least says Herrera. He sailed from Pensacola with the Spanish before turning pirate." Jean-Michel's face turned serious. "The trading posts are spits of land surrounding by marsh and bushes so thick an ax takes an hour to cut through. The trees stand on islands surrounded by a slow-moving sea of thick grass and weeds taller than a man."

"How does anyone live there?"

Jean-Michel laughed. "The men and women are too mean to die!"

10

La Marée Rouge sat as if frozen in place, a brown hulk with round pegs jutting into the sky. Five hundred yards off her bow, a strip of white sand rose from a shimmering blue surface only to be ground up by the gnarled fingers of scrub bushes, stunted trees, and shoots of untamed green grass separating it from a cloudless, pale blue sky. The thin green strip seemed like an illusion to Jean-Michel, a mystical trick luring him into believing the land was solid enough for them to walk on it. He had never envisioned a world so flat.

Isabella cast a quick glance to Jean-Michel standing less than a foot from her on the quarter deck. "I think I prefer the jungles of Saint Domingue."

Jean-Michel kept the spy glass to his eye as he searched the beach, finally letting it drop. He turned to a scruffy pirate standing on the other side of him. "Take a look, Herrera. You know this coast."

The boatswain gave Jean-Michel a tentative look. "Ten years ago." He lifted the telescope to his eye. "Panton & Leslie Trading Company had an outpost on the Caloosahatchee River." He paused. "That'll be on the inside of those sand bars. According to the map; which is old. The water rises with tides as far up as we can get the ship."

Isabella sighed. "No hills. No Mountains. These lands are cursed lands."

"If you can find land," Herrera said. "The mainland is so low that telling the difference between land and swamp is near impossible without a guide."

Juan Carlos stood behind the group as they searched the coast line for a sign of any movement by animal or human. "How do we know if the post is still there?"

Herrera dropped the glass to his side. "Good question, Captain. Not much has survived. The Calusa are a fierce tribe. I heard that Ponce De Leon was attacked twice by scores of Calusa canoes while anchored in the harbor." He scowled. "Ponce De Leon had to retreat. Years later, when he returned, the Calusa attacked him again. He was wounded and died in Cuba." Herrera looked up toward the sky. "I'm going up to the fore top. As flat as this land is, I should be able to see to the Atlantic Ocean from up there!"

The boatswain tucked the spy glass in his breeches, grabbed a rope, and hoisted himself onto the gunwale. He began his ascent, climbing each rung, hand over hand. Herrera swung himself over the fore top, about thirty feet over the deck at the base of the fore topsail. He climbed another thirty feet to the base of the fore topgallant sail. He positioned himself with the glass and decided he was still too low. The final twenty feet put him at the base of the fore royal sail, ninety feet above the deck. All pirate eyes were soon transfixed on the gray silhouette of a figure, a toy sailor against a pristine blue sky.

"There," called Herrera from above, his voice distant. "About a half mile south. I think I see the mouth of a river. We should have twenty or twenty-five feet of draft."

"If it's the right river," Isabella muttered. She walked to the railings and looked over the water. The water was so clear *La Marée Rouge* seemed to be sitting on a bed of coral. A shark emerged from under the keel, its head shaped like a hammer fixed to a thick handle, as if she needed proof their vessel had plenty of draft.

Jean-Michel pivoted to look at the sun, and then down to the water. "It has been a while since I have navigated these waters. Longer than Herrera. Our charts are old. My guess is we have about two feet of rise with the tide. We will have to sail in with the evening tide. We don't have much wind, but we will see if we can get in the right spot before the tide shifts."

He turned toward a lanky pirate with ebony skin. "Sarhaan, we'll set full canvas. With these winds and the shallow waters, we can drag our anchor to take advantage of the right timing."

"I hope that trading post is still there," Isabella murmured. "The last thing we need is to be stranded in a strange harbor and lose another day. I don't like the idea of sending a party into the swamps to scavenge for food, and the fishing is never as good this close in as it is out in the deeper waters."

The bow of *La Marée Rouge* pointed directly into the mouth of what they hoped was Caloosahatchee River. Sanybelle Island stood guard on the north side of the entry—if the maps were correct. On the southern side, they hoped, was Estero Island. Estero Bay was bigger than they thought, extending across the horizon. Herrera had said they would have to navigate north once they passed Sanybelle into what the maps marked as San Carlos Bay.

Jean-Michel looked over to Sarhaan, his arms steady on the tiller. The African nodded as his eyes stayed fixed forward, and the anchor ropes forced the wooden hull to creak under the stress of the tide clutching at their vessel. The anchor, dropped from the stern, kept *La Marée Rouge* in place, letting the tides signal the time to sail into port.

Jean-Michel turned to a clutch of sailors at the front of the boat. He lifted his hand, circled his palm above his head, and the men threw themselves against wooden dowels at the capstan. The anchor rope tightened but failed to move.

The quarter master pivoted to another group of deck hands standing ready for orders. "Hurry, *vite,* to the ropes!" The men scrambled toward the anchor rope and began pulling. Jean-Michel followed the rope's trail to the stern. The current from the incoming tide began to pull at the ship's bulk.

Smoothy stood on the quarter deck, watching the rope grind into the stern gunwale. He shifted his weight and his eyes flashed over to Jean-

Michel. He turned to Isabella, standing next to Sarhaan as she gauged the speed of the tidal current and stress on the ship. He turned his sight back to Jean-Michel as if asking: *Are you going to cut the rope?*

"Not yet," Jean-Michel said, as if reading the crew's mind. He kept his gaze focused on the twisting hemp, eyes darting between the water and the ropes. He calculated the size of the faux bow waves arcing away from the stern created by the tide pushing against the hulk toward shore. "The bottom should be smooth. We did not see any sign of coral or rock when we set anchor."

The deck lurched as *La Marée Rouge* seemed to release from the anchor's pressure, forcing Isabella and Jean-Michel to grab the railing to steady themselves. The hull shifted forward a few feet before stopping again.

Jean-Michel shook his head. "We can't afford to lose an anchor this far out from a major port."

Isabella looked over the stern, the froth of the bow waves growing as the hull refused to budge again. "The tide is picking up." She turned toward Sarhaan. The helmsmen leaned into the tiller, his legs set against an invisible force. "The force is building against the rudder," she warned. Jean-Michel nodded.

Isabella motioned to two other pirates standing near the main mast, watching the actions of their captain and quartermaster. "Quickly, help Sarhaan keep the tiller stable!"

Jean-Michel's glare was fixed on the rope. "Come on," he muttered, as if coaxing the anchor to let loose of its grip on the sea bottom. "*Laisser aller*, let it go."

"*La Marée Rouge* can't take another three hours of this tide against her hull," Smoothy said.

"*Patience,* Mr. Smoothy," Jean-Michel said. "If the rudder holds, she'll be fine. I can feel her stress. She'll let me know when she's had too much."

"If the rudder doesn't hold, we'll be stranded for days, maybe weeks. We can't repair her rudder out here. We may have no choice but to beach her so we can rebuild it."

Jean-Michel nodded, keeping his eyes focused on the reverse bow waves as they fanned out around the vessel. "I appreciate your concern, Mr. Smoothy. Attend to your guns. I have a captain and an experienced boatswain who does not seem too worried. I am not ready to give up an anchor yet."

He looked up into the rigging. Tars lined the yards, waiting for orders. "Let's give her a bit of a nudge; put a little more force against the anchor. Set the fore topsail!"

La Marée Rouge seemed to give up another foot of sand as the sail filled with wind, joining a jib and spanker. Jean-Michel signaled for another sail to drop, and the brig inched forward again. He turned toward the crew at the capstan. "Let's go! Put your backs into it." The hull groaned, refusing to give up another foot of ground, as the sound of the churning water rushing against the stern crested the railing and flooded the quarterdeck.

Isabella turned to Jean-Michel just as her eyes caught the image of Gabrielle walking up the anchor rope. "Get away from the rope!" she ordered.

Gabrielle hopped toward the tiller, now held by three sailors as they struggled to keep it steady.

"Everyone stay as far away from the rope as you can," Isabella yelled. "We don't want to bury a decapitated corpse at sea if that rope snaps."

Gabrielle's eyes widened as she backed across the deck, as far from the anchor rope as she could physically get. *La Marée Rouge* gave up more sand, but stopped again, sending Gabrielle sprawling to the deck. She dug her feet into the wood, pushing her back up against the gunwale and grabbing a set of billets fastened by rope stays.

The brig jolted forward again, prompting another bellow from Jean-Michel to the men at the capstan. A surprised yell from above prompted everyone to look up into the yards. At the top of the main topsail yard, a sailor squirmed and seemed to run in mid-air as two other tars held his arms. In seconds, the sailor was back at his station, ready to unfurl another sail, no doubt thanking God that he was not sprawled lifeless on the main deck fifty feet below.

"Damn, she's stubborn," growled Jean-Michel.

Isabella looked at Jean-Michel, gauging his expression. He still was not ready to give the order to cut the rope.

"She's holding up against the stress," he said, loud enough for Isabella to hear. "She'll come."

Isabella turned away from Sarhaan and his men at the tiller and strode toward the base of the main mast. She lifted the top on a chest fastened to the deck, reached in, and pulled out an ax. She started toward the anchor rope now resting in a deep indentation, splinters of wood ground off the railing.

La Marée Rouge jerked toward the shore again, throwing Isabella down to a knee, the ax tip carving into the upper deck.

"Press on!" Jean-Michel called toward the bow of the ship, raising his arm in a frantic swirling motion at the men at the capstan. "More sail."

The vessel gave another start, pulled up, then nudged forward again. "Keep it up!"

Another lurch, and the brig gave up several more yards before slowing to a near halt, then easing forward toward land.

"The anchor's free! Bring her up before she catches again!"

Another quick jolt, and the brig started to pulse forward. The clacking of the capstan clanked into a rhythm. Sarhaan steadied the tiller as the vessel picked up speed. Minutes later two of the men were no longer at the tiller. Instead, they stood watch, ready to jump to wrestle the ship back onto course at Sarhaan's order.

Isabella heaved a sigh, letting the ax-head rest on the deck for a moment before returning it to its place. Gabrielle lifted herself to standing position. Smoothy let a toothy smile come to his face as he patted Jean-Michel on the shoulder and moved forward to join the men toward the bow.

Jean-Michel checked the sails as the bow centered the boat to the right of Sanybelle Island. He looked toward Sarhaan and then back toward the shore before turning his attention to the anchor rope, now steadily making its way toward its normal resting place in the bow with the help of a dozen seaman.

Gabrielle lifted her hands through her hair. "Is that normal?"

Isabella laughed. "No, thank God!"

Jean-Michel walked over toward Isabella and Gabrielle, an amused smile lightening his expression. "Nothing like a little excitement for entering a new port of call!"

Isabella allowed a thin smile. "You know this ship, *mon amie*."

"I knew she would hold together." Jean-Michel reached for the railing and gave it a strong, playful pat. "She was just testing us."

"Perhaps… a warning!"

The three turned to find the source of the unusual voice which seemed to drop the "r" in his words. None were surprised to see an Asian man of sleight build.

"Omena," Isabella confirmed through a soft exhale.

"Captain-san, a vessel's wood tell us much about what is natural and what is forced."

Jean-Michel's brows dropped closer to his eyes as his face tightened to erase the playful satisfaction it held seconds earlier. "I am sure *La Marée Rouge* was being stubborn. She tests us from time to time."

Omena bowed toward Jean-Michel. "I meant no disrespect, Quartermaster-san."

"Perhaps it was just an anchor caught on rocks on the sea bottom," Gabrielle volunteered.

"Of course," Omena said, bowing to Gabrielle. "I hear stories about this river. Stories of death. Disease. Ghosts who attack in darkness."

"We've heard those stories," Jean-Michel said. "Mr. Herrera knows these waters well. He sailed this gulf and this coast in service to King Charles of Spain as part of His Most Catholic Majesty's merchant fleet."

Omena bowed again. "I see. Quartermaster-san you know all Quartermaster-san need to know."

"Perhaps," Isabella said, looking at Jean-Michel. "But perhaps we should hear your stories, Mr. Omena."

Jean-Michel shot a sharp look toward Isabella. "We'll make sure we have an armed watch at all times. The guns will be primed. We are well aware of the danger. The Calusa Indians inhabited these lands for a long time. They were fierce warriors. But we have been told they were removed from these lands twenty years ago."

"Spain couldn't keep a colony even after establishing a mission here," said the familiar voice of Herrera. "This is a godforsaken part of New Spain."

"Spain no longer controls La Florida," Isabella said. "The British control this territory."

Jean-Michel gave a confident nod to Isabella. "The last of the Calusa were taken to Cuba by the Spanish in 1763."

"Not many of the tribe were left, according to the stories," Herrera said. "The Creeks and Yamasee raided villages, selling most of the Calusa as slaves to grow tobacco and cotton up the coast of the Atlantic."

"I understand," Omena confirmed. "So Spanish colonial government say. But Calusa mean 'fierce tribe.' Fierce tribe not give up."

Herrara's shoulders pulled back, and his fingers curled into a fist. "Are you calling us liars?"

Jean-Michel stepped forward, raising his hand to Herrera.

"I sorry, Herrera-san," Omena said, bowing to the botswain. "I not mean to offend."

Isabella hesitated and turned back to Omena. "Why do you think we may be facing danger in the harbor?"

"Only the British would try keeping an outpost alive on this part of hell," Herrera grumbled.

Isabella leveled a thoughtful gaze toward Omena. "I am sure, Mr. Omena, you did not mean to offend."

Herrera relaxed. "No talk in any port said anything about violent Indian activity in this area of La Florida as far as I know."

"Mr. Herrera," Jean-Michel said, drawing his navigator's attention. "We've picked up headway now that we're under full sail. Check our heading and speed against the charts."

Gabrielle watched Herrera inspect the rigging and yards as he walked toward the bow to get a better view of the channel and their course. "What's with Herrera?" she asked, turning toward Isabella.

Isabella raised her eyebrows. "Pirates and tars are an unpredictable bunch. On land, fighting is in their nature."

"Not on board ship," Jean-Michel said. "The Articles say that fighting will get them ten lashes at the mast."

Isabella nodded. "Everyone signs the Articles when they join the crew."

"Including Omena?" Gabrielle asked.

"The Articles are in my quarters, and his signature is there," Isabella said.

Gabrielle turned her nose as she considered Jean-Michel and Isabella's comments. "I didn't sign the Articles."

"You didn't join us voluntarily," Isabella said. "You saved my life and Juan Carlos's in Port-au-Prince. You came with us so you wouldn't be killed." She turned to Jean-Michel. "We thought it best you didn't sign the Articles. Louis didn't sign them either. It should keep you from the gallows if we are captured."

Jean-Michel winked at Gabrielle. "Besides, we knew you would be fierce in battle. We did not need a contract to know whose side you would fight for."

Gabrielle shook her head. "Why have a contract?"

Isabella smiled. "We need the men on board to do their jobs. They need to know why *La Marée Rouge* rides the waves, and what they can expect from their willingness to join us."

"And what can they expect?"

"Treasure, booty, of course!" Jean-Michel's eyes seemed to sparkle as if he had told a joke that had the entire ship caught up in roaring laughter.

Gabrielle didn't laugh. "This ship doesn't seem to have much treasure, at least not from what I see below. Unless you consider salt and powder a treasure. Your stores are dangerously low. Isn't that why you are making this stop?"

Isabella sighed, turning her eyes out to the western horizon. "We have enough from the merchantmen to turn pretty good coin for our crew. We just needed to make port to sell our stock. Now we are out of the Caribbean, we should have better luck as we get closer to America." Isabella looked at Jean-Michel. "We were certainly richer with gold when flying under Jacob's flag."

"Oui," Jean-Michel acknowledged. "Jacob was much more of a pirate. But we've secured enough booty to hold property across the Carib Sea. Our men are compensated well enough."

"I don't really understand," Gabrielle said, shaking her head. "I hate the French colonials. That's why I am here."

Isabella smiled. "And I hate the Spanish colonials."

"Hah," said Jean-Michel. "Then we are in agreement. We hate all kings and princes." He turned to Gabrielle. "And if you read the Articles, that is truly the only point we hold every signer to. They must be willing to pillage the merchant ships of any power that holds slaves or trades for slaves."

Isabella turned back to Gabrielle. "I don't promise riches in gold and silver. But I promise justice. Even in death."

"But we fight for riches, too," Jean-Michel said, laughing as he walked to the bow to join Herrera and the rest of the crew on deck.

11

Isabella's heart picked up a beat as *La Marée Rouge* passed the desolate, sandy gate of Sanybelle Island on its portside. The incoming tide seemed to propel the brig at an astounding speed of twelve knots despite the light winds. The thicket rising from the beach gave her pause as she wondered what might be watching from inside. A few scraggly trees rose from the bushes, but not more than a few feet higher than the rest of the foliage. What beasts prowled the island?

Above them, seagulls and birds with yellow beaks flew in circles. A long-throated blue-tinted bird swept along the surface and dove into the water, bringing up a flailing fish.

"Twenty feet," called a sailor as he walked from bow to stern with a sounding line.

"Eighteen feet," called a voice a few minutes later as the entire crew gathered on deck to observe the strange rises in sand and gnarled bushes along their sightline. Every hundred yards or so a pine tree would jut into the sky, disrupting the smooth rise and fall of the lower brush.

"Keep to the center of the channel," Herrera instructed from the fore top.

"Can you see the channel?" Isabella called to Jean-Michel, who was perched in the bowsprit, leaning out over the bay as the pirate ship sliced cleanly through the calm waters.

"Oui, the channel is a clear blue. The shallows are green. The channel is opening up once we pass the tip of Sanybelle."

Gabrielle leaned over the side. "The water is so clear. I swear I could step over the rail and walk to shore!"

"Twenty-three feet!"

Isabella cast a smile to her neighbor at the gunwale. "I would wait a few more minutes before I would try that."

"It's so beautiful," Gabrielle giggled.

"What is waiting for us behind those bushes and trees?" Juan Carlos wondered aloud in a somber tone.

Isabella lifted her hand and rested it lightly on the small of his back. "I am sure we can take care of it, whatever it is. Our crew is ready."

Juan Carlos looked down the main deck, noting the muskets loaded but resting next to the crew as they looked out at the widening bay. "We are sailing up the channel now. We'll have to see what holds for us as we go into San Carlos Bay."

"Our main cannon are loaded," Isabella said. "The chasers are loaded, too. We have grape shot ready for close quarters fighting if Indians get too close."

"I've never met an Indian," Gabrielle said. "They were only legends in Port-au-Prince."

Isabella stared into the sea. Gulls and other birds floated peacefully in the bay as the warship passed by. Another heron seemed to walk on water several dozen feet from the beach, a warning of how shallow the waters became. Smaller birds skipped over wet sand, diving their beaks into the mud, and flying a few more feet up the beach before repeating the same attack. The gulls were common enough, none of the pirates noted their presence. "Indians are real enough. I've run into my share, but never in battle."

Gabriella breathed in as her eyes were overwhelmed by a widening stretch of the channel only to see another island extending toward them. "What is that?"

"The chart says Pine Island," Isabella said.

"Legend says that's where the Calusa had their chief city when Ponce De Leon landed," Juan Carlos said.

The water seemed to flow into another distant abyss toward the right, far away from land, daring their little ship to change course and head east.

They turned toward the front of *La Marée Rouge*, diverting their attention from the two slivers of land off the port bow. "Herrera says they attack in canoes. As many as fifty warriors in each one."

"That's if the Calusa are still here," Juan Carlos pointed out, a tactical tone revealing a mental shift to his military training. "They should all be in Cuba. I worry more about the Creek and Yamassee."

Isabella turned toward Sarhaan, his figure more relaxed at the tiller as the vessel's speed helped him guide them into the bay. "Keep her headed due east. Wait for Herrera's signal before tacking north."

The pirate brig glided forward, prompting Isabella to send a quick glance toward Jean-Michel.

"My first trip into the Caribbean toward the equator had the same effect," he said. "The island tides are so shallow I thought for sure we would end up stranded on a beach or at a wharf."

Gabrielle looked out over the water again. "We are moving fast, but we are hardly cutting a wake."

"We just need to keep a few knots ahead of the tide to have enough headway to keep control. In the northern ports—Boston, London, even Cadiz—navigating our way into the bay is much more difficult. And we have no harbor pilot to give us direction."

"We will be lucky if we find anyone in this godforsaken place," said Juan Carlos. "Nothing seemed to survive for long here. If the Indians didn't wipe them out, disease finished them off."

Jean-Michel scowled at the Spanish army captain. "Your happy disposition is inspiring, Señor Santa Ana."

Juan Carlos shook his head. "We should send sharpshooters into the tops."

Isabella looked at Jean-Michel, her expression confirming Juan Carlos's instincts. Jean-Michel turned toward the bow, spotted Smoothy, and then checked to make sure each platform had two tars with long guns at their stations.

Isabella turned toward the bow. The bowsprit was aimed directly at what seemed like a low-lying island, its furthest point soon cresting a line of small scrub trees rising from the beach. She shook her head, marveling at how so much land could be so low to the water. No signs of mountains, or hills. The entire land could be swept away by one major storm.

She looked to the right to see the brig gliding several hundred yards from a southern shore with similar brush along an uneven fence of mangrove trees. The bay continued to stretch out to the left, off their port side, as if they had discovered another uncharted ocean.

A few minutes later and another finger of the bay seemed to open up, the beach they had seen earlier revealing itself as the point of a peninsula. At least, that was what Herrera had said the charts said it would be. Without any land rising from behind the trees and sand, Isabella still wondered if they were really stitching their way through a series of barrier islands.

"Eighteen feet!"

Isabella's heart picked up another beat.

"Fifteen feet!"

Isabella looked toward Herrera, now laying in the bowsprit, his head popping from the water to the beach. "Mr. Herrera?"

"Steady as she goes, capitán! The channel should deepen again."

"Thirteen feet!"

Juan Carlos turned toward Isabella. Her hard, stoic expression didn't seem to calm him.

Isabella forced a small smile. "She draws ten feet at the stern when we are loaded. We've been in shallower water than this."

"Twelve feet!"

Isabella turned toward Sarhaan. He nodded, acknowledging her orders had not changed, keeping his eyes on Herrera.

"Thirteen feet!"

Juan Carlos let out a slow breath. Isabella's smile broadened.

"Thirteen feet!"

She stepped closer to Juan Carlos, leaning in slightly. "I have faith in my crew."

"Twelve feet!"

Juan Carlos turned to Isabella, nodding with a smile. "As I put faith in my men."

"Hard port!"

Herrera's voice carried an urgency that snapped their pirate officers' attention forward. Herrera lifted himself from the netting in the bowsprit. "We'll need to tack up the bay at this point. The mouth to the river looks to be a half mile wide." He pointed to the forward mast. "I am going aloft again to get a better view."

Isabella turned back to Sarhaan. "Take your orders from Señor Herrera."

The retreating sun seemed to push the shadows from the shore and the scrub trees toward *La Marée Rouge*, threatening to overtake the pirate vessel as it continued its slow tack up what they hoped was the mouth of the Caloosahatchee River. Isabella felt the heat beat against her cheeks. *A foreboding sign*, she thought, *of the impending loss of all our wind.* The tide had almost stopped. They would have to lay anchor soon and succumb to the darkness.

"*Mi amor*, men will be on watch all night."

Isabella turned to Juan Carlos and leaned closer, welcoming the touch of their shoulders. "*La Marée Rouge* has never been this isolated from the freedom of the sea."

"Your men are pirates, seasoned by many battles at sea. Your one hundred and fifty men defeated Muñoz and his squadron."

"We are now down to one hundred and ten able-bodied seamen."

Isabella turned her eyes back to the glassy water, disturbed only by the fading power of the bow waves as their progress slowed. "I feel trapped."

"More trapped than Muñoz's blockade of Port-au-Prince Bay?"

Isabella sighed. "I knew our options… and our odds." She turned back toward the shore. "If we can't find the trading post, we have to reduce rations again. We have just seven more days of food at three quarters rations. We can't afford to lose two days chasing swamp ghosts."

Juan Carlos followed her gaze over the water and up to the shoreline. Knots of tall, slender stalks of grass pock-marked the beach, sometimes obscuring the twisting roots of mangrove trees and the solitary columns of scattered cypress trees. Scrub trees formed a line, as if defending the interior from the probing eyes of strangers. What were they hiding?

Silence consumed the brig and its crew as a puff of wind faded and the hull failed to push another bow wave outward. A splash from the forward part of the deck drew Juan Carlos's attention, but Isabella's focus on the shore remained unwavering. The clacking of the capstan confirmed the descent of the anchor into the river. Isabella pulled back from the railing when the capstan stopped just seconds later.

Isabella turned toward the bow, spotting Jean-Michel consulting with Herrera by the capstan. He turned to look at her.

"Is everything okay, Bella?"

Gabrielle's voice was soothing, even if the tone was uncertain.

"The river is very shallow."

"Have we run aground?"

"Not yet."

Gabrielle looked at Isabella, her expression asking the next question.

Isabella didn't smile. "We might find ourselves stuck in the morning."

"Isn't that dangerous?"

"If a trading post truly is nearby, we will be fine."

"And if it's not?"

Isabella paused and looked at the pirates lining both railings of the *La Marée Rouge*. "Muskets are loaded, knives are secured, watches are set. No pirate will sleep far from a weapon tonight."

Gabrielle nodded. "We won't be caught by surprise this time."

12

Isabella struggled to breathe as she tried to sort out the spectacle unveiled by the next day's rising sun. All she remembered from the night before was staring at the ceiling as she waited for the first hint of gray from sunrise. Juan Carlos's steady breathing and calm body did little to comfort her once he had fallen asleep.

But the tableau wrapping *La Marée Rouge* from all sides on the river was dumfounding: Twenty canoes by her quick estimate, with a dozen or two armed Indian warriors in each. Many held long poles with bright white tips, spears no doubt. The arch of the rods bending back over the warriors was held with disciplined strength as arrows pointed at an upward arc at the brig and her crew. Isabella searched for the telltale sign of a musket barrel or other powder-type weapon. "Where did they come from?"

"Certainly not from our ship!" Jean-Michel said.

Isabella breathed in deeply, her eyes scoping and scanning each object, its men, and their weapons. The warriors were covered with no clothing except a breech cloth that extended down their front, their bronzed skin exotic against the twinkling sparks dancing across the receding water set off by the morning sun. Most had faces and arms painted with red, blue, and white streaks. Many had what appeared to be leather arm bands, and a few had feathers tied to headdresses of various designs and sorts. "When does the tide turn again?"

"Based on our charts? Two hours."

"Long enough for us to escape into the Gulf of Mexico."

Jean-Michel paused, dipping his head over the rail to look at the water. "*Peut-être,* if we didn't have to navigate shoals, and Herrera had a better memory."

"*Disculpe, capitán,*" Herrer apologized. "I was here ten years ago. I was not even the navigator—"

"*No te preocupes,* Señor Herrera," Isabella said, hoping her tone, if not her words, would calm him. She needed him sharp now. "The sand moves with the wind and tides. We have learned that La Florida is a changeling."

She looked out over the river, unsure of whether she should give the order for her line of pirates to pull their triggers... or wait. "Who was on watch?"

Jean-Michel stood silent.

"Warriors arrive middle of night," said a steady, matter-of-fact voice behind them.

Isabella's head snapped toward the sounds, her brain registering Omena's broken English in an instant.

Omena's eyes were fixated on the canoes and warriors resting in the water before him, as if Herrera, Isabella, and Jean-Michel were little more than ghosts frustrated with their destiny. His small, agile body was calm, his hands empty of weapons. At least conventional ones.

Isabella turned back to the makeshift blockade of canoes and Indians. "Why didn't you warn us?"

"Men on watch. They sound alarm if Indians attack."

Isabella shook her head.

Jean-Michel sighed. "We had four men on deck at six bells. Plus a man in the main mast top."

The pirates watched the canoes as if they were frozen in place despite the ebb of the tide. Warriors adjusted long poles in the water to steady the boats and what appeared to be paddles to keep them in place.

"What do they want?"

Isabella glanced up and down the gunwales, noting the weapons each sailor held. Gabrielle was striding toward their group, one hand firm on the grip of a sword with the other holding the blade close to her side as she snaked her way through the crowded gun deck.

"Patience, Señor Herrera," Isabella said. "I need a confident pirate now, not one worried about whether he will see his treasure at the next port of call."

"What do they want?" Gabrielle asked as she came to a stop between Isabella and Jean-Michel.

Jean-Michel shook his head. "I don't know. No one has come forward yet."

"Who are they?" Gabrielle's question seemed more curious than fearful.

"I've not worked with American Indians," Jean-Michel responded.

"They've been watching us all morning. They were there before sunrise." Isabella turned to Gabrielle. "Where is Louis?"

Gabrielle hesitated, as if unsure she heard the question correctly. "Asleep."

"Wake up Doc, if he's not already awake. Tell Louis to join him on the lower deck." Isabella sighed and shook her head. "They should prepare for another battle. Louis is much safer there in case we are attacked."

Isabella focused on her friend, raising her hand to touch her arm. "Stay with him. We have no experience fighting warriors like these. I don't need to worry about a ten-year old boy running around the deck if they board us."

Gabrielle paused, opened her mouth slightly, but then turned to descend into the nether decks where only the powder monkeys and wounded and dying were welcomed during battle.

Isabella began to walk the deck. She inspected the first cannon and looked at the crew. "Are you ready?"

The gun captain nodded. "Loaded with grape shot."

Isabella counted ten canoes on the port side, four more directly off their bow, ten on the starboard side, and three forming a makeshift wall in the river off the stern. "Twenty-seven canoes, with twelve to twenty warriors in each. Three hundred and fifty warriors?"

"Oui," Jean-Michel confirmed. "Well, perhaps more. Three hundred and seventy-five by Herrera's count."

Isabella began to tap the hilt of her sword. "We are outnumbered four to one."

"We have faced worse odds."

She turned to Jean-Michel. "We don't know this enemy."

"They fight with bows and arrows. We have grape shot and muskets."

"They have bows, arrows, pikes, and weapons we can't see."

"Warriors have blow guns," Omena said from behind them, "and other weapons."

Jean-Michel set his jaw. "Omena! Step forward."

Omena appeared in front of Jean-Michel and Isabella, bowing to them both. "Yes, Captain-san. At your service, Quartermaster-san."

Isabella tried not to appear surprised at Omena's quick and virtually silent movements. "Blow guns?"

"Yes, Captain," Omena said, bowing. "Many warriors have long sticks for blowing darts. They are good weapon for long distance. Darts have poison tip."

Isabella nodded. "I have heard of these weapons. My mother and her sister used to speak of the Indians in the hills above Santo Domingo with weapons such as these."

"Yes, captain. These weapons used in Japan as well."

"Have you used these weapons?" Jean-Michel's inquisitive tone revealed a deepened concern about their new enemy.

"Yes, monsieur. They very good. I do not know poison used in West. In Nippon, poisons kill very fast."

Jean-Michel paused, peering at the Japanese. "You have not used these weapons in these seas and islands?"

Omena bowed. "No, Quartermaster-san."

Jean-Michel nodded, as if his brain were connecting pieces of a puzzle. He pivoted toward a group of sailors clustered around Sarhaan and a few others at the tiller. He spotted Herrera behind Sarhaan and raised his hand, letting his fingers act is if they were pulling him into the group of officers. "Do you recognize these Indians?"

Herrera shook his head. "No. When I sailed in from Pensacola, we harbored in the river at the trading post. The traders were Spanish. I didn't go ashore, but none of the party mentioned Indians."

Jean-Michel cursed under his breath.

Herrera stepped to the gunwale and looked at the Indians in the closest boat. "Strange looking Indians. They've painted their faces. Warriors are just wearing breech cloths, no leggings, no tops..., shell necklaces..., bird feathers in their hair..., topknots for their hair." He paused. "*Dios bueno en el cielo!*" he said, making the sign of the trinity across his chest. "Calusa!"

Jean-Michel grimaced, a slight turn of his head toward Omena.

"Mr. Omena," Isabella said, her eyes trained on the war canoes. "You know about their weapons. What do you know of their tactics? Why haven't they attacked?"

"I do not know, Captain-san. They are patient. Like ninja in Japan. They wait all night and not move."

Herrera's pointed to a cluster of Indians on a platform held up by two canoes fastened together. "That's the leader. He's in the biggest canoe and surrounded by warriors. Maybe we can ask him."

Energy seemed to flow into Isabella's body. She gripped her sword.

"Excellent idea, Señor. Herrera," she said turning to the Japanese. "Mr. Omena, please go below and summon Captain Santa Ana."

13

"No offense, Mr. Herrera," Isabella said as she looked more closely at the double canoe, "but I think we will need someone with better Spanish if we are going to communicate with our new friends and the Calusa leader."

Herrera spit into the river below, without taking his eyes off the warriors, bows at their ready, just a few yards away. "No, offense taken, *mi capitán.*"

She put a hand on his shoulder. "I still want you nearby. You are the only one with knowledge of these Indians. We need that experience."

"I hope the army captain's Spanish is good enough," Herrera said. "The Calusa seem to know something's up." Herrera pointed to movement among the warriors in the canoes.

"Let's stay calm. Keep our guns below the gunwales. Keep movement to a minimum." Isabella looked up to the main and fore mast tops, forty feet in the air. Each had four pirates with at least two muskets each—one to shoot, and one to load. "Steady up there! Fire only on Herrera's orders!"

Scattered, "Aye, captains," confirmed they heard and understood.

Juan Carlos stepped over toward the clustered officers. He smiled at Jean-Michel. "The gun deck is quite nice in the morning when it's not taken up by men in hand-to-hand combat or obscured by the smoke of battle."

Jean-Michel chuckled, and swept his arm out across the river toward the river-born army of Calusa Indians. "As you can see, my dear land captain, we thought a change of pace was in order. We did not want to start the battle until after you had arrived on deck and had a full breakfast!"

Isabella shook her head. "Yes, we were quite focused on protocol this morning." She pulled Juan Carlos toward the gunwales. "As you can see we have a problem."

"Bows, arrows, canoes," Juan Carlos said, shaking his head. "Not much of a fight if we take the first shot."

Isabella sighed. "We haven't found the trading post, yet. The river stretches north, but it's too shallow for us to follow. We would have to lower the cutters and row our way up with the tide. If we fight, the chances of us wiping them all out are small. The last thing we need is to have them picking off our men from shore with their darts and arrows, stranded while we wait for the next tide."

"I agree with *mi capitán,* Señor Santa Ana," Herrera said. "The Calusa were supposed to be enslaved and moved to Cuba years ago. As you can see, not all of them went."

"You are sure they are Calusa?"

"Si, Señor Santa Ana. You can tell by the markings on their faces. Stripes of blue, red, and white. They use the grasses from the marsh to make arm bands and necklaces and use the shells to show their rank and family. The long white feathers in their hair? They are from the long-legged birds that walk in the swamps. They have long necks with sharp, orange beaks. The French call them *aiegrette,* the silver heron."

"You seem to know a lot about these Calusa," Jean-Michel grumbled. "But you've never seen one?"

"I am not worried about seeing one," Herrera said in a low voice. "I am worried about fighting one."

Juan Carlos inhaled a heavy breath. "I saw the canoes from Isabella's cabin. They seem to be very patient."

Herrera lifted a hand and pulled it through locks of hair, matted by sweat. "I was told the tribe was ruled by a king, but the last king died fifty years ago. They've been raided by other tribes for the last one hundred years."

Juan Carlos's eyes shot toward Herrera. "You are sure these are Calusa?"

Herrera raised his eyebrows. "As close as I can be. My knowledge is based on what I have heard, and what I saw when our ship stocked up at the trading post when I sailed on the Spanish merchant ship. That put us in this river about 1771, before the American rebellion. Rumors were a group of Calusa refused to move to Cuba when England took over La Florida in 1793. Our captain did not want to stay around any longer than needed."

Juan Carlos nodded. "Then we must be very careful. If these Calusa remained behind, they must be independent and fierce."

"My captain did not trust the Calusa. He sent the boatswain ashore on a cutter with the newer deck hands. The quartermaster thought the risk was too high."

"Calusa means 'fierce warrior,'" Jean-Michel reminded the group as one hand tugged at his beard. He looked toward Isabella, as if asking for orders. "Should we invite them aboard?"

Isabella shook her head. "I think they are waiting for me to go out and meet them."

Jean-Michel levered to the side, looking at Isabella as his face turned into a grimace.

Isabella lifted her palm toward Jean-Michel, as if warding him off. "We have to make contact. They are waiting for us to make the first move. Look at how close they are. If we fired our cannon at them now, the shot would clear their heads. Those canoes would be on our hull in seconds, and four hundred Indians will be climbing onto our deck. If they are as fierce as the Carib and Arawak, we would be lucky to survive with one quarter of our crew, barely enough to sail out with the next tide."

"It's too dangerous," Juan Carlos said. "We don't know anything about them."

Isabella shook her head, checking her sword, and relieving Herrera of a pistol he had lodged behind his back. "That's why, Capitán Juan Carlos Maria Lopez de Santa Ana, you are coming with me!"

Juan Carlos secured himself on a bench as the cutter drifted from the hull of *La Marée Rouge*. The forward sailor, a man more weathered than his youth foretold, dropped the bowline, and the tars above pulled it back onto the main deck. Juan Carlos steadied himself with his healthy arm and flexed the hand and wrist extending from the wounded shoulder.

A deck hand in the rear of the small boat pushed the stern into the river with an oar and let the blade fall into the water as its shaft rested between wooden dowels. A few strokes in the slow ebb of the river, and the cutter was carrying the small party of pirates toward what they believed—or hoped—was the leader of the Calusa warriors.

The Indians remained quiet as the small launch approached, but the hardness in their stares showed they were alert. As each tug of the oars pulled Isabella and her crew closer to the warrior leader, Juan Carlos began to disentangle the silent web of communication that kept the bands of water-born warriors harmonized. Individual Indians were assigned different parts of the boat, and their focused look suggested a level of discipline he admired among his best-trained soldiers. Their arms lay near their sides, but high enough that hand signals would be visible to the others. Bows were loaded with arrows, and at least one was trained on each of the six passengers in the boat as they glided forward.

Juan Carlos felt perspiration pool on his scalp as the sun pounded the top of his head. The sweat seeped into his hair until it overflowed and a steady stream rushed down channels over his temples and cheeks. He lifted his knee under his hand and began to lift his arm to wipe the water from his brow but stopped. He quieted his body, hoping to keep an Indian's arrow targeted at his chest content and unmoved in the bow.

He looked at the warrior, noting his bare chest, toned torso, and hair pulled into a top knot. His pull on the bow string was steady, despite the tension of several dozen pounds against the limb making up the bow. The black, blue, and red stripes drawn from his nose across the cheekbones to his ear seemed to jump off his face in defiance of the even bronze tone of his skin.

Good, the army captain said to himself. These were well-trained warriors, comfortable in a fight. A trained adversary was a professional... and predictable... one.

Juan Carlos's eyes scanned the full body of the warrior and his heart skipped as they descended into the canoe. The warriors and their arrows were deadly enough but the glint of another weapon sent his heart racing. Flint lock rifles lay just below the gunwale of a canoe, their presence betrayed by a spark of sunlight glancing off steel barrels.

The Calusa are a warrior tribe, Juan Carlos reminded himself. Even pirates commanded by the legendary Pirate of Panther Bay would be praying for their lives if something sparked a full-blown battle with this band of warriors.

The cutter slowed as the sounds of oars pulling against the water ceased. Juan Carlos diverted his eyes to the front of the boat. Isabella was standing, her head bound by a maroon bandana, her hand up, the signal for her crew to pull their oars. The cutter continued to drift forward, as Isabella and the apparent chief of the Calusa raiding party faced off in silence.

His army instincts kicked in as he flexed the grip of his hand and checked the interior of the boat. Each of the six muskets was placed near the foot of a sailor, along with a pistol, allowing them to be retrieved in seconds. Isabella's sword was at her side, and he could see the slight bulge of a pistol lodged in the small of her back under her shirt. He resisted the temptation to check the hunting knife he secured in his breeches.

Juan Carlos chuckled at the futility of defending themselves at this point. Each arrow would find its mark well before a muzzle could be brought to bear on an attacker. He heaved a sigh, trying to calm his heart. They would have to talk their way to safety.

"*Buenos dias gran jefe!*" Isabella called in a sure voice to the chief's canoe.

The Calusa canoe was sturdy, thick, and long, cut out from a tree trunk. Herrera had referred to the trees as swamp cypress. But Juan Carlos had seen pine trees grow as big and round in northern Spain and throughout Portugal. As he looked at the shore and the water creeping under shrubs, billowing out from the shore, he began to understand the swamp. Scrub trees rose as a second line of defense against intruders. Spanish moss thickened the branches, bending them toward the ground.

He had seen trees on Puerto Rico and St. John large enough to make a canoe this size, but nothing in this area. So far.

The chief, or the man they assumed was the leader, stood on the platform of his double canoe, looking at Isabella, a firm grip on a staff. If he looked at anyone else, Juan Carlos couldn't tell, because his eyes stayed focused on Isabella. He was bronze skinned like his warriors but wore a headdress, a leather band wrapping his head with egret feathers framing several plumes of what looked like a hawk or eagle. His mask was painted from ear to ear, leaving holes big enough for eyes to peer through the darkness at his victim. Only one other warrior, the one sitting next the chief, had more than one feather fixed to his hair knot. The chief was armed with a blade extended down his side, secured by what appeared to be a leather belt that fixed his breech cloth in place.

"We mean no harm," Isabella said, this time in English and lifting her hands palms out.

The chief continued to glare at Isabella. Juan Carlos's fingers began to tingle as his quickened heartbeat pushed more blood into his limbs.

"We need supplies," Isabella said, again in English. "We need food and water. We are looking for a trading post. We were told we could find it in the San Carlos Bay. At the mouth of the Caloosahatchee River."

Juan Carlos used his eyes to search for any sign or movement that could indicate an attack by the chief's warriors. The chief stood silent, as if fixed in place.

Isabella turned to look at Juan Carlos. "Captain Santa Ana? Can you please stand... slowly... and join me?"

"*Si, capitán.*" Juan Carlos used small, deliberate moves to lift himself from the bottom of the cutter, stand, and walk up to Isabella. He was surprised at how little his new vantage point helped in assessing the Indians and their leader. "Perhaps we should head back to *La Marée Rouge.*"

Isabella lifted her hands, palms out to the chief again. "We can trade for supplies: rice, meat, fish, fruit, wool. Can you help us?" She brought her arms to her chest, crossing her forearms as if embracing herself.

A few more moments passed, but the chief remained an immovable statue. Isabella continued to look at him, searching for a response of some sort and made a decision. "Let's head back to the ship," she said out loud. "Oars in!"

The sailors dropped their wooden blades into the water, a move that triggered a lift of the chief's arm.

"Oars up!" Isabella called. She looked back the chief. "Trade? Will you help us?"

The chief looked over to Juan Carlos and lifted his arm, pointing at the Spaniard's chest.

"I hope he's not telling them to shoot me," Juan Carlos whispered under his breath. Isabella's silence told him more than her words could. "Calm yourself, Isabella."

"I am the captain of *La Marée Rouge*," she hissed.

"Right now we have a score of arrows pointed at us. I think it might be wise to keep your temper in check. We are not facing Muñoz or Rodriguez."

"Capitán Santa Ana," Isabella said, loud enough to carry across the water, "you may address the Calusa chief."

"*Gracias mi comandante*," Juan Carlos responded. He stepped closer toward the bow, making sure he didn't step in front of Isabella.

The chief looked at Juan Carlos. He turned his chin up as he faced him. "*¿Usted es el líder?*"

Juan Carlos felt Isabella's body stiffen. He was sure her hand was snaking its way to the pistol lodged in under the sash behind her.

"He speaks Spanish!" she said in English, the indignity soaking her words.

"Yes," Juan Carlos responded in a low voice. "But I would not assume he does not know English, either. Or French."

The Indian nodded at Juan Carlos. "*Estoy hablando con usted, capitán.*"

"He also knows your rank," Isabella whispered.

"Easy, Isabella," Juan Carlos said. His head spun, checking different pockets of his memory for something that might help. Portugal, he remembered. His first battle on the border with Spain with the insurgents. How many prisoners did he interrogate? Forty? Fifty? His head slowed with each discovery of another memory pocket, another snippet of his work interrogating prisoners from the battlefield and villages. Each memory crystalized another lesson, guiding him forward.

He turned to Isabella and bowed slightly. "Captain, may I have permission to speak to the chief."

"*Estoy hablando con usted, capitán!*"

Isabella kept her gaze fixed on the chief. "How dare he—"

"Give me permission again, Isabella. Quickly!"

Isabella drew in a deep breath and brought her hands to her front. She pulled the hilt of her sword forward, careful to keep it in its sheath. She placed her free hand over the handle and turned to Juan Carlos. "*Sí, capitán,*" she replied as she continued in Spanish, "you have permission to speak to the great leader."

"*Gracias mi capitán.*" Juan Carlos let out a long breath and turned to the chief. "*Gran líder, vuestra Alteza, el capitán Isabella es nuestro líder.*"

The chief sent a sharp look toward Isabella. "*¿Una mujer?*"

"Si, great chief, she is the captain of *La Marée Rouge*. According to our laws, the captain of a ship is the undisputable leader." Juan Carlos scrutinized the chief's reaction for any hint that he knew he had just lied, but the mask hid any emotion he might have.

The chief looked at Isabella and back to Juan Carlos. "Where is her husband?"

"She is not married," Juan Carlos said quickly. "She is captain of this ship by her own right."

The chief stood unmoving.

Juan Carlos was close enough he could sense the blood course through Isabella's body and the slight twitch of her fingers as they eased around the hilt of her sword. He recalled the placement of the spears and long guns in each of the canoes as they passed by. He noted again the distance of the bows and arrows. Each Calusa stood steady and focused. Any move—

Isabella bowed her head. "If you cannot help us," she said in Spanish, "then we will leave and head back to sea."

As she lifted her face to look at the chief she sensed his body relaxing. He lifted an arm, and each bowman lowered their weapon. He looked at Juan Carlos. "What do you need?"

Juan Carlos let out a deep sigh. "Food. Meat, fruit, mostly. Fresh water."

The chief gave a quick nod. "What do you have to trade?"

"We have salt."

The Calusa leader seemed to consider this. "We want gun powder, bullets, and rifles."

"Our supplies are very limited," Juan Carlos said.

The chief looked over to *La Marée Rouge*. "Ship has many guns. Cannon. Many sailors. Many muskets."

Isabella turned to Juan Carlos and gave him a slight nod.

"We may have extra rifles, gunpowder and bullets for the great Calusa warriors."

The chief turned to an Indian standing next to him. The man was about the same height and, like the others, dressed in little more than a breech cloth. Three layers of necklaces wrapped around his neck, their shells draping over his chest, with grass, braided arm bands around his upper arm. The chief gave him an order in a language Juan Carlos did not understand. The chief turned to look at *La Marée Rouge*. "A barrel of salt. Fifty rifles. Powder and bullets for one-hundred rifles. We will take all now."

Juan Carlos heard Isabella catch her breath.

"Great chief," he said, fearful Isabella would speak too soon, "if your warriors approach the ship without our orders, they will be shot."

The chief stood impassive as he looked at the small band of pirates. "Then you will die."

Juan Carlos nodded. He began to notice a throb in his shoulder and heard the soft shuffle of feet behind him. The pirates were shifting their positions. He hoped they had the sense to keep their weapons out of sight, for now. "It will be a great death. An honorable death."

The chief signaled for his canoes to advance on the ship as the warriors lifted their arrows toward the pirates.

"Twenty-five rifles, powder and shot for fifty rifles now," Isabella interjected. "The rest and the barrel of salt when we finish the trade."

The chief tipped his head before Juan Carlos could translate. "Twenty-five rifles now. Powder and bullets for seventy-five rifles now. After trade, powder and bullets for twenty-five rifles and barrel of salt."

Isabella paused. Juan Carlos stood next to her, beads of perspiration now leaching together through his shirt. The sun was well above them, beating down, turning their small boat into a small oven as the sun's rays invaded the wood and radiated over their bodies.

Isabella nodded. "The final payment is given only after we've seen and inspected all the supplies."

14

The powder and shot took less than a half hour to load into the Calusa canoes, despite the urgent complaints from Jean-Michel and Smoothy about trading away such a large share of their armory. Within an hour, Isabella, Gabrielle, Juan Carlos, Patrick, and three other trusted pirates were being ferried up the Caloosahatchee River, the sun high over their heads.

Jean-Michel objected to Isabella going deep into the swamps to finalize the trade, but he could present no better alternative. Isabella and Juan Carlos had negotiated the trade. Isabella convinced him he was much better off commanding *La Marée Rouge* in the event the bargain fell apart. They would need a quick escape.

As the Indians paddled up the river, their small boats showed the benefits of their design; they seemed to fly through the water despite a deeper carve to the hull. The boats broke water twice as fast as four pirates could ever hope to travel pulling at the oars of one of the small launches. The speed and stability surprised the pirates, given the power the Indians put into poling and paddling their way up the river.

After an hour of steady paddling, the canoes started to pass through various types of swamp grass, lilies, and other plants. The canoes appeared to skim the river bottom, enticing Juan Carlos to dip his hand into the water to check its depth. A shout from one of the warriors prompted him to pull his hand back into the boat. The Indian continued to yell at him, his voice raised and tone piercing through the air like a pirate swinging into battle from the rigging as he boarded a resistant merchant ship.

He looked back at the Indian, who was pointing toward the shore just ten feet away. A long lizard-like creature lay half submerged in the water, its scales creating a menacing ripple along a line easily ten to twelve feet in length. He watched the animal in fascination, having time to note the teeth jutting out from its jaws and the narrow snout protruding in front of the monster's eyes before they turned a bend in the river.

Gnarled, green bushes and branches lined their path as the river narrowed. Near *La Marée Rouge*, the river was wide enough to allow all the canoes to head up river at once, dodging islands of sawgrass as it poked up through the shallows. Now, the shrubs and small trees extended over the water, preventing more than two or three canoes from traveling abreast of each other. The branches and foliage provided a welcome respite from the sun, but the thick air continued to press down on Juan Carlos and the other members of her crew.

The river seemed to take a new turn every two hundred feet—hard left, then right, then a smoother curve to the right, then left again. Juan Carlos's heart sank as he realized he would not be able to navigate back to *La Marée Rouge* without the help of an experienced guide. He guessed the sun was now more at his back than beside him, meaning they must be heading east.

Around another bend, a turn to the right—south? he wondered as the river changed again. The brush began to pull back. The river bottom seemed so close he couldn't imagine how they had avoided running aground. The sand began to rise around the boat, the brush fading into more clumps of sawgrass. Minutes later, the waterborne caravan left the thickness of the forest, entering a vast prairie of grass reaching six feet or more into the sky, and the banks of the river pulled away. Then, dead ahead of their canoe cavalcade, a green wall of sawgrass seemed to rise against them, a barrier to a world beyond.

As they approached, Juan Carlos noticed a small channel had been cut at a beach head. A thick batch of grass growing over the water's surface hid the opening. From the river, which had now narrowed to a creek, the channel looked like a thick, wild thicket, impenetrable without a machete or other blade.

But the Calusa poled directly into the mass. The blades separated at the bow, and they pushed on, the boat slowing just a little before the grass thinned. Now the canoes picked up speed, and Juan Carlos saw solid earth rise one to two feet above the water on both sides. The rises looked as if someone had packed dirt and grass on top of a wall, possibly made up of tree limbs, creating boat access deep into the watery prairie.

Isabella stood up in the canoe as it continued to push forward at what seemed like a break-neck speed. Juan Carlos looked behind him to verify that Isabella remained in the procession. "Nothing," she called out as she turned to look in all directions. "Small trees behind us, a few clumps of trees in the distance. Nothing else but this swamp weed."

Gabrielle stayed low in her canoe but raised her head to call out to her friends. "The swamps around Port-au-Prince are similar, but the land rises into the foothills. I see no mountains or hills."

"Si, it's like a desert, but with water and grass instead of sand."

Isabella lifted her sleeve to her forehead. "It seems as hot as a desert."

The Indians poled through the grass for what seemed like several hours, the sun at their backs, the landscape now featureless, except for the earthen works that charted a maze only a swamp denizen could fathom. Juan Carlos looked up at the sun, noting its position.

"East," Isabella said.

He looked at her. "What?"

"We're heading east. At about five knots. We started going south, but we turned east. We're about twenty-five miles into the swamp."

Juan Carlos nodded. He noted the turns in the channel and the few markers on land. He had no way of finding his way out of this labyrinth. He hoped a minotaur did not live at the center because he had no thread to guide him to safety.

Isabella heaved a sigh as she saw the small island of trees appear on the horizon. She figured the canoes had traveled at least thirty miles. The

Calusa did not seem to notice or care. *They must do this every day*, she thought. She scanned the horizon, failing to see anything she could use as a marker.

She shifted her weight, careful to keep herself centered, her movement dislodging sweat-soaked wool from her stomach and breasts. She rolled her shoulders, hoping a pocket of air would give her skin a respite from the humidity fueling new waves of perspiration over her body. As they drew closer to what must be the tribe's village, she noticed more Indians along the canals, playing children brought to a standstill by the parade of canoes and their unusual freight.

The children wore nothing, except a woven belt, perhaps stitched from the weeds and stalks of swamp grass, adorned with shells based on their large coin-sized shape and bleached color. A few of the older children wore breech cloths slung around their waist in a fashion similar to the men. None of the girls wore clothing above the waist, exposing their chests as their unbraided hair cascaded down their backs. Older women, perhaps sisters, mothers, and aunts, gathered up the children with mild urgency as the canoes passed. They cloistered them behind earthworks that now rose high enough to obscure everything except their shoulders and head. Isabella smiled as she thought of the impracticality of her pirate garb under the sweltering sun. She lifted a hand to unfasten two more buttons on her wool blouse.

Isabella looked behind her again to check on Gabrielle, noting the small brimmed hat she had snatched to shield her from the sun. Jean-Michel had objected to her joining the trade mission, but her gut told her that another woman in the trading party would give her leverage with the Calusa and reinforce their peaceful purpose. They wouldn't know her ferocity in battle. Gabrielle would be her trump card if the negotiations failed, and they needed to escape.

Isabella peered around the bodies of the five warriors poling their canoe forward, sure that Juan Carlos was just as irritable. She pressed her hand against her sword, confirming for the hundredth time its place at her side. They had followed through on their bargain. Powder and bullets for seventy-five muskets. Twenty-five rifles. Soon, she would see whether the bargain was a good one—or one more suited to Faust and the devil.

The warriors continued the unspoken rhythm, their poles propelling the alien visitors through the canal and toward the trees. The trees rose into the sky, gray tubes capped by thin layers of limbs and leaves rising higher than the main mast of Isabella's pirate brig, over one hundred feet. Each stroke of the pole uncovered new texture. Blue green clumps of Spanish moss hung from low-hanging limbs, the type of tree unclear through the lush, brilliant green brush. Soon, the massive wooden fingers at the base of the trees revealed their cypress origins. Beyond the cypress, pine trees rose as slender, unadorned stalks, only the top twenty feet sprouting limbs to form a leafy bulb held together by unruly clumps of green pine needles. What lay under those canopies? Isabella wondered.

The native boats at the lead seemed to disappear into a thicket of green brush resting atop a gray foundation, an illusion created by the slight bend in the canal, she soon realized. The thicket was made up of vibrant ferns mixed with Spanish moss draping off the limbs of cypress trees, sitting on a base of gray trunks clawing deep into the mud, well below the water's surface. The canoes turned to trace the outer circle of the forest cluster, its size obscured from a distance by the vastness of what seemed like a featureless swamp prairie.

Isabella's heart quickened as the fullness of the forest before her eyes was revealed. She could hear the crackle of large fires but searched in vain for smoke. Despite the watery carpet they traveled, the fuel for these fires had long dried. The knocks of tools landing against hard wood were now as clear as the sun beating down on them. She resisted a temptation to shake her head, a dangerous signal of disbelief among people with such a fierce reputation.

She glanced over to the warriors sitting in her canoe, noting the calmness of their perch and the casualness of their grips on the weapons.

She drew in a breath, sure what she saw now was not what the truth would be.

The muscles in her throat contracted, a futile attempt to find enough saliva to swallow, and she took in another breath. Where was the village? Where did all the children and women come from? She looked away from the island forest, seeing nothing but bunches of two, three, sometimes, a half-dozen trees rising above thirsty grasses growing from the mud. This forest, this village, must be massive, but invisible to all except the most adventurous foreigners.

She turned back to the island and noted the gentle slowing of the canoe. She looked toward the lead canoes and saw them make a sharp turn, exposing the full length of the boat and its travelers before disappearing into the island. As her canoe approached the turning point, she saw an open space carved out of the thicket, a channel now visible that reversed direction just beyond the outer perimeter. As their boat turned into the channel, she felt the presence of eyes watching from the forest and bushes, although nothing was visible to her.

Isabella ducked, an immediate reaction to an unexpected low whistle. She looked toward the outer trees just in time to see the shaft and feathers of an arrow disappear into the water. Giggles and laughter erupted from the leaves and brush, as a warrior behind her yelled toward the trees. His tone and inflections conveyed a scolding message, and Isabella was sure his words provided more clarity about the acceptability of their behavior to the arrow's owner. The warrior shouted something in a sterner tone but less angry spirit, and a more measured but youthful voice responded. A hard drive of the pole pushed the canoe forward, causing a large ripple as its bow cut through the still water.

Another two hundred feet and the channel opened. A wide beach spread before her with scores of canoes lined up on its shore. Juan Carlos, Herrera, Gabrielle, and four other pirates stood among several warriors as the boats unloaded. Beyond the canoes, Isabella counted more than a dozen large structures, huts, or lodges—*chikees* she thought she remembered Herrera call them—bordering another canal leading to a very large round building at its end. Poles held the structure up, many appeared to be high enough to support a roof six or seven floors above the ground. Some *chikees* had walls, but she couldn't make out the materials. The sun illuminated ordered, disciplined lines in the weave of palm leaf thatched roofs.

The canoe nudged onto the beach. Four Indians jumped into the water with such skill the boat remained motionless in the water. Isabella rolled to her knees, putting both hands on the gunwale to steady herself, but an urgent, insistent voice stopped her. She looked up at an Indian, his hands in a frantic wave, a clear message for her to stop. Six warriors pulled at the canoe until it was out of the water. The warrior looked at her and said something else she didn't understand but decided it meant she could get out of the canoe.

She stepped onto the sand and walked over to the band of foreigners.

Juan Carlos looked around and laughed. "Someone needs to update New Spain's accounts! *Claramente*, not all the Calusa made it to Havana."

Herrera turned to Isabella, his eyes narrowed as they darted from side to side. "Capitán, I don't like the looks of this. These Indians should not be here."

Isabella nodded.

Gabrielle stepped closer. "Where is the trading post?"

Isabella turned to Juan Carlos. "Did you talk to the chief?"

Juan Carlos shook his head. "No one said a word… except to keep me from being eaten by a crocodile." Any thought of laughing at Juan Carlos's quip was suppressed by the foreboding mood that seemed to hang with the trading party as they surveilled the strange village.

The pirates turned to an assembly of a dozen warriors unloading the powder, bullets, and rifles from the canoes. One warrior, several loops of shell necklaces hanging from his neck, three large feathers extending from his knotted hair, inspected each box and bag. Each Indian waited for his permission before moving the supplies toward a *chikee* about three quarters of the way up the road.

"Keep a close eye on where those supplies go, Señor Herrera," she said as she watched the unloading. "Just don't make it too obvious."

"Welcome to Tanpa, captains, my friends!"

112

The band turned toward the voice and saw the chief from the San Carlos Bay taking his last steps toward them. "We also call our village Nueva Calos. *Por favor*, come with me. I will introduce you to our Paramount *Cacique!*"

Isabella turned to Herrera, his raised eyebrows communicating his confusion. Juan Carlos gave her a slight shake of the head. She turned back to the chief and bowed her head. "*Gracias, el jefe.*"

The chief turned and led the group of foreigners toward the round building at the end of the canal leading from the beach as Isabella covered the hilt of her sword with her hand.

The chief had the pirates stop at the base of the large round building. Juan Carlos could see the thatched walls, knitted together by palm leaves which looked like rows of sowed braids. The weaves seemed to pull him closer to the thatch, the intricacy capturing his focus.

"It's palm thatch," Isabella said.

"Si, but the weave is so complex. It's a marvel."

Isabella looked at the walls and nodded. "Many buildings on the islands have this type of construction."

"Spaniards prefer wood plank and brick."

"Not everyone has the luxury of the wealth to fire brick or the labor to rip lumber to build homes." Isabella squinted at the wall. "Thatch works with the right palm leaves. Keeps water and bugs out."

Gabrielle turned to look at the walls. "We didn't have anything like this in Port-au-Prince. Stone and lumber were the materials for our buildings with iron heated for joints. *Encore*, the weave is impressive. I don't think I could learn how to thatch a wall that finely without years of practice."

Isabella nodded. "Tradition. Mother to daughter, father to son, over generations." She reached out to touch the weave, the tightly connected stems and leaves bringing back memories of her mother teaching her similar skills in Santo Domingo.

Herrera turned back to look down the wide canal connecting the large, round *chikee* to the beach. More than fifty canoes now lined the sand. "Why do you think they have this canal?"

Juan Carlos joined him by his side. "My guess is ceremony. I do not see a military purpose."

Herrera pointed to the different sides of the canal. "Unless the village was cut in two by some army. They could defend the rest of the village using the canal as a moat. The water would slow anyone charging across it."

"I agree, but the canal is not very wide. No more than three canoes could navigate its length." Juan Carlos paused, his silence conveying deep thought. "The canals we followed flowed from the river. Miles of canals. Our best army engineers would be amazed at how well constructed they are. Yet I don't see any tools from the Continent."

Gabrielle looked around the side of the building and returned to the group. "This village is so well hidden. The canals. The canoes. These lodges. None of our buildings except the fortresses and colonial palaces were built like this in Port-au-Prince."

Isabella nodded. "Not giving the Calusa the respect they deserve could kill us."

Juan Carlos kneeled, inspecting the poles holding the round *chikee* up above them. "Why so high? The village is in the middle of swamp too big to flood from rains. Tides?"

Herrera chuckled. "Too far in for tides." He pointed to the packed sand underneath their boots. "No signs of flooding." He looked around the village. "I would say varmints of various kinds." The others stayed silent. "I've heard this part of La Florida has mountain lions, wild pigs, and lizards with monster teeth—crocodiles. I saw a few of those crocs on the way in. They have tails strong enough to cut a long boat in two with one whip. Their jaws will snap a man in half."

"*C'est terrible!*"

Herrera laughed. "I am sure you didn't see many of them in Port-au-Prince."

"*Mais oui,*" Gabrielle said, a quiver in her voice. "We have crocodiles in the swamps around Port-au-Prince. But I have never seen

114

one. My parents just warned me of them, and I heard of them attacking hunters at night."

Gabrielle gasped. "*Regardez!*" The group turned to see Gabrielle pointing up the steps outside the main entrance to the big house.

Isabella caught her breath.

"*Pardonnez-moi Sainte Marie.*"

Rising twenty feet above the foreigners were four poles. On their tips were the severed heads of four men. By the leathered look of the skin, hollowed cheeks, and missing eyes, the men had been dead for a long time, weeks or perhaps months.

"Two of them are white men," Herrera said in a low voice.

Isabella paused. "The other two are Indian." She rested her palm on her sword, letting her fingers tap around the grip. "Do we know which building holds the rifles, powder and shot?"

"The third building up from the lagoon on the right side of the canal," Juan Carlos confirmed. "I am sure they store other muskets there as well."

"I don't think these men were killed as part of a sacrifice," Isabella said. "At least, not one I know of from the spirit healers of the mountains on Hispaniola."

"We are not on Hispaniola," Gabrielle reminded the group. "We are in a new world."

Juan Carlos turned away from the piked heads and looked at Isabella. "I don't know if that should give us hope... or prepare us for something very dark."

15

Each step leading to the threshold of what they assumed was the Calusa leader's house seemed to toll a warning. The building rose above the hard-packed sand, held up by two and four-foot-thick poles made from pine trees to shoulder its weight. Worn wooden planks dulled the clacking from their leather-soled boots, robbing the small band of pirates of any sound that could in some way herald a grand entrance. Hands glanced off the handles of pistols and knives cloaked by wool shirts and bound sashes.

The chief who guided their canoes into the swamp appeared at the portal. He raised his hand. *"Espera aquí."*

Isabella, at the lead, halted and the other pirates closed ranks.

The chief lowered his hand, his eyes unfocused as he looked out to the small bay, as if he could look through Isabella and her band. "The Paramount Chief is ready to see you. All who address him are expected to show their respect by kneeling before him and lifting their hands to him." The chief lifted his hands in front of him, palms up. "You will talk only after he responds."

The chief turned, and he appeared to step into an abyss.

The band stood in place. Isabella let the chief disappear into the darkness before she stepped forward behind him, and the remaining pirates followed her into the black.

Isabella listened for the chief's footsteps as they passed through the wooden threshold insulated by the woven thatch walls. She remembered the wood-framed buildings of her cabin on the Santo Domingo plantation. A shallow shiver rolled down her back as she recalled how the moisture from the trees around their clustered slave quarters seeped through cracks and holes left unattended. The inside of this Calusa building, in contrast, felt dry and comfortable as they moved inside the space.

Her eyes adjusted to the gray, and the full size of the great hall emerged. Her fingers closed around her sword. She took in a deep breath and let it out, counting as her lungs emptied, trying to calm her muscles and grip. Scores of Calusa warriors created human walls funneling them through a grand hall. The chief was taking them through a gauntlet.

Light seeped in from windows fifteen feet or higher above them. The Indians didn't wear armor, or any clothing other than the leather or finally woven breech cloths falling from their waist, and belts holding shell-tipped axes and conch hammers within easy reach. Their faces were covered by wooden masks with haunting images framed by triangles and scythe-like blades around the eyes. Some evoked images of animals, mostly predators such as wolves, falcons, panthers, and alligators. Shell necklaces draped over their chests. Their hair was pulled back to reveal faces lined with red, white, and blue stripes from dye extracted from local plants. Their stern looks gave no illusion of their purpose or actions if called upon by the chief.

As the pirates adjusted to the interior, the light dance of lanterns began to fill space as they progressed deeper into the leader's house. As more light filled the room, the long shafts of muskets became apparent among some of the warriors, triggering a jump in Isabella's chest. She had just given this tribe enough powder and shot to wipe out a small town.

The chief in front of her obscured what was directly ahead, but she saw an Indian woman sitting on the left at the end of the hall, her yellow-brown skin evident in the light. Her arms were crossed, as if ready to pronounce judgment when called. Shell-laced bands adorned her forearms and ankles, her hair held up by a carved rod fastened with more shells. A regal expression seemed to project a seriousness to what was about to happen.

"The Paramount *Cacique's* wife, I think," Herrera whispered in Isabella's ear.

The chief stopped and kneeled. As his head and torso dipped, Isabella saw a man on a raised platform sitting on what was clearly a throne. A wood carved headdress, lines and angles painted in ordered intricacy, extended to the ceiling. Only his stern, piercing eyes were visible below the headdress and above painted stripes leading at angles from his ears to his mouth and nose, not that much different from the chief that led them to this village deep in the swamps of La Florida, now kneeling in front of him.

A web of leather lace at the base of his neck held one of the largest sand dollar shells she had ever seen, larger than the width of Jean-Michel's closed fist. Centering it with a necklace framed by a fish-bone cross, his upper torso projected an elegance that stood out from the others among the warriors and chiefs. The design and placement alone erased any doubt they were now in front of the Paramount *Cacique* of the Calusa.

The Paramount *Cacique* focused only on the chief kneeling before him, revealed now as a chief of authority. He nodded, said something in his native language, and the chief stepped aside to stand next to the woman. Another warrior stepped toward the chief holding a headdress, kneeled before him, and placed it on him. The headdress was decorated with feathers Isabella recognized as those from a hawk, extending from a wooden crown that rested on his head. A line of small, round sea shells fastened by some type of thin rope or string descended down both sides of his face, the last shell resting on the top of his shoulder.

"The Military *Cacique*," Juan Carlos whispered in her ear. She resisted the temptation to nod, unsure of whether any movement would be considered a sign of disrespect.

The Paramount *Cacique* looked at the pirates, his eyes shifting from one head to the other, then fixing on Isabella.

She stepped forward, kneeled, and stretched her arms up to him palms up. "We come in peace… and to trade."

The Paramount *Cacique* sat silent and resolute.

The Military *Cacique* spoke in what she now recognized as their native tongue. The Paramount *Cacique* nodded.

After a pause, Isabella spoke again. "We have given the Calusa twenty-five long guns plus powder and shot for seventy-five guns."

The Military *Cacique* translated again. This time the Paramount *Cacique* nodded and acknowledged the words with his own.

Isabella's heart slowed, relieved that at least they were communicating. She hesitated, expecting the Military *Cacique* to translate the Calusa language. She felt the air thicken around her.

"The Paramount *Cacique*," the Military *Cacique* said, his words deliberate and slow, "thanks you for your tribute."

Isabella's chest tightened. Tribute? She looked over to the Military *Cacique*. "We are here to trade."

The Military *Cacique* nodded once.

"We are in need of supplies," Isabella said. "Water, fish, meat, fruit."

The Military *Cacique* turned to the Paramount *Cacique*. The two exchanged several words before the Military *Cacique* turned back to Isabella. "The Paramount *Cacique* would like to know what you have to trade for these supplies and how much you are offering."

Isabella's heart raced as the blood flow quickened through her arteries. Her eyes hardened. "We have already provided twenty-five rifles, powder and shot for seventy-five guns."

The Military *Cacique* nodded. "And the Paramount *Cacique* has thanked you for your tribute. Now he is ready to begin discussing your terms for a trade."

She felt how the shift in tone and language had also prompted movement from Juan Carlos and her party. She heard Juan Carlos order the others to calm down, more through his tone than her ability to hear the precise words. She kept her eyes on the Military *Cacique*. "May I consult with my quartermaster? He keeps track of all our stores."

"The captain of the ship approaches the Paramount *Cacique* for a trade, but she does not know with what she has to trade?"

She bowed her head to the Military *Cacique* and retreated from her kneeling position into her group.

"We are eight against four hundred," Herrera said in a hushed voice.

Isabella kept her eyes turned to the wood planks separating their band of pirates from the hardened mound of sand and shells below them. "How much powder do we have?"

Herrera huffed. "Not enough to fight off another attack by Muñoz at this rate."

"That's not what I asked," Isabella hissed.

Herrera sighed. "We agreed to another trade of twenty-five rifles worth of powder and shot. We've got fifty more muskets left on the ship, not enough to arm all our men. We trade the rest of the powder out, we'll have about four shots per cannon, maybe a few rounds for the muskets."

Isabella sighed.

"Cap'n, we got to get out."

Isabella turned her face to look at the source of the husky voice she rarely heard. "I know Patrick. We're outnumbered. We need to be clever to get out of this."

"And calm," said Juan Carlos. "We have no way of escape if we stay in this chief's lodge. The first thing we need to do is get out of here. We need a better plan than sitting between a Paramount Chief, his wife, a Military Chief, and hundreds of armed warriors."

Isabella nodded and turned back to the throne but hesitated when she saw who had joined the Paramount *Cacique*. Another much older man kneeled next to him. Isabella's heart skipped. Black ink around the older man's eyes created the illusion of a large, cat-like predator, a black panther, watching them from the darkness. Had the Military *Cacique* seen the scarlet flag of another panther slung on the mast of the *La Marée Rouge*?

Three long, colorful feathers extended upwards from the warrior's head, perhaps fastened by the knot of hair that had been pulled back behind his head. Scores of shells of different sizes and shapes hung from a thick pearl linked necklace, while a woven matt hung from his waist like a breechcloth with designs of diamonds, squares, and triangles of different colors. He held a long pole, longer than a fully-grown man, with a large conch attached to the top, the spiral tip facing toward her like the end of a battle ax.

Isabella stepped forward, kneeled again, lifting her palms up to the Paramount *Cacique*.

"The shaman says you are filled with a strong spirit," the Military *Cacique* said from the side of the throne.

Isabella nodded. "I have strong faith."

"It is not a Christian faith."

"The Paramount Chief knows about Christianity?"

The military *Cacique* laughed. "All Calusa know about Christians. The stories of the ships carrying Christians to our villages and towns are part of our tradition and heritage."

The images of the severed heads at the entrance to the lodge flashed before her. "Two of the heads on the pikes at the entrance are white."

"You observe much, captain. They were evil men, men who did not respect the traditions of the Calusa."

"The heads of the Calusa as well?"

"Perhaps you know less than you think. The brown skinned heads are those of Yamassee."

"The Calusa are at war with the Yamassee?"

"The Calusa will never be at peace with Yamassee. They have contract with English to capture Calusa and sell them to whites who farm in the North."

Isabella paused, letting her head dip. She closed her eyes. Scenes of Europeans and Indians armed with guns, blades, and clubs unfolded before her eyes as slavers crashed through shoulder-high grass cloaked by a blue-gray morning mist to seize unsuspecting Calusa men, women, and children. These images yielded to the gnarled talons of flames clutching at the sky over Santo Domingo as she felt her mother's body fall limp in her arms and her last breaths took her spirit back to Lasiren, the spirit of the ocean. Her world, the planation she had known all her life, a cauldron of evil and darkness, was consumed with the devil's own inferno as she ran for her life. The sounds of gunfire, the screams of boys and girls she had known as a child, the blood curdling, vengeful chant of

Gamba as he chased these images into a rising Tsunami of darkness that followed her for two years.

Isabella fell to the floor, her palms down on the hard surface. Then she lifted her face to the ceiling. She heaved in air, bringing her arms up, extending her hands to the cypress rafters holding the thatch room in place.

"Aiyiayiahi, Aiyiayiahi, Aiyiayiahi," she chanted in a low, rumbling tone that rose in a crescendo and silenced the room. Feet shuffled around the pirates, but arrows were held to their bows and spears close to their warrior owners.

Isabella continued her chants, "Aiyiayiahi, Aiyiayiahi, Aiyiayiahi. Aiyiayiahi, Aiyiayiahi, Aiyiayiahi."

She dipped her head again, bringing her arms down and crossing them on her chest, her palms flat against her shoulders. She drew in a full breath of air, a heave that seemed to lift her to her feet and opened her eyes. The Paramount Chief seemed unmoved. A smile appeared on the Shaman's face as his eyebrows narrowed his eyes to focus on Isabella. He announced something in the native language. Feet shuffled again, but the sounds seemed to fade into the background.

"Shaman says you filled with spirit."

Isabella's nod acknowledged the Military Chief. She brought her arms down, letting the back of her left hand fall into a cup made by the palm of her right hand. She extended her hands, one on top each other, to the Paramount *Cacique*. "*Tepe*," she said, her voice strong and directed.

The sound of the Calusa word startled the Paramount *Cacique*, the blink only visible to those focused on the pupils of his eyes shadowed by the brim of the mask.

"I was a slave," Isabella intoned, looking into his eyes.

The Military *Cacique* directed his next words to the Paramount *Cacique*, triggering a series of exchanges between the chiefs and the shaman. The tone seemed to adopt an edge.

A female voice rose above the words, and the exchange stopped. Isabella turned to see the woman sitting next to the throne rise and step toward her. Isabella examined the sophisticated weave of the mat that hung from her waist and the necklaces more clearly. She wore nothing above her waist, her breasts exposed like the other women and girls in the village. Five petals extending from the center of a necklace revealed the round shells as sand dollars, but they were large—four or five inches wide. As she approached, the carved edges around the circle became clear. She paused just long enough to recognize the skill and patience needed to convert the remnants of a sea urchin into such an exquisite pattern without damaging the shell.

The woman approached Isabella and looked into her eyes. She said something in the native tongue. She said something else, this time directed at the shaman based on his movement. He responded. Then she turned to the Paramount *Cacique*. Her words, still in the native language, were direct and unwavering.

"The men are to stay here. You are to go with Chosa," the Military *Cacique* announced.

16

Gabrielle's chest tightened. Isabella tried to object to the separation from the men, but her protests were ignored. Now they were isolated.

"Where are they taking them?" Gabrielle asked as they followed Chosa down the steps of the lodge.

Isabella didn't respond, but Gabrielle thought she saw a short, brief shake of her head.

Each step Chosa took seemed to lighten the air around them. Children at the bottom of the stairs parted as they peered at the two, dark-skinned women, one with wavy curls flowing to her shoulders from a red bandana, and the other with a brimmed hat shading her eyes and covering tight matted curls.

Isabella had never seen so many children in one place, and she looked behind her to see them collect into a pulsing trail leading back to the lodge.

"*Bonjour mes enfants,*" Gabrielle said, resisting the temptation to touch one of the nearer children on the head. The strange words seem to create another foot of distance between the leaders and the women.

"Don't worry, I won't hurt you." She chuckled in a low voice. "I reserve my pain for the Spanish and French."

Gabrielle felt Isabella's hand clasp around hers. Isabella dipped her head toward her and then pitched a nod toward Chosa. "Sssh. We don't know what she can understand."

Gabrielle acknowledged Isabella's warning with a quick squeeze but laced her fingers through hers as they continued to follow the Paramount *Cacique*'s wife.

The women approached another building, rectangular in shape but raised above the ground by about four feet. They followed the wood steps up to a narrow porch and entered the building.

Torches lit up the inside of the building, the flames controlled by poles located deep in the interior. A hole in the roof, well over twenty feet above them, allowed the heat and what little smoke the flames generated to escape into the evening air.

Gabrielle looked around, noting the woven mats along the floor evenly spaced in sections along the edges. Like other *chikees*, the lodge did not have walls, allowing a breeze to sweep through the building. In the middle of the floor was a work area with pestles for grinding seeds or other hardened food, bowls, trays, and what looked like a mallet of some sort.

Chosa turned to Isabella. She then looked at Gabrielle. She turned back to Isabella and pointed to her. "*Cacique?*"

Isabella hesitated at first, then nodded. "Captain. *Cacique.* On the water."

Chosa seemed to smile and pointed to Gabrielle. She spoke several words in the native language, but neither the pirate nor the rebel could understand a word. She lifted her hands up as if catching the entirety of the lodge and swept her arms in a circle.

"I am sorry," Isabella said, shaking her head. "*Lo siento, no entiendo.*"

Chosa stepped toward Isabella and put her hand on her chest and said another word with a smile.

"Thank you," Isabella said. "*Gracias. Merci.*"

Chosa turned with an abrupt pivot and brought her hands together in a series of loud claps. She shouted more words in Calusa, and the sharpness of her pitch prompted Isabella to step back.

Gabrielle stepped closer to Isabella. "What do you think?"

"I think if they wanted to kill us she would not have brought us here. This looks like a place people live, work, and sleep."

"What about the men?"

Isabella shook her head. She reached for Gabrielle's hand again. "We'll find them."

As soon as Chosa's hands stopped moving, several women entered the lodge. Chosa turned to Isabella and with a gentle sweep of her arm signaled for them to sit on mats close to a work station.

Gabrielle wished for the hammock swung over her cramped space on *La Marée Rouge* as soon as her butt felt the mat underneath. The designs were detailed, like everything else the Calusa had made, and colorful. She wondered what plants or rocks generated the reds, blues, yellows, and grays that made up the triangles, squares, diamonds and other shapes embedded in the woven reeds.

Someone brought a bowl over and placed it in front of her. Inside she could see the white flesh of scaled fish. She looked up to Isabella, and their eyes met. With a raised eyebrow, Isabella seemed to say "okay," and they started picking the pieces apart and eating them. Gabrielle's throat seemed to rebel, refusing to let the boiled fish any further than the back of her tongue. She looked back to Isabella, who seemed to be enjoying the food.

Isabella laughed. "Eat up Gabrielle! I think you're too used to the fine dining of a pub in Port-au-Prince!"

Gabrielle shook her head. Her cheeks bulged in and out as she maneuvered the fish until finally she jutted her jaw out and lifted her face toward the ceiling to force it down her throat. "I've been forcing your grub down my throat for almost two months!"

Isabella laughed again, lifting a piece of fish up between her fingers. "Our hosts did the courtesy of boiling the fish so it falls apart in my hands! This is how we boiled fish on St. John, in Panther Bay." She sighed before putting another mouthful in her hand and savoring the delicacy.

"I agree," Gabrielle said. "It's much better than the dried beef and hard tack on *La Marée Rouge*." She dribbled another piece of fish into her mouth. "It's really not bad. They must boil it in saltwater, because that's about all I can taste. I wouldn't mind some chicken, though."

Another bowl filled with oysters provided a second course. Gabrielle looked up to the Calusa woman who served the food to her and smiled. "*Merci.*"

126

Once done with the oysters, a ceramic plate was brought out with a slab of white colored muscle twice the size of two fists but shaped like a ham hock—a ball of meat on the end of bone. The meat was drier than the boiled fish, clams, and oysters, the orange and darker tinge signs of being cooked over a fire.

Gabrielle smiled. "Queen Conch!"

"Ha!" chuckled Isabella. "So you do like seafood."

Gabrielle sighed. "My father was a good cook. I am sorry he spoiled me."

Gabrielle looked around the tray and bowls and found a bone fashioned into a rectangular blade. She picked it up, inspected it, and saw that the bone had been carved into a cutting blade. She reached over and cut off a piece of the grilled conch and placed in in her mouth. "*Merveilleux,*" she hummed.

She cut off another piece and offered it to Isabella. Isabella slipped the sliver into her mouth, rolled it on her tongue, sucking on its mild taste and swallowed it. Isabella nodded. "I like the grilled conch. Still very chewy... hard on the jaws... but the taste reminds me of clams."

Gabrielle leaned back on the floor after she finished, her legs still crossed on the mat. She sighed. "I hope the men were able to eat like we have tonight."

She heard Isabella sigh next to her. "I just hope it was not our last supper."

Gabrielle breathed in, closing her eyes, letting her hand reach over to Isabella. Isabella opened her palm, and their fingers clasped together in a fine weave.

Isabella's eyes popped open, wondering what woke her. She lay still, scolding herself for falling asleep. The memory of her capture on St. John by Rodriguez's pirate hunters suddenly ticked her heart up to a dangerous pace. A sweat broke out across her body as the images flashed through her brain. She had awoken, in a start, under the palm leaves near the beach after her narrow escape from the mutiny. Her breathing became short as she remembered the ambush and being taken to El Morro. She would not let that happen again; she had vowed to herself. She would keep that vow now, even if it meant death.

Isabella drew in a deep breath to calm herself and listened. She was not under palm leaves now, but she was under an alien roof. The soft shuffle of feet seemed to ring in her ears, but how far away she could not tell. A muffled voice seemed to carry urgency to set off more shuffling.

Isabella unlaced her fingers from Gabrielle's hand and moved her palm up her arm to her face. She felt the twitch of Gabrielle's arm as she woke. Isabella placed her palm to gently cover her mouth. Gabrielle's hands come up to hers and pulled them away. Isabella thought she could hear the rise and fall of Gabrielle's lungs as the shuffling feet became more intense.

The scuffle of skin on wood covered the movement of her right hand as it checked for her sword by her side. The sheath was pinched between the floor planks and her thigh, making it almost impossible for her to draw it for defense. She would have to roll into a new position.

A shadow danced across the ceiling as the fading flame from a torch tracked its origin. The shadow left the light, but not its sound. The body was coming closer.

Isabella narrowed her eyes to little more than slits, hoping she would have enough illumination to give her warning. The feet transitioned from a scuffle to slow deliberate steps, heavier as the body closed in. Isabella let her arm relax against Gabrielle's body, and moved her other hand off the hilt of her saber.

A woman's body emerged over her, hesitated, then hovered. The woman's hair flowed over her shoulders and breasts, obscuring any light from the torch. She descended toward Isabella, an arm suddenly holding something large above her.

Isabella shot her arms up toward the body, using her left arm to block the woman and the object, thrusting her other arm under the woman's armpit. Isabella's weight threw the woman off balance, and the two rolled.

Isabella had the woman on her back, one arm pinned to the floor. She moved her free hand to clasp her attacker's mouth shut as she let the full weight of her body immobilize her. The woman shook her head, trying to loosen Isabella's grip.

She sensed Gabrielle roll onto her knees and lunge toward them. Gabrielle lifted a bowl above her head.

"*Arrêtez!*" Isabella ordered in hushed breathe. "Gabrielle wait!"

Isabella glowered into the terrified eyes of the woman. "You are a white woman!"

The woman's eyes glistened with tears as she tried to nod under Isabella's cupped hand.

"Shhhh," Isabella said with a soothing voice.

Gabrielle lifted her head to look around the room. "*Je ne vois personne,*" she whispered as she kneeled next to them.

Isabella nodded and turned back to their attacker. The woman's eyes darted to Gabrielle's voice, the frightened tears transformed into confused panic.

"*Silence,*" whispered Isabella in French. "*Êtes-vous Français?*"

Isabella relaxed her fingers just enough to let the woman respond with a vigorous nod.

"*Bien,*" Isabella said continuing in French, her voice more serious than urgent. "I am going to uncover your mouth. Do not yell. Or I will have to kill you. Do you understand?"

The woman nodded, the quick rise of her lungs the only remaining evidence of her fear of death.

Isabella removed her hands. "What is your name?"

The woman sucked in air. "*Je m'appelle*, Marguerite."

Gabrielle leaned over, letting her face come within inches of Marguerite. "Are you Calusa?"

"*Non, non,*" she pleaded in French. "I was captured along with my children. They will not let us go."

"Slaves?"

Margeurite's face fell, and she shook her head. "I... I... I don't know. I only know a few words. I don't know how to escape."

"How long have you been here?" Isabella asked.

"I don't know. Our ship ran aground after a storm. The Calusa killed all the men. They killed all the boys old enough to work the ship."

Gabrielle rolled over on her bottom, resting her arms on her knees. "What about the women and children?"

"My family was the only one on board the ship."

"How many were in your family?

"Just me," Marguerite said, "and my two sons, Pierre and Jean. Pierre is thirteen years old, but he looks like he is ten or eleven. Jean is not two years old yet."

"And your husband? Was he killed by the Calusa?"

Marguerite shook her head. "He died months ago from the Fever in Saint Domingue."

Gabrielle looked at her. "You are from Saint Domingue?"

"Oui, my husband was a trader. Our ships traveled between Bordeaux and Port-au-Prince. We were afraid. We knew the *gens to couleur* and slaves were planning a revolt. We wanted to get out. But he died before we could arrange passage. It took me three months to get out of Port-au-Prince."

Gabrielle kneeled down beside the woman. "You were a trader? What is your family name?"

Panic returned to Marguerite's eyes.

"I am from Port-au-Prince," Gabrielle reassured her. "My family ran *Le Coq Fantôme* in the colored section of the city."

Marguerite's eyes relaxed. "Oui, *Le Coq Fantôme*. My husband, Pierre, mentioned it. He would sometimes recruit deck hands from your family's Inn. He liked to sign on the *gens de coulour*."

"Then I may know of your family," Gabrielle said.

"Our family name is Lafitte," Marguerite said. "My husband was Pierre Lafitte."

Gabrielle nodded. "My father knew your husband. He did not let everyone recruit from his inn. He thought your husband was fair."

Isabella lifted herself off of Marguerite's body. "I am sorry; *je suis désolé*. I thought you were attacking me."

Marguerite smiled. "I am sorry. I was cleaning up after your dinner. I was following Chosa's orders. I did not want to wake you."

The three women covered their mouths as they tried to muffle their laugh. Isabella lifted a hand to her face as she dusted her breeches. "The Calusa have been very welcoming."

Marguerite straightened herself and looked at Isabella and then Gabrielle. "Do not trust them," she said, a quiver in her voice. "They sacrificed two sailors from my ship to their gods."

Isabella looked at the French woman, naked except a deerskin breech cloth attached to her waist. "Where are your clothes?"

She looked away from Isabella and Gabrielle. "They took them. They say I must live like Calusa now. They will use my clothes and all my belongings to trade with other Indians."

"The Yamasee?" Gabrielle asked.

Marguerite shook her head with vigor. "Never the Yamasee. Or the Creek. Or the English or Spanish. Only the tribes native to this area of La Florida, the Ai and Tequesta."

Isabella leveled a skeptical glare at the Calusa prisoner. "How do you know so much? You said you only know a few words?"

The French woman shook her head. "Young boys are still naïve enough to think we are not enemies. Pierre is a smart boy. He is friends with several boys in the village. He has learned much of their language already."

Gabrielle shook her head. "We are French." She turned to Isabella. "She was a slave. Why would they want to kill us?"

"You are foreigners," Marguerite said, rolling over on her knees. "They do not trust any foreigner. The Spanish forced them to give up their traditions and religion and moved them to Cuba. The English allied with the Creeks and Yamasee to hunt the Calusa and enslave them."

"The French?"

"They trust no one."

Isabella ran her fingers into her hair. "We have to escape."

Marguerite looked at them. "You have to take me and my children with you."

Gabrielle leaned over, cupped her hand behind Marguerite's neck and touched her head. "Of course. We are a ship of refugees and outcasts.

Criminals, revolutionaries, and former slaves. To keep you off the *La Marée Rouge* would not be civilized."

Isabella stood up, tapping dust from her breeches. "Well now that you two have fallen in love, you better get permission from the captain."

The Pirate of Panther Bay turned to Marguerite and made it official: "*Bienvenue à bord* La Marée Rouge." She looked over to the threshold of their *chikee*. "If we get out of here alive."

17

Morning broke, but Isabella didn't need to be woken. Her brain churned most of the remaining night, reconstructing the buildings, the village layout, and counting warriors as best she could. Getting out of the hidden Calusa sanctuary would be the easiest step in what seemed now to be an impossible quest to navigate the swamps and canals back to *La Marée Rouge* alive. Even if they made it, they weren't assured of escaping San Carlos Bay, past Sanybelle Island, and into the gulf. And then they would have to contend with Muñoz.

Isabella rolled on her side, watching Gabrielle as her legs and arms seemed to twist her awake. She lifted herself on her elbows, looking around the floors. Scores of Calusa women and children now occupied the mats. She checked each body from her place near the center of the room, searching for the pale skin of the French woman Marguerite. Maybe she would also get a glimpse of her youngest son.

Bodies started to move, and Isabella lifted herself to a sitting position. The air was already thick as beads of perspiration began to percolate under her shirt and under her nose. The Calusa were practical. Who needs clothes in this climate? She unbuttoned her shirt, a futile move to coax what little air circulated in the room onto her skin.

She leaned over, bringing her lips to within a few inches of Gabrielle's ear. "Wake up," she whispered. "I'm heading outside."

Gabrielle's eyes blinked open, and she murmured a response. She lifted her hands to her face and dragged the palms down to her chin as she nodded an acknowledgement.

Isabella straightened herself, letting the extension of her shoulders stretch her back and legs. She breathed in. Her lungs pulled the blood through her heart and into her arms and hands. The clack of her boot's sole rang across the room, stopping her. She pulled her boots off and carried them to the threshold.

She and Gabrielle must be in the lazy lodge, because the village was bustling with the rising dawn light. She looked back inside the hut. Many of the women were up. They must have been letting the foreigners sleep.

Fires were lit, raging across logs as Calusa men worked to hollow out a new canoe. Another went to work skinning a deer, its head hanging from a noose fastened to a branch of a cypress tree. The meat would no doubt be a welcome delicacy for someone's dinner. The hide might be even more valuable, either to trade, or as clothing, or protection from the elements.

Isabella turned toward the small inlet that served as the port for the fleet of canoes. She started to count them and realized more than half were already out of the village. The warriors were not out in the estuaries at the fisheries. Where were they?

She turned back toward the Paramount *Cacique's* lodge, the *maśuhoma*. That's what Marguerite said the tribal lodge was called. The smaller buildings were "*ri*." The chief's lodge dwarfed the other *ri*s in the village, and its regal rise dominated every other building in the village. She examined each of the other buildings, looking for signs of where the Military *Cacique* or the village *cacique* might live. The buildings, all rectangular in design, with peaked roofs except the Paramount *Cacique*'s, seemed to be assigned to families or subclans within the tribe. Which was Marguerite's *ri*? Where were Juan Carlos, Herrera, Patrick, and the others?

Isabella moved to the edge of the stairs, looking back toward the Chief's house and paused as she saw Chosa looking out over the village. She lifted her hand as a morning greeting, but the wife of the Paramount *Cacique* turned and disappeared into the lodge.

She remembered the shaman the night before. Why was he smiling? Why did Chosa intervene? The Calusa trust no foreigners, Marguerite said.

"*Bonjour, capitaine!*"

134

The high-pitched voice of a young boy pulled Isabella back to the front of her lodge. She looked down to see a white boy, black hair pulled back behind him as thick waves seemed to dangle and sway into his eyes. He dressed in the traditional breechcloth and waist sash of the Calusa, the rest of his body covered only by the deep, red and brown skin of a European overexposed to the sun. "You must be Margeurite's oldest son, Pierre."

"*Oui capitaine! Ma mère* told me of your arrival!"

Isabella started down the steps. "And did she ask you to come fetch me?"

He smiled. "*Oui capitaine*! She is down by the water, preparing the fishing nets."

"Well, I am happy to follow my guide. *Allons-y!*"

Pierre led her toward the beach following the side of the ceremonial channel. Other boys turned as they approached, passing over Pierre until their eyes fixed on Isabella. Isabella kept her eyes forward, noting the movements of the children and men from the corners of her eyes.

The morning sun revealed new mysteries in the ground as they approached the bay. The bleached white fragments of sea shells created a coarse foundation for their walk. The pathway was hard, and she felt the leather soles of her boots slip with each step. She looked down at the bare feet of her guide, his gait fast and sure. "Do you miss your shoes?"

Pierre giggled. "*Non capitaine.* After one week, my feet are tough, like the other boys. I slipped too much with my boots. I fell too much as we played games—warrior games—around the village. *Ma mére* worried I might get a disease. But now I play and hunt with bare feet."

"Hunt?"

"Oui!" Pierre's voice lifted with pride. "Last week I shot a deer!"

"A deer? You have a gun?"

"*Malheureusement*, non," he sighed. "Only the warriors use the guns. I shot the deer with an arrow. We tracked it for two hours. We had to shoot it again before it finally fell."

"Just you and the boys?"

"Oui! Hugo was with me. And other boys."

"Another French boy?"

135

Pierre laughed. "No, he is Calusa. I could not pronounce his name in Calusa then. It sounded like Hugo to me, so that's what I call him. He is fifteen. Next year he becomes a *ñoka*!"

"A *ñoka*?"

He looked up at Isabella, his eyes steady and focused. "A warrior—*ñoka*. He will go out and fight with the men to protect our village."

As they approached the bay, Isabella saw older men loading nets and women inspecting shells fastened to the ropes. Sinkers. Several of the women used long, white dowel-like tools to weave the nets together. Another was breaking apart pieces of wood, using the pointed end of a giant conch attached to a wooden handle. Their entire world revolved around the shells and the sea. Shell Indians, she mused.

"What else do you hunt? I see fish nets and other water traps."

Pierre seemed to pause, letting the crunch of the shells beneath his feet churn thoughts through his brain. "We have very dangerous animals that only the warriors hunt. I have seen them bring back panthers. One time, I saw a bear. Sometimes the warriors do not come home from the hunt…."

Pierre's voice trailed off.

"You have come back each time," Isabella said, coaxing her voice to be bright.

Pierre stayed silent as he stayed deep in thought as he continued to lead Isabella to the bay.

"Did one of your friend's father die on a hunt?"

Pierre shook his head. "Fathers are very experienced. They come back."

Isabella waited a few more steps. "Did all your friends come back?"

Pierre shook his head.

Isabella stepped up to his side, putting her hand on his shoulder. "Sometimes bad things happen to good people. I have been through many battles. I have friends that did not survive."

Pierre sniffed, and lifted a hand to his eye.

"I have lost two people in battle that I loved very much," she said.

136

Isabella's slowed, letting the grip on his shoulder slow the young boy to a stop. She kneeled beside him and looked into his face. His eyes glistened from the tears he refused to let free. "You must miss him a lot."

"He was my best friend."

Isabella looked around the village. The trees rose above the buildings and busy fishing port, a giant natural citadel protecting the Calusa from the outside world. "This is a very difficult place to live."

Pierre sniffed again. "I could have saved him."

"How? You are just a boy. What could you have done?"

"He was attacked by a crocodile."

Isabella shook her head. "Crocodiles are very dangerous. They lived in the swamps and lakes of Santo Domingo where I grew up."

The tears finally broke. "I did not know it was a crocodile. *Ma mére* told me to stay out of the swamps in Port-au-Prince because she said they would eat me."

"I am sure you could not do much. Crocodiles lie in wait, hunting prey. The live underwater and stalk you. They hide in the tree roots and in the sawgrass."

Pierre shook his head. "I thought it was *el lagarto,* not a crocodile."

"*El lagarto?*"

"Alligator," Pierre said, nodding, pulling back his tears with a deep breath. "The alligators usually run from us. Sometimes the boys will throw sticks at them."

Isabella cocked her head. "They tease them?"

"But it was a crocodile, not an alligator. And he was big, much bigger than you. He attacked Sinaesta. He pulled him into the swamp and rolled him until he drowned."

Isabella closed her eyes, keeping her hands on Pierre's shoulders.

"We tried to help him but we didn't have weapons."

"You could not do anything without a gun. Or a strong blade with a tip well placed. Crocodiles are very dangerous. Their skin is too thick. I only know one person who has ever survived a crocodile attack."

Pierre looked at her, his eyes asking the question.

"He was a boy, older than you, who I cared very much about. His name was Gamba. I knew him on Santo Domingo where we were slaves harvesting sugar for trade. He was very brave, but he survived because he had a knife, and he knew where to cut the beast. He carried many scars from that fight."

"We are not taught how to fight crocodiles. But they teach us to stay away from them."

"That is very good teaching," Isabella said, pulling Pierre closer. He wrapped his arms around her. She let him press his body against hers and felt the gentle pressure of his hands against her back and shoulders.

Pierre than pulled away, his expression confused and concerned.

"What's wrong?"

"Your back," he said, lifting his hand and wrapping his fingers over her shoulder.

Isabella nodded, but kept her gaze on Pierre's eyes, struggling to keep her own tears hidden behind her eyes. "Those scars come from many places. The overseer's whip on the plantation. I was also captured by the Spanish and tortured in their fortress, El Morro."

"Why did they torture you?"

"I stood up for myself on the plantation. That was my first crime, and that was enough for fifty lashes at the post. I escaped. That would have been good enough for another fifty lashes, but I found a pirate ship to take me on. The second crime is enough to get me hanged and whipped. I was captured and got the lashings but they didn't get the satisfaction of hanging me." She smiled at Pierre. "I have much more life to live. You see, I have a prophecy to fulfill."

Pierre's eyes glistened with anticipation. "A prophecy?"

Isabella nodded. "I was told the prophecy by my mother, and it was confirmed by a priestess high in the mountains of Saint Domingue. My Christian friends say I have been called. I know it in my heart. So, you see, I have much more to do before I die."

Pierre smiled, but then his face descended into a serious expression. "You must hate the Spanish."

Pierre's innocent statement jolted Isabella. She thought of the torture her mother received and the flames consuming the plantation in the slave revolt she sparked. Jacob had saved her months later, but he was an American. And a pirate. "I hate Spain," she said. "I hate slavery. I hate what the Spanish have done to my family and friends. For a long time, I hated all the Spanish. Then I found one to love. He taught me that our hearts are not controlled by a king, or an overseer, or a plantation owner. He taught me that whether to love or hate was my choice. And I found one Spaniard to love. He was the one who saved me from El Morro. So I do not hate all Spaniards. I stop the evil and hope their hearts will follow."

"Will Sinaesta's mama and papa love me again?"

Isabella sighed, bringing her lips to Pierre's forehead. "I hope so. You deserve love. You have a good heart. You loved Saneasta. Your mother loves you." She looked into his eyes, lifting her hand to his cheek. "I have learned everyone has a heart. That heart is worth loving. I have learned that all hearts are valuable and should be protected, and that your spirit is eternal."

Pierre smiled. "The Calusa do not believe that. They believe we have three souls. When we die, one of our souls is in our eye and never leaves. It's in that really dark round part of our eyes. We can go to where we buried our friends, and we can talk to them because their soul is in their body."

"Huh," Isabella said. "That is a new type of religion. What happens to the other souls?"

"They leave the body. One lives in our shadow and is gone. Another is our image that we see in water, or a mirror that reflects our face. That soul goes into an animal like a fish or a beaver."

Isabella gave an uncertain nod. "What happens when the fish with your soul is caught and eaten?"

"It goes into another smaller animal."

Isabella brought her hand to her chin. "Well... all animals die."

Pierre shrugged his shoulders. "I guess sometime that soul is gone altogether."

"I think I like my God idea better," she said, standing up and shaking the dust from her pants. "Some who follow the Christian beliefs think when you die you go to heaven and you spend eternity with God. He knows we make mistakes but believes we can redeem our souls through a pure heart. He believes all persons have a heart that can be saved and become good. That is why He loves us all. Even a slave with the scars of a hundred lashes who now captains a pirate ship."

"Do you believe in this God?"

Isabella put her arm around Pierre as she nudged him back toward the bay. "I am not sure. He is much more complicated than I thought. Before I met this Spanish man, I don't think I would have liked him. But if my heart can be turned so I can embrace and love a Spaniard, maybe I should think more about this Christian God. I do believe all souls can be redeemed. I see it every day on my ship."

"So the Christian God will let me into heaven even though I could not save my best friend from the crocodile?"

Isabella pulled Pierre close, slowing their gait. "I am sure the God you believe in loves you, Pierre. He knows you did everything you could. Sometimes, bad things happen to good people. The truth is we all have a heart, and a soul, and a loving God would want to see you grow and be happy and make the world better. Sinaesta's death was very sad for you and everyone who knew him and loved him. But I am sure a God worth believing in would like you to see life in your friend's death. Breathe life into his memory and spirit by making him proud of the man you will become."

Isabella saw Marguerite and greeted her with the lifting of her hand. She looked at the other men and women, and wondered if they believed in a God, or some other spirit, that would allow them to grow and become better mothers, fathers, sons, and daughters. She wondered if her God would get her pirates out of what her gut said was a trap.

18

"You slept well?" Marguerite asked with a smile.

Isabella nodded and returned the smile. "About as well as could be expected after our night time interruption." She looked at Pierre who was now busy sorting through nets and shells. "He's a very special boy."

Marguerite shot a quick glance at Pierre and showed Isabella a shy smile. "I wish he were mine, but he was my husband's son. His mother died in childbirth. My son, Jean, is eighteen months old. He was less than a year old when his father died. He barely knew him."

Isabella looked around. "I never knew my father. Or at least my mother never told who he was, although there were rumors. Where is Jean?"

"I am sorry you never knew him." Marguerite stopped her work and looked up at the line of *chikees*. "Jean is up with the older village women. They watch the very young ones while we work to prepare the nets and go out to the estuaries for the day's catch."

"Many of the canoes are still here. I would expect them to be out much earlier than now."

Marguerite nodded. Her features were less fine and her face more rugged than was apparent under the glow of the torches the night before. She was fit, and her hands worked the nets nimbly. She looked around, her eyes low and unobtrusive. "Something is different. The women have been more quiet than usual. I am not sure what is going on."

Isabella kneeled down to a net, picking up the woven rope. She examined the precision order of the shells at the bottom of the net. She looked up, turning her head to observe what appeared more a klatch than a work detail. "I didn't do much fishing growing up. Sugarcane fields are far from the bays and coasts."

Marguerite's eyebrows turned up as she checked another section of weights. "*Gens de couleur* are skilled at fishing."

Isabella's eyes picked up a young Calusa woman several feet away, watching her. "I was not a free black," she said to Marguerite.

The comment snapped the French woman's head up, locking their eyes.

Isabella smiled. "I am a runaway slave."

"But you speak... your French accent—"

"I had very good teachers."

"You must have studied among the house slaves."

"Spanish is my second language. My childhood was spent on a plantation in Santo Domingo. French is my third language, and English a fourth."

Marguerite's hands stopped. "You're African?"

"I was born on the plantation in Santo Domingo."

"But... how... did you...?"

Isabella pointed to the net. "Is this what you did in Port-au-Prince? Maintain nets so the men could go out and fish?"

Marguerite shook her head, diverting her attention back to the net. "Of course not. My husband was a merchant. He owned two vessels before he died of the Fever."

Isabella peered through the net, its shell weights holding the line taut between her fingers. "Yet here you make nets..., very well I think."

"I do this because I have to," she said, her jaw becoming stiff and her hands becoming more deliberate.

"You do this because you have no choice."

Marguerite's eyes glanced up at Isabella before setting herself back on her task. She pushed a set of nets to the side and started to replace a shell on another net.

"You have not forgotten your skills and knowledge from Port-au-Prince. But bookkeeping and trade accounts do you little good... here. Where you are born, and your lineage, may determine where and how you are born, but you are more than the place and your family history."

Isabella joined Marguerite on the net, examined the bleached shells, and walked over to a small pile of shells sorted by size and type. She picked up three that were of the same type that appeared to be weights on the nets.

"Did you learn all this wisdom and language on the plantation?"

Isabella chuckled. "No, we were whipped if anyone taught us Spanish. Some of our African language survived the great passage. Some of our religion. Santo Domingo had a few free blacks, and as a teenager, I would sneak out at night and join them."

"That must have been very dangerous."

"Twenty lashes if I was found out. Fifty if they thought I was trying to escape. I was always back in our family quarters before dawn."

"I would have run far away."

"Where? We were on an island and slavers made port every day." Isabella stopped for a moment to look up at the sky. "Besides, they would have killed my mother, probably tortured her first, if I ran away. They wouldn't believe her if she said she didn't know where I went"

Marguerite stopped and looked at Isabella. "Why did you escape?"

"The slaves... my family, our friends... revolted. The plantation burned to the ground."

Marguerite reached over and covered Isabella's hand. "I am sorry. Are you the only one who escaped?"

Isabella nodded. "Two months later, I was on a pirate ship." She looked up to Marguerite, a sparkle returning to her eyes. "You will be amazed at what you can learn after five years on a pirate ship."

Marguerite smiled. "A pirate ship? My husband hated pirates. He almost lost two of his schooners to pirates. Their loss would have wrecked our family."

"My family was dead," Isabella said, keeping her eyes and hands weaving the shells through the woven rope. "I would have been hanged if I stayed on land. What would monsieur Lafitte have done if I had tried to sign up to work his ship?"

Marguerite's hands slowed.

Isabella huffed. "He would not let me on his ship. A merchant ship was no place for a girl, he would say. If I didn't have papers—and I had

143

nothing to prove I was free—he would have turned me in to the plantations. Then I would have received another set of lashings. If I survived the infections, I would have been sent to the fields. I am sure I would have died or been killed, if I didn't bear children."

The two women finished the net and folded it over onto the growing pile.

Marguerite stood, lifting a hand to wipe her brow and fastened a stray hair. "France is changing."

Isabella smiled as she shook her head. She remembered the meeting she and Jean-Michel had with Governor Bellecombe in his palace. They met on the hills of Port-au-Prince the night before D'Poussant stoked the flames of revolution in *Le Coq Fantôme*. The governor of Saint Domingue agreed not to arrest her or her pirates, but *La Marée Rouge* still had to fight her way out of the Spanish blockade of Port-au-Prince Bay on her own. One brig against a Spanish squadron. "So I have been told," she said.

Isabella stood and took a silent count of the fishing canoes. "I count twenty canoes."

"The Calusa have over one-hundred canoes. Only the ones they use for fishing are kept in the cove."

Isabella's chest tightened. "Fishing canoes?"

Marguerite nodded. "The fishing canoes have a wider bottom for storing fish and nets. The canoes used for hunting and battle are narrower and a little deeper. They are built for speed and quickness."

The pirate's eye darted from canoe to canoe, assessing the design for agility. The canoes that carried the warriors into the mouth of the Caloosahatchee River were different. They were cut deeper to hold a line under a strong paddle. The canoes transporting her to the village would not have stored fish or nets very well.

"Marguerite," she said with a low, soft voice. "Do you know where my men slept last night?"

Marguerite shook her head. "Maybe the lodge next to the Paramount *Cacique*'s house. That's usually where they keep white men."

Marguerite's eyes snapped up to catch Isabella's. Her jaw dropped as her eyes darted around to the others on the beach as if she was about to say something but closed her mouth. She stepped close to Isabella. "Where is Gabrielle?"

Isabella's eyebrows dropped, reflecting the sudden clarity of her thoughts. "Still in the lodge."

Marguerite turned to look at the beach. She spotted Pierre with several other boys at the water's edge inspecting a canoe. "Pierre!" She waved him toward her. "*Viens ici!*" Pierre looked at her but didn't move. Her hand became more instant. "*Maintenant, vite!*"

Pierre shook his head, said something to two other boys at the canoe, let his shoulders drop, and plodded toward his mother with his eyes on the sand.

"What?"

"Come with me and *Capitaine* Isabella. We need to check on her friend, Gabrielle."

"Why do I have to go? We were going to fix that canoe."

Marguerite's eyes popped up to Isabella and back to Pierre. She nudged him toward the lodge. "I may have another task for you."

"But I want to work on the canoe. I need to know how to work on them if I am going to be a warrior."

"Oui, but we need to check on Gabrielle and her other friends. They have been sleeping too long. They need to be up and working like the rest of us. We need to check on your brother Jean as well."

Pierre let out a long sigh that matched a disappointed grimace as he lingered behind the two women and the trio marched back up the canal toward the lodge. The sun was higher and beat down on their shoulders, their shadows no longer threatening the steps to the buildings that sheltered families and children from the night. Isabella kept her head forward as her eyes took stock of the men, women, and chores. The women seemed to slow under the late morning heat, while the number of men seemed to be fewer.

"Most of the men are hunting," she said. Isabella's words were intended as a question rather than as an observation that needed to be checked.

Marguerite directed her head around the work area of the lodge. "Most are hunting or fishing. But…." She turned to look back toward the lagoon. "Too many fishing canoes are still here."

Isabella gripped the hilt of her sword, steadying it as they continued toward their overnight lodge.

Just as Marguerite set her foot on the first step, Gabrielle moved out of the gray interior.

"*Merci!*" she called down to Isabella once she spotted her.

The sarcasm in Gabrielle's voice forced a small smile across Isabella's face. "I thought you needed sleep after all that food you ate last night."

"The food was good, but not good enough to miss all the activity outside." Gabrielle surveyed the village from her three-foot-high perch. "You can see much from this vantage point when you do not have hills or mountains to interfere."

Isabella nodded, stepping up to her height before turning. "They've moved mud and dirt to create an island out here."

"Pierre," Marguerite said, her hand leading the boy's shoulder in to the lodge, "go check on our brother." Pierre paused for a brief moment, but relented, shaking his head as he went through the roughed-out wooden frame making the doorway. "He has such an adventurous spirit. He wants so much to be out with the warriors. Learning to hunt. Preparing for another attack."

"Another attack?"

Marguerite's statement turned both pirates toward their hostess. Marguerite's eyebrows raised. "The Calusa always are ready to be attacked. The Yamasee and Creek have been raiding the Calusa villages with the English for more than one hundred years, as well as the Ai, Mayaimi, Jeaga, and Tequesta tribes. Men, women, and children have been taken to the north to the plantations."

"But the Spanish were supposed to have taken the last Calusa to Cuba more than twenty years ago."

Marguerite laughed. "Look around you Isabella and Gabrielle."

"But how have they survived?" asked Gabrielle.

Marguerite shook her head. "I was little more than my husband's bookkeeper, wife, and mother to Pierre and Jean. You must be very confident in your ability to find your way back to your ship through these swamps and forests. I would not last an hour before I would be eaten by a crocodile, bear, or panther."

Gabrielle glanced at Isabella. "I have no idea how to get back to the ship."

A memory of Gamba standing over a wild boar in the hills of Santo Domingo flashed before Isabella's eyes. He stood on top of the dead carcass, the base of his spear fashioned from a straight tree limb lodged against it bloodied side. He was resourceful.

"I learned to hunt with the boys on the plantation," Isabella continued. "I can handle a panther or boar. A bear is more difficult. But a well-placed shot or deep blade will kill it. Crocodiles…, that's a different matter."

Gabrielle rolled her eyes. "You do not know how to kill a crocodile."

Isabella turned to Gabrielle. "I have never faced one with a weapon."

Gabrielle used her arm to sweep the area in front of them. "Crocodiles are everywhere around here."

"If we make noise," Isabella said without a hint of doubt. "They will run."

"None of that does me much good," Marguerite huffed. "I can't fight, and my husband did not train me on weapons. I would never find my way out of here even if I had a place to go."

Gabrielle placed her hand to Marguerite's bare shoulder. "I know this has been difficult for you. No one expects you to try to escape."

Marguerite placed her hand over Gabrielle's but continued to look at the canal linking the Paramount *Cacique*'s quarters with the lagoon. "This life is not what I expected, for me or my sons."

"Marguerite," Isabella said, turning to her. "Was the trading post gone when you were captured by the Calusa?"

Marguerite hesitated before answering. A slow, deliberate nod confirmed a thought. "We had heard a trading post was at the mouth of the Caloosahatchee River. Our ship ran aground about a four-hour walk south of the river. Our captain had intended to see if the post had any new skins. Mainly deer and mink, from what he said. After we were captured, the Indians marched us to the river, but I did not see a trading post. I did not see any other white people other than what remained of our crew."

Isabella began to descend to the shell-hardened ground below the hut. "I'm going to look around. I have to find out where they are keeping Juan Carlos and the others."

Gabrielle began to follow Isabella, but the sound of her boots on the wood steps prompted Isabella to turn around. She lifted her hand to place it firmly on Gabrielle's hip. "Stay with Marguerite," she said in a low voice. "Make sure Pierre and Jean are okay, and don't leave them if you can help it."

Gabrielle cocked her head as if asking a silent question.

Isabella gave her a reassuring nod. "I am not sure what is going on in this village, but I haven't seen the men all morning. The Calusa took battle canoes out this morning, not fishing canoes." Gabrielle's expression hardened. "I'm going to look around a little more. If we split up, they will not worry about us, believing that we are comfortable in the village."

"I don't trust Chosa," Gabrielle said.

"I don't either," Isabella said, keeping her eyes focused on Gabrielle's. "I will look around to see what I can find."

"Do you think they went back out to *La Marée Rouge*?"

"I don't know. We are strange people in a very strange land." Isabella took in a deep breath. "Be prepared to leave quickly. Hopefully, if we have to leave, we won't leave until night. Then I can let the stars guide us back to the ship."

Isabella could tell Gabrielle still didn't understand. "Just stay close to Marguerite and the boys. I'll be back in an hour and report what I see."

Gabrielle turned to go back up the stairs.

As Isabella continued to the pathway, she caught a glimpse of Chosa standing on the front deck of the *maśuhoma*. She forced herself to keep her eyes focused on the ground.

Dear God, she said to herself, please just give me until dark.

19

Isabella approached the edge of the canal, kneeled down and tested the hardness of the ground. The shells, bleached white by the sun, had been ground into the sea wall to create a hard, resistant surface. A cannon would have trouble destroying these ramparts. The Calusa, however, wouldn't have to worry about cannon. No army could bring a cannon across or through these swamps, and no White man's navy would have a boat shallow enough to navigate the canals and carry the weight of artillery.

She looked at the trees rising up on the other side of the ceremonial canal and behind the lodges. Cypress, mangrove, and pine. All the trees rose straight up toward the sun, their trunks rising into thick impenetrable canopies that obscured everything inside. A perfect place to hide warriors… or snipers. Perhaps the Calusa would trade for tar and turpentine, her naval stores.

She shook her head. *La Marée Rouge* was long overdue for scraping her hull. Jean-Michel had already noticed barnacles and other crusty travelers had shaved a knot or two off her speed. They were barely keeping ahead of Muñoz. They needed that speed. Careening her hull would let them caulk her seams with the pine tree resin to make them watertight and the tarring would make her fast again. She smiled as she remembered Jacob tutoring her on the fine points of maintaining a pirate ship when she stepped foot on *La Marée Rouge* years earlier.

She closed her eyes and brought her hands up to her lips. She remembered the warm touch of his hands, the soft tug of his lips on hers.

She inhaled, fighting back tears. Thank God for Jean-Michel. Jacob's loyal friend was her salvation as captain of his warship.

The American pirate had laughed when she asked why he had named the pirate ship "Red Tide." The name Blood Red Tide was too dramatic he had said as he downed his third tankard of rum at the Wooden Anchor in Charlotte Amalie. Carl gave her a wink from across the table before getting up to break up a brawl between two English sailors and a French marine, all three of whom could not hold a mug to Jacob.

"I need my words to suggest just enough poison to scare my prey into submission," he had pointed out. Her heart quickened as she relived Jacob's death on the quarter deck of *La Marée Rouge*.

Isabella didn't understand at the time, just weeks after the plantation, her home, burned, the life of a pirate was like rebirth as a newborn. She knew, somehow, that this rogue of an American was not as roguish as he pretended. She also learned soon enough that Jean-Michel was not about to let the young pirate captain squander the stakes his father had laid out for him to placate his wayward son.

Isabella's breath wavered as she let out the air, the last bits of oxygen, trying to turn away the treachery that ended her new love's life before they really had a chance to start. Thank God for Jean-Michel and the treachery of a brave young Spanish Army Captain in service to His Most Catholic Royal Majesty King Charles III.

She had experienced tragedy and rebirth more than once. She kept rising after each death.

The words seeped into her brain as if they started far away in the recesses of a deep cavern, gained voice and rushed to escape, shocking Isabella from her dreamy state. She turned her head to see Chosa speaking to her as she kneeled. She rose from her crouch and bowed her head.

"The wife of the Paramount *Cacique* asks what spirits you pray to."

The soft female voice seemed disembodied from the powerful partner to an Indian chief who commanded hundreds of warriors and families in this village. Isabella found its source, a young woman, most likely in her mid-teens, standing just behind the Chieftess. Long black haired flowed over her torso and covered her breasts, a triple looped shell necklace pulled close to the base of her neck. The necklace included fully formed and exquisite examples of sand dollars, but none as large as the chief's. Her eyes seemed to look beyond Isabella as she focused on the Spanish words she formulated in her brain before forcing them through her mouth.

Isabella hesitated, unsure if she understood the request. "Spirits?"

The teenage girl, hesitated before dropping her head in one movement. "Si, what spirits. You see spirits in trees? In ground? In shells? In ocean?"

Isabella's head clouded, preventing any thoughts from navigating a path to a verbal response. "I am still searching for my spirits."

The girl paused. After a few moments, she said something to Chosa in Calusa.

After Chosa responded, the girl refocused her eyes on Isabella. "You have three souls," she said. She pointed to her eye. "One is in the round circle of your eye. This soul sees all and never leaves you. We can always talk to this soul. The other is the spirit of the body, which lives in another animal when we die. The third soul is our warrior soul and carries us through the day."

"Si, I have heard this explained to me." Isabella hesitated, then looked at the girl. "Do you have a name?"

The girl's face seemed to tighten and her eyes widened.

"Perdón, yo era grosero. I did not mean to be rude." Isabella turned back to Chosa. *"Cacique* Chosa, may I ask the girl her name?" Isabella turned her eyes back to the girl, raising her eyebrows and nodding toward Chosa. The girl's mouth opened, and her eyes seemed to reveal panic.

"It's okay," Isabella reassured her. "Translate my question to *Cacique* Chosa."

The girl continued to look at Isabella as she translated the question. Chosa's expression did not change when the girl finished, but the pause in her response made Isabella wonder if she had blundered. Chosa responded, and the girl's expression relaxed. She nodded one time as she said "Si" to acknowledge permission had been granted. "My name is Śeha."

Isabella looked to Chosa and smiled. *"Gracias."* She turned back to the girl. "Śeha, does your name have a meaning?"

Śeha translated the question to Chosa. Isabella guessed she must have explained how she would respond to the chieftess based on the length of the words. Chosa nodded. Śeha looked at Isabella. "My name is given to me because I observe and see all that is around me, and I explain what I see to our *cacique*."

Isabella nodded. "You translate the world to the language your people understand."

Śeha nodded.

"I was raised by my family to believe in many spirits," Isabella explained. "We have spirits of the ocean, of death, of life. My mother believed the spirit that embodies me is the Queen of the Ocean, Lasirene."

"Then your spirit has much in common with the Calusa."

Isabella smiled. "Our people were forced to cross the ocean as slaves. I am from Hispaniola. An island east of Cuba."

Śeha translated the words, and Chosa seemed to ask several questions.

"Chosa would like to know why you are with white men."

"White men…, the white men with me… are my friends."

"Chosa says white men cast spells on the Creek and Yamassee, convince them they are better than the Calusa."

Isabella nodded. "Some white men are that way. Perhaps most, I do not know. The white men that enslaved me and my family are that way. And I fight them."

"Then Chosa wants you to fight white men with Calusa. She see you are… umm…. *ra*? Umm… fierce and… umm…. *Śi*… brave. *Ra… śi*. Fierce and brave. With Calusa you can build fierce nation. She sees Calusa spirits in you."

Isabella looked at Chosa. *"Gracias, Cacique* Chosa." She turned toward Śeha and nodded. She turned back to look into the eyes of the chieftess, the principal wife of the Paramount Chief of a proud warrior nation. "Thank you for such a compliment. I honor and respect the Calusa and their spirits."

She paused to let Śeha translate. Chosa smiled, lifting her shoulders as she finished.

"But these men have been with me for many years. They have been loyal."

Śeha pinched her lips as she heard Isabella's comments. Her eyes dipped to the ground and away from Isabella as she translated the response. Chosa's back straightened as Śeha finished, and her eyes fixed on Isabella's.

"*Cacique* Chosa says that white men are evil and turn Indian against Indian. They make Calusa slaves and force families to leave the land of their ancestors. They take Calusa's land to live in Florida."

Isabella nodded. "I agree, some white men are bad and very evil. But not all white men are evil. The men with me saved my life from evil white men."

Chosa looked at Isabella for several minutes before Śeha had a chance to translate again.

"*Cacique* Chosa says that white men cannot be trusted. You have blocked the truth from the spirits."

Isabella chest began to tighten. Where was Juan Carlos? Herrera? And the others?

"Please tell *Cacique* Chosa that I understand the pain and suffering her people have experienced at the hands of the white men. I have fought the evil men from my ship, which is now waiting for my return at the mouth of the Caloosahatchee River. But I have also found white men of honor."

Śeha kept her eyes to the ground. Isabella thought she could see her breathing pick up its pace. Her words stumbled at first, but soon began to flow. Chosa stood resolute as she heard the words.

"*Cacique* Chosa says that Calusa who do not see the evil of white men will become corrupt themselves. Calusa will fight the evil and burn their eyes so their souls cannot live on. They will be forever surrounded by darkness until their soul animal is just an insect."

Isabella recalled the heads on the pikes, the eye sockets devoid of eyes. Were they blinded before they were executed?

Isabella looked over to Śeha, her glare forceful enough to bring her gaze back up from the sand and to lock their eyes. She turned back to Chosa. "I understand our presence here in this village may be unsettling. We are grateful for the hospitality of the Calusa people, especially to *Cacique* Chosa and the Paramount *Cacique*. However, if *Cacique* Chosa believes we are not welcome in the village, we can take leave and return to our ship."

Chosa remained steadfast before Isabella as Śeha translated.

"Can *Cacique* Chosa let me know where our companions are? We would be grateful if we could take our leave of the Calusa people as soon as is reasonable for the *caciques*."

Chosa turned, cutting off the translation, and strode toward the *maśuhoma*. Śeha cast a quick glance over her shoulder as she followed her chieftess, panic and concern evident in her eyes.

Isabella's brain buzzed. She turned, careful to keep her gait steady and deliberate. Each step seemed to reveal another angle to a cold reality that seemed hidden by a spell cast by the chieftess.

As Isabella approached the *chikee*, Gabrielle stepped out into the sunlight, lifting her head in an invitation for the sun to work through her cheeks and face. She opened her eyes and noted Isabella's return.

Isabella looked up. Gabrielle's expression tensed as their eyes caught each other's. She turned back into the lodge as Isabella's foot stepped onto the first plank.

"We need to leave."

Isabella's words were stern, prompting Gabrielle to pause as she was arranging pots, vases, plates, and other utensils around the fire pit. She looked at Isabella. "What are we going to do about Juan Carlos? Herrera? The others?"

Gabrielle caught Isabella's eyes flashing around the inside of the hut, finally settling on a long fishbone blade extending out from under a pot. She signaled for Gabrielle to pick it up.

"I think I know where they are located." Isabella's words were clipped and steady, the same tone Gabrielle had heard when the pirate captain was preparing for battle.

"We need to move fast."

Isabella turned her head as if searching for something or someone, and then stopped to focus on the far end of the hut. Gabrielle followed her gaze to see Marguerite holding a small child in her arms as she talked with several other Calusa women. Isabella turned back to Gabrielle and nodded, and she followed her march over to the cluster of women.

As they approached, the Calusa chatter stopped.

"*Pardonnez, Madame* Lafitte," Isabella said in formal French, using a very deliberate tone. She looked at the bundle and recognized it as child a little over a year.

"*Excuse moi*," the pirate continued in French. "Is this Jean?"

Marguerite smiled, her expression showing surprise at Isabella's tone. "*Oui, le nom de mon bébé est Jean.*"

"He's beautiful," she said, continuing in French. She lifted her hands toward the child. "May I hold him?"

Marguerite nodded. She placed him in the cradle Isabella's arms created as her smile broadened. "A pirate who knows how to hold a baby?"

Isabella smiled as she looked into Jean's face, the toddler's round eyes wide and cheeks puffing as he peered into the strange visage. "Bonjour, monsieur Jean Lafitte," Isabella cooed, lowering her voice into a smooth, wispy tone that flowed with the seductive cadence of a native French speaker. "You have a wonderful mother and a strong and brave brother."

She looked up and smiled at Marguerite. "Is he walking?"

"Not yet, thank goodness. I think he would walk off the edge of the floor if he did! He is trying. He is standing, but not well. So not long."

"As a girl coming of age on a plantation, I held many babies and raised many young children before they went into the fields." She looked over at the Calusa women. She smiled, and their faces relaxed. Isabella seemed to have passed a test, and the women turned their attention to other tasks.

Isabella turned back to the baby. "You are going to be a strong man," she said looking into Jean's face. His eyes sparkled and a smile lightened his face. She continued in a silk-lined tone as she talked to the cherubic child. "I will see to it. And your brother will grow to be a strong man and friend. But Tanpa is not a place you will be allowed to grow up."

Marguerite looked at Gabrielle, fear now replacing the surprised comfort in her expression as her lips parted. Gabrielle lifted a hand to her chest, her forefinger waving off any words Marguerite was thinking of saying.

Isabella started to rock Jean, and the infant's eyes begin to droop. "Too many Spanish missionaries, too many broken promises, too much suspicion."

"My friends are Calusa," Pierre said, his confidence giving his words an edge that turned the heads of the other Calusa women.

Gabrielle looked at Pierre, pulling his eyes away from Isabella. "Of course they are. But you are not one of them."

Marguerite put her hand on Pierre's shoulder. "Patience, Pierre. Watch your tone with Gabrielle and Isabella."

"Do your friends speak French?" Isabella asked, her tone sweet and even.

"Non," Pierre said. "They are teaching me Calusa."

Isabella reached over and touched Jean's nose, eliciting a playful gurgle from the infant. "Have they asked to learn French?"

Pierre turned his eyes away and toward the thatched walls of the hut. "Non, they said I needed to become a Calusa *ñoka* first."

Isabella's heart quickened, and she tried to hide the heavier, steady breaths she was using to calm her muscles and steady her brain. "How many white men are in Tanpa?"

Marguerite shook her head, and she lifted a hand to her forehead. She closed her eyes. Her grip on Pierre's shoulder became more firm. "Pierre," she said as she focused on her voice and words. "Do you have your knife, bow, and arrows nearby?"

"Oui."

"*S'il vous plaît,* go get them. Act like you are getting ready to go for a hunt. Come back to us."

156

"Mais...."

"Silencieux, aller vite. Go... go."

Pierre opened his mouth, but another firm squeeze from his mother and a stern look from Gabrielle sent him off.

Marguerite looked at Gabrielle, knowing that Isabella was listening to every word. "Are we in danger?"

"Gabrielle and I are in more danger," Isabella said, keeping her casual tone. "I just had a revealing conversation with Chosa, the wife of the Paramount Chief. The Calusa do not trust any white men."

Gabrielle nodded. "Isabella and I are African."

"But I am white. My children are white. Why am I alive?"

Gabrielle looked at Jean, fast asleep. "Because you are a woman. And maybe because you are a mother."

"Why didn't they kill Pierre and Jean, then?"

Gabrielle shook her head.

"I don't know," Isabella said raising her eyes to meet Marguerite's. "Based on what Chosa told me, I am now convinced that Pierre and Jean will not be allowed to join the warriors. They will be used for other purposes, if they are allowed to live."

"What purposes?"

Isabella shook her head and looked over to Gabrielle. "I don't know for sure, but I am worried that the men who came with us are in grave danger as well. We are all in danger now."

Gabrielle nodded. "What is our plan?"

Isabella pursed her lips, as she sunk into a deeper thought. "I don't have a complete one yet. I think we need to stay together and find the men."

Isabella looked at Gabrielle. Her next words made Gabrielle's heart leap in her chest. "You need to be ready to lead Marguerite and her boys through the swamp and back to the ship."

20

Marguerite had said the men were held in the *ri* next to the *maśuhoma,* but this no longer made sense to Isabella. She had seen the powder and shot put into the lodge two down from the Paramount *Cacique*'s temple. If they didn't trust white men, why would they let them sleep anywhere near the most important structures in the village?

The warrior standing guard over the *ri* made it clear he was not going to let them get any closer.

"He says you're not permitted into the building," Pierre confirmed.

Isabella put her foot on the first step leading to the *ri,* triggering another warning from the guard. This time his orders were reinforced with the pointed end of a spear targeted at her chest.

Isabella nodded and raised her hands. "*¡Yo sé!*" she said hoping Spanish might help. "We are looking for our friends. Our comrades."

"*Quelle langue est-ce?*"

Pierre's question was so natural and simple, Isabella hesitated and then tried to keep herself from laughing.

"*¡Es español!*" Marguerite said.

"The Calusa speak Spanish?" Pierre wondered out loud, his voice indicating more confusion than revelation.

"*Apparemment pas cet Indien!*" said an exasperated Marguerite. A tiny, muffled voice came from within a swaddle of cloth in her arms. She looked at Pierre. "*Silienciex!*"

Gabrielle leaned down to Pierre's ear. "Some of the Calusa speak Spanish. But they do not speak French."

"Why?"

"La Florida has been occupied by the Spanish colony for over two hundred years. The French have not travelled to this part of the territory often enough for them to learn your language."

"I didn't think they spoke anything but Calusa."

"*Silienciex!*" his mother hissed.

Gabrielle pulled Pierre closer, wrapping the crook of her arm around under his chin with her arm pressed against his chest. "Let's see if Isabella can get us into the lodge."

Isabella brought her next foot to the step, repeating her objective in Spanish, but the warrior kept his spear pointed at her chest.

"*Ra ñoka kuhpe ri?*"

The warrior's eyes shifted to Pierre.

"*Śeha ri?*"

The warrior grunted something in Calusa.

Pierre stepped over to the warrior. "*Ra ñoka śera ri?*"

The boy's words seemed to incense the guard, shifting the point of his spear to Pierre. The boy gasped, and the guard moved his tip toward his chest. Isabella grabbed the shaft just below the tip, pivoting her body as a fulcrum so her other arm pressed against the spear. She turned again, tacking the shaft to her body and pulling it forward a few inches. Caught in mid thrust, the Calusa guard fell forward, tumbling to the ground. Isabella jumped on top of his chest, pinning the guard's arm with the shaft of the spear and locked it against his neck.

Her head spun as the Calusa warrior glared at her, the muscles in his face taut and hardened by the defeat. She kept her gaze on him. "Gabrielle, look inside the lodge. See who is inside."

Gabrielle's boots tapped up the steps in a quick clip. "No one is in the lodge!"

"That doesn't make sense," Isabella hissed. "Pierre. Can you ask the warrior what he was guarding?"

"Umm, I will try. That is a hard question for me." She heard the light steps of Pierre's bare feet come up to her side. "Umm... *śera* ... umm ... strangers... *kuhpe ka ri*...."

The guard seemed to ignore Pierre's words.

"Isabella!" Marguerite's tone was urgent. "The villagers are looking at us. *Rapidement!*"

Isabella cursed to herself. Where could Juan Carlos and the others be? She peered into the face of the guard. "*Maśuhoma?*" A slight softening of the warrior's eyes confirmed what she suspected. "They are in the house of the Paramount Chief!"

Gabrielle's heart raced as she followed Isabella up the steps into the *maśuhoma*. She steeled herself for the inevitable clash that would come as they ran into the jaws of the Paramount *Cacique*'s guards brandishing a spear from one of his disarmed warriors. She watched as women and children, along with a several older men, clustered at the base of the lodge. She checked for the knife behind her back, and gently nudged Marguerite forward, the infant Jean snuggled into a deerskin harness around her front.

Her eyes adjusted in seconds rather than minutes as they crossed into the grand opening of the tribe's temple. At first, all she could detect was the pulsing bodies in front of her. Each step, however, seemed to create jagged lines of humans framing a corridor. Soon she saw the walls of the gauntlet were made up of warriors with spears and bows, their heads and torsos framed by the glow of torches along the sides of the hall. She wished she could see what lay ahead of them. Even the figure of Isabella advancing toward the throne was obscured by the shadows and narrow gauntlet.

A suffocating feeling of entrapment wrapped around Gabrielle as their small group made its way down the corridor. Gabrielle could see Chosa sitting to the chief's right. The shaman sat on the *cacique's* left. Where was the Military Chief?

"Great *Cacique*," Isabella said as she approached, her voice muffled to Gabrielle's ear. Gabrielle stepped closer so she could see the Paramount *Cacique*, but she now found the shaman blocked from view.

Isabella stepped forward, kneeled, and lifted her hands palms up to the chief. "We greatly appreciate your hospitability and that of your wife and the people of the village. But we have a long journey north along the coast of La Florida. We humbly request your permission to complete our trade so we can sail north."

A young woman with long, flowing black hair stepped from the shadow of Chosa and began translating Isabella's request. Chosa stood unmoved, while the chief appeared to contemplate the request.

"Séha," Isabella said looking at the girl, her tone noticeably more familiar and soothing. "Please tell the Paramount *Cacique* we would like to reunite with our colleagues from the ship and take our leave."

Gabrielle shifted her attention to Chosa, and nodded in silent recognition. The girl must have translated for Chosa when she met with Isabella earlier this morning.

Séha translated Isabella's statement, and Gabrielle noticed Chosa shift her weight on her stool. The shaman stood and walked over to the Paramount *Cacique*, saying something in a low voice. The words seemed to unsettle the girl. The chief nodded, and the shaman returned to his station where a drum sat as if ready to conjure spirits into the room. The chief looked at Isabella and began speaking in Calusa. Gabrielle saw Pierre suddenly look up at his mother, then slip his hand in hers.

Séha turned her eyes down to the ground, gathering her thoughts. "The Paramount *Cacique* appreciates your willingness to barter but does not believe you can make these trades."

Gabrielle rubbed the palms of her hands against her breeches.

"I have a ship at the mouth of the Caloosahatchee River," Isabella said. "She has more powder and shot for your guns. We can include long guns if you wish. But we need to set sail soon with the tides. I would like to consult with my crew."

The chief turned to the shaman and issued what appeared to be a series of commands. Then Séha looked at Isabella, her eyes now anxious. The shaman stood and disappeared into a darkened chamber behind the chief. The *cacique* turned to look at Chosa, who nodded, before he looked back to Isabella to make another statement.

"Umm… the chief has heard that you defeated one of his warriors," the young translator said, her eyes turned to the ground. "For this he will be punished."

"Great *Cacique*," Isabella interjected. "The warrior threatened a young boy. I acted out of instinct. I should have been more measured in my approach. Please do not punish the guard for my impulsiveness."

The chief sat unmoved after the translation. The group stood silent, waiting for another sign from the Paramount *Cacique*. After a few moments, Isabella continued, "Great Chief, I respectfully request that I be reunited with my crew. We will take our leave, and never return to these lands. I will also follow through on the bargains I make."

The girl translated Isabella's words with what appeared to be more optimistic confidence, but the chief's gaze hardened and his eyes seemed to darken from the furrow of his brow. His next words were forceful. The girl appeared to take careful stock of their meaning before translating them for Isabella.

"The Paramount *Cacique* says further trade will be impossible. You have committed a grave sin against the Calusa and showed you do not respect us. You will have to pay tribute to the Calusa before you can go free."

Isabella's shoulder's stiffened. "I have to get back to my ship and her crew. I am her captain." Isabella's words seemed to drop into the base of her neck, producing a low, deliberate and stern tone. The full meaning of her statement was not lost on the Calusa girl as she struggled to muster the courage to translate them to the chief.

The chief did not wait for the full translation. "Five years of labor with the Calusa will be your tribute!" he roared in Spanish.

Gabrielle felt a sudden emptiness in her lungs, as if all the oxygen had been sucked out of her body. She began deep, steady breaths. She dropped behind Isabella and brought a hand up the inside of Marguerite's arm. How many warriors were in this lodge?

Marguerite leaned over to Isabella's ear, whispering several words, but Gabrielle could not hear them.

Isabella stood resolute. She turned her head away from the Chief and toward the translator. "Śeha, where are my men?"

The chief rose from his throne, his eyes glaring at Isabella.

"Por favor, look at the Paramount *Cacique* when you are speaking to him," Śeha pleaded, her voice high and anxious.

Isabella turned to Marguerite, Pierre, and Gabrielle. "Gabrielle, Marguerite," she said in French, "when I pull my sword from its sheath, charge the space where the Shaman disappeared. The men are there."

"But—"

Isabella snapped her head back to the Paramount *Cacique*. "Śeha! where are my men?"

Isabella's actions seemed to ignite flames in the chief's eyes. The Paramount *Cacique* lifted his staff high toward the ceiling.

Gabrielle grasped Marguerite's elbow, nudging her toward to the side. "Trust Isabella," she whispered. "This may be our only shot at freedom... and life."

"But—"

A firm squeeze on her elbow prodded Marguerite into silence. "For Pierre and Jean."

Gabrielle turned her attention back to Isabella just as she stepped toward the chief, pulling her shoulders back and lifting her chin.

"I was born a slave and lived under the overseer's whip for most of my life," Isabella said. She turned toward Śeha, as if speaking directly to the young girl. "I will never again submit to any man's hand or weapon."

Śeha's jaw dropped. The Paramount Chief looked to his side, an apparent signal to someone else in the room.

Isabella pulled her sword, the glint of the exposed blade flashing in the light.

Gabrielle shoved Marguerite and Pierre into the darkness, as Jean ejected a thunderous wail into the room.

Gabrielle knew from the shouts and clattering behind them that chaos had consumed the void they created. She pushed any thoughts of

Isabella fighting to her death from her mind, forcing her eyes to focus in front of her now. At least Isabella had bought them a chance.

"*Vite! Vite!*" Gabrielle urged as they barreled into the gap in the wall. She kept her hand pressed against what she hoped was Marguerite's back, betting that Pierre was scrambling in front of her.

Isabella's instincts were right. They lunged from the main room and careened into a smaller chamber, but the light was too dim to see much more than the shapes of a woman and a young boy in front of her.

Gabrielle pushed at their backs, forcing them further into the room, and they crashed into yet another chamber. Another step and they tumbled forward over an invisible barrier.

Gabrielle dropped her shoulder and rolled, untangling legs and feet, as she flipped from her back onto her belly, and then up to kneeling position.

"*Kuči!*" bellowed a deep foreign voice.

The warrior's urgency sent Gabrielle into a forward summersault, an instinctive reaction to avoid a projectile of some unknown type. She used the forward thrust to bring her to her feet, but her face slapped into a prickly wall of swamp-grass thatch. She ducked, her cheeks scraping against the wall as she turned toward what she thought would be the middle of the room. She brought her knife up just in time to deflect a spear into the woven grass behind her. She locked the shaft under her free arm and jutted the knife into a body in front her, sparking a wretched scream.

The body crumbled against her as she retreated, looking around the room. She faced three other Calusa warriors, spear tips pointed at her, ready to advance. Behind them she caught a glimpse of several white men—three, four, she couldn't tell how many—kneeling with their hand and arms bound. She caught a flash of a man at the end of the row of captives flopping forward.

Gabrielle grabbed the shaft of the dead Indian's spear and fell forward, pivoting to use the weight of her falling body to pull it loose from the wall and rotate it toward the advancing warriors. She held the shaft with two hands, converting into a staff, and spun it to knock the Calusa spear tips away from her body as she advanced into them.

The three warriors held their ground and began to push her back against the wall when a wail pierced through the clamor.

Shuffling feet behind the warriors caused the Calusa to hesitate. A warrior's face twisted in agony, and he fell to the floor. The flash of a conch fell into the back of the head of another warrior, and he fell as well. The disruption gave Gabrielle the moment she needed to summon enough energy to push against the last remaining warrior. He retreated but let out a sudden screech as his eyes widened and mouth opened, a panicked realization of imminent death as a white arm locked around his neck. His head snapped back, and the warrior dropped to the floor as all force abandoned his body.

Gabrielle's brain snapped image after image, trying to assemble the puzzle pieces into a complete picture. Four..., no five..., Calusa lay dead on the floor, their figures tracked by pools of blood around their torsos and abdomens. Marguerite stayed huddled in a corner, little Jean's cries muffled by the shield of her body. Pierre stood, as if shocked into a bewildered pose, a bloodied shell knife in one hand and a frayed rope in another.

Muffled screams and distant thuds thumped beyond the walls of their chamber filling their room with the sounds of an ongoing struggle in the main temple.

Juan Carlos jumped over to Gabrielle as Herrera cut through the ropes of a third pirate. Three others were scraping ropes from their wrists and legs, as a fourth lay face down on floor, a dark red stream of liquid flowing from his neck.

"Gabrielle, we need to move quickly!"

She nodded as the last few details of the scene registered. "The shaman is dead?"

"Yes," Juan Carlos nodded. "As soon as you and that woman came through the door, he slashed Silvio's neck." He turned to search the room, and his eyes fell onto Pierre. "That boy acted like a seasoned soldier! He cut my ties just as the shaman finished Silvio."

"We need to go!" Herrera jumped over a body. "Out the back door before the rest of the tribe comes after us."

Gabrielle grabbed Juan Carlos's arm. "Marguerite!"

The perplexed looked on their faces told her they didn't understand. She pointed to Marguerite. "She's a white woman! She and her boys have to come with us."

Herrera started to shake his head.

She turned them to face Pierre. "Her son…, Pierre…, may have saved your lives! We would all be dead if he hadn't cut your bonds."

Juan Carlos waved at Marguerite. "Come on! We need to get out of this place!"

Marguerite shook her head. "Where will we go? The Calusa are everywhere!"

Herrera grabbed Pierre and pushed him toward a door further back in the room, then grabbed Marguerite by the arm.

"*Non! Mon bébé!*"

Herrera swore in Spanish and pushed her and toddler out of the room.

21

Isabella's plan, as thin as it was, did its job: She had lunged low toward the Paramount *Cacique*, luring him into bringing the staff down to defend himself against her blade. As the rod fell, she shifted to the side, allowing her to pivot behind him. She snaked the blade around his back and under his arm so that the sharp edge rested against his neck and her other arm was free to lock it in place. The chief immediately fell to his knees, yelling something in Calusa.

"Stop!" Chosa's voice rang through the temple.

"*Kuči!*" the chief ordered, which Isabella now knew was a command to kill her.

"No!" Chosa yelled again. Chosa turned to the warriors in the room, most with spears pointed toward the chief and a few with bows set to let loose their arrows.

Isabella held her breath. "Any movement and your Paramount Chief will die! *Cacique kuči!*"

Chosa stepped in front of her husband, her hands raised against the warriors in the room.

Isabella could not understand Chosa's words, but the warriors held their ground and gave her a few more seconds to invoke the next step in her plan. If she had one.

Isabella pulled a deep breath into her lungs. "Aiyiayiaha, Aiyiayiaha," she chanted into the *cacique's* ear. "Lasiren calls me into this world. Binta. Binta. Binta."

The Paramount *Cacique* barked something toward Chosa who turned her attention back to the chief.

Isabella breathed in and exhaled a deep breath that crossed the *cacique's* ear as she sent "Aiyiayiaha, Binta!" in a series of low, rumbling chants toward Chosa.

Each time the chant reached her, Chosa seemed to weaken.

Isabella leveled her eyes, focusing her stare into the dark irises of the chieftess. Chosa locked on Isabella. The queen raised her arms to the ceiling as she began her own chants. The sounds conveyed a higher pitch with a smoothness that sliced through the air. Isabella's mantras slammed into Chosa's chants; the air around the chief seemed to twirl and twist. Particles of dust and sand swirled up from the floor, beams of sunlight producing glints and sparks that morphed into a funnel.

Isabella felt the power of the priestess, high in the mountains of Saint Domingue. Focus my will, she said to the beam. Channel my will! Streaks of purples and blues formed in the column, turning and swirling into tufts and locks. Isabella's mind cleared, becoming more focused even as her body, hands, arms, and body registered every twitch of the chief's moves. The blues turned and twirled into locks.

Isabella felt Chosa's chants, even if she couldn't hear them, as the chieftain's wife battled for control, perhaps for her life. The warriors stood motionless; all the energy in the temple seemed to be pulled into the vortex of twisting strands of purple.

"Aiyiayiaha, Binta," she chanted, allowing the words to flow over the crest of her lips. "Aiyiayiaha, Binta. I am With God."

Isabella lifted the blade into the neck of the chief. She sensed Chosa's chants become more frequent and urgent, but she concentrated on her steady, deep, rhythm. "I am With God," she said, loud enough for the Paramount *Cacique* to hear. "I am With God."

The chief began to lift himself from his kneeling position, moving upward with the blade. Purple strands darted and churned and whirled in the air around them, stretching to the ceiling before turning to the earth and wrapping themselves around Chosa and the warriors.

As the Paramount *Cacique* rose from the floor, Isabella brought a knee up into the small of his back. The chief's back arched, his face now fully exposed to the ceiling. She bent her leg into the crook of his knees, keeping their two bodies in balance.

168

"See the power of my God," she said into his ear. "Feel the power of *my* God!"

The beam of sunlight now captured the two figures, one African and pirate, the other chieftain of a lost tribe of proud warriors. The air around them calmed.

"The Prophecy is true!"

Isabella's voice barreled through the room, obliterating all the energy and power created to block her will.

"I am Binta! I... Am... With... God!"

She pushed her knee into the back of the chief as she released the blade to let his neck and head shoot forward. The Paramount *Cacique* tumbled into the room, the force of her strike driving him toward Chosa as he sprawled out in front of the warriors.

Isabella dropped to one knee, bringing her sword's blade in front of her. She looked into the mass of warriors, holding the flat part of the blade forward. The whistle and whoosh of a dozen arrows was drowned out by the knock of their tips burrowing into the throne behind her. Two arrows dropped harmless in front her, victims of the impenetrable defense of her steel blade.

She rose holding her blade in front of her. "Stop!" Her voice consumed the room. Warriors hesitated as they fumbled to reload their bows. She stepped forward, one palm forward, the flat part of her sword facing the warriors.

She looked down at the Prominent *Cacique*, his expression blank and void. "Stop! *¡Parar!*"

Isabella looked over to Chosa.

The Chieftess's eyes flared with anger. She lifted her arm toward Isabella. "*Kuči!*"

Isabella looked over to Śeha, but the young girl had retreated to the walls. She peered at Isabella through hands that shielded eyes widened by fear.

Isabella brought her sword down. She looked at the warriors, her eyes making contact with each body. "Stop," she said. "*¡Parar!* Let me go with my people in peace. We will leave you to your life."

169

Chosa let out a high-pitched scream. Isabella saw her arm go up, a weapon in her grip. Isabella ducked, bringing her blade up to deflect the attack. But her weapon arched away and across the temple of the fallen Prominent *Cacique*. The chief fell over, blood spewing from a gaping wound created by the pointed end of a conche hammer. She turned the weapon toward Isabella. "Kill her! *Kuči.*"

The warriors stood, their Paramount Chief's lifeless body serving as a barrier between the Calusa army and Isabella. Isabella brought her blade up in front of her torso and face, tip pointed to the ceiling. "Let me go with my people. In peace. *Déjame ir con mi gente. En paz.*"

Isabella felt the air part in front of her, and she swiveled just as Chosa's hammer arced into the space that would have been her body. She stepped back, as Chosa swung again. This time Isabella charged into Chosa, avoiding the arc of the conch again. The momentum of Chosa's swing spun her around Isabella's body and she tumbled to the floor.

A pain seared through Isabella's shoulder. More arrows swooshed past, their points lodged into the wood and thatch around her. She jumped toward the throne, empty of the Calusa leader's body, as the warriors advanced on her.

Chosa stood, yelling commands, her tone urging her tribe to attack.

Three warriors with spears charged, but Isabella dodged their points by retreating toward the back of the throne room. She grabbed one of the spear shafts, and pulled it toward her, bringing the warrior within striking distance of her sword. She lifted the blade, bringing it down on the warrior's arm. A searing scream came from the body as it rolled away, leaving a hand still attached to the shaft.

Urgent yells swamped the agony of the wounded warrior as a row of Indians advanced on Isabella. She swung an arcing cut at two other warriors and fell backwards into the wall behind her.

Isabella was grateful for the engineering ingenuity of the Calusa Indians as she felt the wall behind her give way. The shaman had disappeared through the threshold of a doorway only visible to those close to the throne. She had figured the wall behind the throne was solid. Now, as she tumbled backwards through thatch, she thanked them for giving her a few more seconds to conjure up a new plan.

She tucked her sword close to her body as she finished a backward roll. As the momentum of the fall brought her to her feet, she saw the hole she backed through was well hidden. She retreated into the space. The bowls, utensils, shells, and skin bedding confirmed that this room must be the living quarters for the Paramount *Cacique* and his wives.

She let her eyes dart from place to place as she surveyed the room, finally resting on a dark mass of sticks toward the back. As her eyes focused, the sticks became rods. Then the rods revealed their true identity—muskets.

Isabella sprung toward the cache of arms, pulling a gun from the pack. She inspected the flint, rubbing her thumb across the hammer and frizzen, and into the pan that would hold the powder to fire the gun to expel any dirt or obstruction. The guns were clean, ready to fire. She scanned the stacked firearms, stopping her count at a dozen.

Thumping and pounding from the heels of bare feet pulled her attention to the front of the room as she snatched a powder horn. She poured powder into the pan and closed the frizzen. Isabella leveled the barrel, prayed it was loaded, aimed at the part of the wall she hoped would lead the warriors into the room, and fired.

The smoke obscured her view, but the kick of the musket was convincing. Like pirates, the chief was always ready for a fight. She dropped the spent firearm and reached for another. She leveled the loaded barrel at the entrance to the room just as a warrior's head emerged and pulled the trigger. The Indian fell to the floor, and she pulled another gun from the stack. She didn't wait for another Indian to show his head and fired into the thatch. She pulled another gun from the stack, trying to subdue the questions popping through her brain about why the Paramount *Cacique* would have loaded muskets in his room.

Isabella's heart skipped as she looked back toward the door, and she saw five warriors charging her. She fired, dropping the lead Indian, but could see more appearing through the threshold into the chief's room.

She turned and started toward the back of the room when she found herself skidding across the floor as a thunderous boom shook the *maśuhoma* amid a crescendo of rapid fire pops and cracks.

22

Juan Carlos's head snapped toward the temple lodge as the noise inside its walls seem to rise in a sudden wave. "*¡Con rapidez!*"

"I know, *capitán* Santa Ana! I am going as fast as I can!"

Herrera passed two more pistols to Gabrielle, tucking one in her shirt while handing the other to Pierre.

"I've never shot a gun before," he said in French.

"*Pas de problème,*" Gabrielle responded. "Just give it to me when I need it." She picked up a leather flask sitting on a barrel, its splintered lid testifying to the recklessness of their efforts. She handed the pouch to Pierre. "Be careful with this. Any spark will blow us up."

"Faster, but be careful. The lodge is about to explode!" Juan Carlos' voice was more urgent.

"We're almost done," Herrera said, tucking a musket under his shoulder as gunpowder dripped out of another tanned pouch in a thick line. "Leave, *capitán!* Get to the woman and her children. This whole half of the village is going to blow up once I strike a flint against this powder."

Juan Carlos retreated toward a back door to the lodge, pressing Gabrielle and Pierre in front of him. "*¡Vamos!*"

Gabrielle shot an impatient look toward Juan Carlos. "Remember who saved your life in Port-au-Prince!"

"*¡Lo siento! Pardonne moi,* but we need to leave this lodge fast."

173

The pirates almost tumbled over each other as they abandoned the Calusa armory of room powder, munitions, and muskets.

Several feet closer to a thicket of bushes and trees, Marguerite waved them over. "Pierre can show us how to escape to the canoes through these woods."

"*Bueno.*" Juan Carlos turned to Gabrielle. "Go with Marguerite."

Gabrielle eyes hardened as she pursed her lips. "I am going after Isabella."

"Go with Marguerite," Juan Carlos insisted. "I'll go after Isabella."

Gabrielle pointed to Juan Carlos's shoulder. "You are still injured. What good are you going to be if she has to slow down for you?"

"Let's go," Marguerite insisted. "*Vite, vite.*" The bundle in her arms began a muffled complaint. She looked inside the fur-skin wrapping and shook her head. "He was fine when you were inside the lodge. Let's go, he will calm down once we are moving."

Gabrielle grabbed Juan Carlos by the arm. Juan Carlos blinked with a wince. "See? Go with Marguerite. She needs someone who knows how to protect her. I am more mobile. If Isabella can be saved, I am in a better position to help her."

Juan Carlos looked up at the back of the lodge. Herrera was taking his last steps, backing out of the threshold. Juan Carlos nodded. "Take Herrera with you. I'll get Marguerite and the boys to a canoe. We'll head back through the canals. "West." He looked up at the sun, and then back to Gabrielle. "If you get separated, the sun should be behind you in the morning and in front of you in the afternoon."

"*Bien. Merci. Allez!* We will see you soon, *mon ami.*"

Marguerite was right: as soon as their group started moving, Jean quieted down, content to ride the up and down waves of a steady gait through the swamp forest. Pierre seemed to dance through the thick brush, over the roots of mangrove trees dipping into the marsh, and trunks of pine trees rising dozens of feet into the air. He would stop every fifty feet or so, waiting in silence for the others to catch up, even though his anxious eyes darted around them, looking for traps or some indicator they would be discovered.

Even with the brush and trees serving as a buffer, the force of the exploding lodge knocked everyone to their feet and sent splintered wood and flaming thatch raining down around them. A plume of black smoke billowed up from the location of the armory, flames pushing it higher into the sky as a nearby *ri* erupted in orange, yellow, and black. A gray cloud settled around the lodges and trees as ash flittered to the ground and a canopy of smoke smothered the village. A heaviness descended into Juan Carlos's chest. Could Isabella have survived being so close to the explosion?

He pulled Marguerite to her feet as fast as he dared, knowing that a trip or stumble could injure the child in her arms. "*Lo siente*; I am sorry. We need to move on quickly."

"*Vite, vite!*" Pierre urged, his hands waving as if he were scooping the stragglers up in his arms. "*Les canoës sont devant nous.*" He pointed forward. "*Les canots…* the canoes!"

"*Si, si!*" Juan Carlos nodded, careful to keep Marguerite balanced as they stepped over another mangrove root protruding from the sodden dirt.

Juan Carlos looked up, hoping Pierre had not disappeared too far ahead. Instead, he was looking down the barrel of a musket held by a white man.

23

Isabella flailed, kicking her feet to regain her balance as the lodge floor settled. The sharp, pungent smell of gun powder cloaked the room, provoking a torrent of tears to stream down her face. She squinted, bringing her arms up to clear her eyes, but the scene behind her remained blurred. She reached up, checked to ensure her bandana remained on her head, and pulled it down over her eyebrows to shield her face and eyes.

Isabella dug the soles of her boots into the floor's planks and started to push and claw her way toward what she hoped was the back of the room. The smell of spent powder lessened, but dust was now coating her throat. She belched coughs with each gasp of breath.

Yells and screams behind her pushed her forward. More pops punctured the air around her. A wave of heat swept up her back. The thuds of bare feet pounded behind her, then around her as she lay below the din of voices.

Isabella turned on her back and let out a scream as a scorching heat seemed to burrow into her skin. She pulled her sword across her chest and continued to scoot toward the exit and out of the inferno. One dark figure lept over her, its path marked by a weaving trail of flickering light. Another crack and she heard something fall to the floor behind her.

One more push of her boots, and a force clutched both of her shoulders and pulled at her. The floor disappeared beneath her.

Isabella felt the weightlessness of a fall, but not the impact of a hard surface. Instead, something twisted her torso so that she found herself arched over something softer.

"Go!" yelled a voice, and she began to bounce as an erratic pulse of air beat against her cheeks. The air helped clear her eyes, and she realized she was on someone's shoulder. But who? She was lying across the shoulders of someone wearing a linen shirt. She lost count of the steps that heaved her body up and down but the noises from the bedlam behind her lessened. Just as she felt her back was going to snap, the shoulder she was riding dipped and she spun to the ground on her butt.

Isabella grabbed her bandana and brought it to her eyes, letting the cloth soak up the tears and dirt.

"I am sorry captain."

The voice was familiar. She wiped her eyes and recognized the gaunt face of Sarhaan.

"What?"

Sarhaan knelt beside her, his eyes looking behind them and to the sides. He raised his finger to his mouth, as he brought a musket up to his chest and began to reload.

"You are supposed to be with the ship!"

"Please, Captain, be still. It is… muy loco… crazy!"

Isabella rubbed her eyes again and wiped her face. Her vision cleared. She rolled over onto her knees and tried to focus on the scene surrounding her. Sarhaan had brought her to the edge of the forest; a tangle of briars and brush obscured them from the Calusa village… or what was left of it.

They were behind the *maśuhoma*. The angle allowed them to see the backs of the lodges that served as the Indians' quarters. Black smoke billowed from a fireball on the far side of the temple, the remains of what had been a *ri*. The temple itself was now engulfed in flames. On the ground, warriors scrambled, some shooting arrows into the trees that enclosed the village, others trying to regroup, and a few running toward the canals. A carpet of bodies, some still on fire or smoldering, lay below the temple lodge as flaming timbers fell, creating what would soon become a pyre.

Isabella looked at Sarhaan. "*¿Juan Carlos?*"

Sarhaan looked at her. Isabella's heart sank.

"*¿Herrera?*"

Sarhaan shook his head.

She closed her eyes and took a breath.

Sarhaan rested his hand on her shoulder. "We have seen no one except you since we arrived."

She lifted her hand to her eyes, straining to focus on their survival, to hold back another wave of tears. "How many did you come with?"

"Twenty-four."

Isabella's head snapped up. "How many are left on *La Marée Rouge?*"

"Forty-five."

"Who was left in command?"

Sarhaan smiled. "Smoothy."

The tears vanished from her eyes as she tried to picture the gunner's mate in charge of a pirate ship. "Not Jean-Michel?"

"He led us to rescue you. He took half of the party to the other side. We were supposed to meet at the large lodge. But a cabin on the other side exploded. We could not get there. They must store their powder in that building."

Isabella's stomach felt heavy, as if a giant ball of lead had settled inside. Herrera and Juan Carlos would have destroyed the Indian armory if they had gotten that far. "Gabrielle? She was with a white woman and her children."

Sarhaan shook his head.

A scream nearby focused their attention as a pirate fell to the ground, an arrow extending from his chest. The crack of muskets and sounds of lead passing near their heads coaxed them deeper into the thicket.

"Captain, our boats are just a few hundred yards down this path. We need to get back to the ship!"

Isabella shook her head. "We can't leave without Juan Carlos or Jean-Michel."

"Jean-Michel was very clear with his orders. If we could not meet at the lodge, we were to retreat back to the ship."

"We are not leaving without Jean-Michel or Juan Carlos!"

Sarhaan shook his head. "We cannot win. There are too many Indians. We have weapons but they will overwhelm us. They are a fierce tribe."

Ra, Isabella reminded herself. The Calusa word for fierce. Chosa had said she was fierce.

Isabella pointed to the burning *maśuhoma*. "This is a fierce, warrior tribe. Just as the Spanish had found them. But their primary chiefs are dead and their temple is destroyed. We will have no better opportunity than right now to find Juan Carlos, Herrera, and the others."

Isabella lifted the hilt of her sword so Sarhaan could see its worn grip.

Sarhaan gave an exasperated nod. "Yes, Captain. At your command, on land and sea."

24

Gabrielle and Herrera pushed through the vines and thicket as they circled back toward the temple lodge. They stumbled along a path skirting the inner edge of the canal surrounding the village. The water was an effective moat as well as a snarling trap for the unwary.

"We have to swing wide," Herrera said in a low voice as he pushed a vine out of their way.

Gabrielle coughed. "The smoke! I can barely see."

Herrera reached back and grabbed her arm. "Let me lead you. We will enter from behind the lodge and—"

Herrera jerked Gabrielle to the ground and climbed on top of her as a whoosh tore through the woods followed by deafening cracks and overwhelming heat.

Gabrielle screamed as she felt flames singe the back of her hand.

Herrera yelled and rolled off her. "Get back!"

Gabrielle looked up to see fireballs leap from limb to limb high above them. She looked down to see Herrera's back light up with sparks and smoke as flames ate away his clothing. She dropped to her knees and started pulling at roots and grass, dislodging dirt and sand.

"Roll!" she yelled. "Roll to me!"

Herrera rolled over his back, screaming with each turn. The dirt seemed to have doused the sparks. Gabrielle scooped up the loose dirt and sand. She starting throwing it over Herrera, letting the mound grow until even the smoke from the smoldering fabric could not escape.

"How hurt are you?"

Herrera cursed. "I don't know!"

Herrera cursed again as he lifted himself onto his knees and felt the palm of his hands.

Gabrielle tried to lift him. "Can you walk?"

The navigator stumbled to his knees, nodding, and patting the sand and dirt from his sleeves. He pointed toward the *maśuhoma*, engulfed in flames. "We can't get anywhere close to that lodge now. Isabella has either escaped or has burned with the Indians in their temple."

Gabrielle struggled to breathe as her heart seemed to pound its way out of her chest. Her knees weakened as her mind drew blank. She wanted to scream, to call out. She opened her mouth to nothing but silence, the crackling of burning limbs overwhelming her ears, the heat of the fire pressing against her eyes.

She felt the embrace of arms wrapping around her waist and the pull of a force that lifted her from her feet.

"Isabella!"

25

Isabella counted eleven pirates in her band as she led them through the woods. Finding the path skirting the village in the brush was difficult, even though she knew it had to exist. Invisible to anyone in the village or approaching through the swamp, she suspected the children shooting arrows at her as she entered the lagoon were perched in sentry posts connected by this path.

The Calusa were more than warriors. These paths, like the canals, the lagoon, and this village, were marvels of engineering. The Calusa molded their environment to serve them, even without the ropes, pulleys, and tools fashioned from the furnaces of the colonial powers. They were far more sophisticated than the absentee lords that ruled her plantation on Santo Domingo. The Spanish overseers struggled to keep water flowing through the plantation's mill even though an idle plantation would result in financial ruin.

As the pirates came abreast of the beach, Isabella brought the band to a halt. She looked out over the lagoon, counting a dozen canoes resting on the sand. A clutch of warriors kneeled next to the boats. At least one seemed to be holding a long gun.

Her band was just across from the finger of land that obscured the village from the outer canal. She had a clear line of sight into the water entrance. Where would Jean-Michel take his pirates? Where were Juan Carlos and Herrera? Gabrielle? Marguerite and Pierre? Her heart sank as she thought she might not find them all. Someone would be left behind.

"Captain," a pirate whispered from behind her.

She turned to see the full, rounded, bronze face of one of the newer recruits.

"The Indians are in pursuit. Followed us into the woods. Fifteen minutes, I'm guess'n', before they be all over us."

"Thank you, Phillip." Isabella looked back down the path. "Take four men and set up a defense about one hundred feet up the path. If they get within distance, fire. Don't worry about accuracy. Slow them down and keep the arrows as far away as possible. Hopefully, we'll have a way out in ten minutes."

She turned back to the beach.

A series of shots rang out from across the lagoon.

"Someone's still alive," Isabella said under her breath.

Sarhaan tapped her on the shoulder and pointed to a group of Indians on the far side of the village about halfway toward the flaming lodges and *maśuhoma*. "They must see Jean-Michel."

And Juan Carlos and Gabrielle? Isabella turned back to her small squad. Eleven pirates, as seasoned as they were, would not be enough to hold off a hundred or so Calusa warriors. Their muskets could not load fast enough, and their knives could not hold off the arrows. But where were the other warriors?

She turned to Sarhaan. "Have you seen other Calusa warriors? The village held many more when we arrived."

Sarhaan sighed as he looked out over the lagoon. "Several hundred warriors attacked our ship in the middle of the night."

Isabella felt her heart flip.

"Jean-Michel had double sentries. He did not trust the Calusa to leave us alone."

Isabella shook her head. The Paramount *Cacique* never meant to uphold his end of their bargain. She remembered Chosa's words earlier that afternoon. She tried to bring her into the tribe, knowing that her warriors were already fighting *La Marée Rouge*. She was testing her loyalty to her crew. "When did they attack?"

"At the full height of the moon. We heard a shot from the flying top. The night was quiet. We thought someone was anxious. Then Murray fell to the main deck, an arrow through his heart. They had used the spark of his gun to target their arrows."

Isabella tried to imagine scores of Calusa warriors scaling the sides of the ship and overwhelming her crew. "How did you survive?"

Sarhaan let a smile crack his somber face. "Jean-Michel was prepared. He had oiled rags and tied them to rods to make torches. He stayed up on watch. As soon as Murray fell, he lit the first torch and sent it into the bay. Soon dozens of torches lit up the bay like lanterns warding off demons. We could see the canoes, and we fired."

"But how did you defeat hundreds of Calusa warriors?"

"Ha ha, Smoothy is very good. The cannon were loaded with double grape shot. He had the gun ports shaved to lower their sites and give his gun captains a better angle."

Isabella smiled. He could not have used cannon balls; they would have rolled out the muzzles before the charges could ignite.

Sarhaan sighed again. "It was a long night. We still lost many good deckhands. Doc is very busy." He turned his eyes down to the dirt. "And Louis."

Isabella tapped Sarhaan on his knee. "We have come a long way since that day on St. John after the mutiny."

"I am sorry, Captain."

"You did not know the village had turned. You did not know about the trap. Or that Rodriguez would use Jean-Michel as bait to capture me."

She turned back to the lagoon. "You can tell me the rest of your story when we finish writing ours by escaping from this hell hole. We'll call it the Battle of Caloosahatchee."

Two pops came from the trees on the other side of the lagoon, followed by a third.

"The Calusa are closing on them," Sarhaan said, urgency mounting his voice.

"What was Jean-Michel's plan if you could not reach the temple?"

Three more pops came from across the path, preventing Sarhaan from responding.

"I heard six shots." She turned to Sarhaan. "You said Jean-Michel had a dozen of our crew?"

Sarhaan nodded. "They had muskets and pistols. Each carried a knife and blade as well."

"Better armed than a boarding party!" Isabella smiled. Jean-Michel expected his plan on land to be tough to execute. "The Calusa must not be charging them. They are not shooting too many rounds."

The sound of another shot made its way into their position. Sarhaan pointed to a cluster of pine trees on the other side of the beach. "There."

Isabella covered her eyes with her hand and squinted. Another shot rang through the air, and this time she saw the flicker and puff of smoke. She looked back up toward the line of Calusa running into the woods. She could now count about ten Indians near the canoes. "Jean-Michel is laying cover fire. They are retreating. Where would he have tied his boats for escape?"

Sarhaan directed her eyes toward a point that seemed to go through the center of the finger of land that protected the inlet.

The Indians on the beach started to move and spread out among the canoes. "Ugh," Isabella grumbled. "More Calusa! They seem to climb out of the sand."

A crack from a musket shot through the woods.

"We cannot wait," Sarhaan said.

"Where did you tether your boats?"

"They are down the path. We tied to trees in the canal on the outside rim of this island."

Two more shots crashing through the foliage signaled the pirates that their time had run out.

Several volleys from guns across the lagoon announced the start of a more serious skirmish. The Indians were using the canoes as a defensive line, with one Indian reloading guns while the other fired into the retreating group of pirates across from Isabella and Sarhaan. Several hundred feet away, the trees and brush swayed with advancing Calusa as powder ignited, producing more pops and cracks.

"We need to create a distraction. They need more time to get to the boats."

She turned to her helmsman. "Have four of our men shoot at the Indians on the beach. Then signal for Phillip to fall back fifty feet."

Sarhaan turned down the path to alert the picket.

The first shots from her side of the lagoon turned the Indians on the beach toward them. One lifted himself to pivot back toward their position and fell to the ground as shots rang out from the other side of the woods. The Indians fired again, this time in both directions. The bullets drifted high into the trees. Two more Indians fell on the beach as the area around the lagoon seemed to be overwhelmed with clumps of smoke created by spent gunpowder.

Footsteps and breaking wood turned Isabella's head back up the path where her pirates continued to load and reload their muskets. An arrow sliced through the leaves, but lost momentum and dropped to her feet. Sarhaan came bounding down the path, tapping pirates on their shoulders as a signal for them to fall back toward the captain.

Two pirates turned the barrels of their guns up the path as the others retreated. A Calusa warrior appeared behind some brush, and one fired. Arrows swished through trees. Isabella ducked, although she knew the twigs and leaves provided little protection. Another crack from a musket, and she heard a yell and a curse from a pirate.

"Go, go!" someone yelled.

Phillip and two other pirates broke from the foliage and sprinted past Isabella.

"How many of our crew are still up the trail?" she asked, keeping her focus on the path.

"Just two more."

"Once you see them, fire two shots on either side of the path. That might keep a few of their heads down. Who was hit?"

Another shot, this time with a higher pitch, triggered a wave of sweat in Isabella's palms. More arrows cut through the brush. "A pistol. They're getting closer. We will have to run for the boats."

Phillip inched up to Isabella. "We cannot hold this position. There are too many of them."

"As soon as Sarhaan gets to us, retreat to the boats. We will send another volley of bullets into the Indians, and then join you. Have our guns reloaded so you can cover us."

Feet trampling down the path revealed Sarhaan bounding toward them.

Isabella tapped Phillip's shoulder. "Go!"

Phillip turned and signaled for four other pirates to follow him.

Sarhaan ducked as another volley of arrows seared the leaves and branches around them as he slid to a stop next to Isabella. A musket boomed over her head, prompting her to duck. A hand grabbed her shoulder and pulled her back. "Get to the boats, Cap'n. We'll cover ya!"

Another musket cracked above her. Isabella scrambled to catch her balance and turned to run. Her brain just registered the crackling path of another volley of arrows when a numbing pain pounded into her side, throwing her into an uncontrolled forward stumble.

She gasped, unable to inhale, a blistering throb in her side. She lifted her arm, only to find herself paralyzed in agony with each move of her muscles. An ache now spread from her back to her torso.

She reached around her side, grasping for the location of the wound, when her fingers hooked its source: the shaft of an arrow buried in her flesh.

"Pull it out!" she yelled.

She tried to push herself down the path, unable to hear or focus on anything other than the pain. Breathe in, she commanded herself, breathe in. Each breath allowed another layer of sounds to register in her ear, even as the pain continued to burn through her brain.

Someone grabbed her shirt and started pulling. Another spate of agony consumed her as she felt the shaft of the arrow bend against the pull of her shirt. She cursed, trying to bring her legs underneath her as the force pulled her down the path. Cracks from muskets and pistols filled the air, blotting out the sounds of descending arrows and spears even as she saw them dig into the dirt next to her. She felt a wooden beam scrape down her torso to her legs and feet as she dropped onto a plank floor.

Arrows burrowed into the wood around her with thuds and thwacks. Another force pushed her up against the gunwale, and she felt the boat float into the water, rocking as men scrambled inside. The boat jerked forward. At first haphazard, unpredictable, the oars quickly settled into a steady, rhythmic pattern. The cracks from muskets faded, becoming less steady and predictable. Soon, all she heard were grunts, foreshadowing another thrust of the boat through the water.

The pirates stacked in three rows of four, firing rounds in three directions as they fell back through the woods. Juan Carlos staggered the shots but maintained a rhythm that allowed each pirate to focus, load, and prime their muskets. Each volley forced the advancing Calusa to pause, giving them more time to retreat to the canoes.

Jean-Michel guided Marguerite toward the canoes, assigning a pirate to guard her and the youngest of the boys. He turned to the older boy. "*Comment t'appelle-tu?*"

The boy's eyes seemed vacant, unable to focus.

"What is your name young man? *Tu es français, n'est-ce pas?*"

Pierre looked down at the breech cloth slung around his hips and his bare feet. "I am not dressed like a Frenchman."

"It's not what you're dressed like that makes you French. What's in your heart?"

Pierre looked up at Jean-Michel. "I am not a Calusa in my heart, but I am not sure if I am French."

Jean-Michel laughed. "Well then I have the perfect place for you. *La Marée Rouge* is full of men who have hearts searching for a place."

Pierre looked over at his mother. "*Je m'appelle Pierre.*"

Jean-Michel checked to make sure Marguerite was secure in the canoe. "*Bien,* Pierre. Stay here with your mother. Guard her with your life. We have more work to do here before we can leave. Be ready to paddle hard when you get the signal from me or Captain Santa Ana."

An uneven volley of shots pulled Jean-Michel's attention back to the battle unfolding in the woods. He launched into a jog back up the trail into the thicket and skirmish.

"Cover them!"

The urgency of Juan Carlos's command set off several rounds of muskets up the trail as he pulled pirates along the path. One pirate was dead, the wounds of two others severe enough he worried whether they would make it back to *La Marée Rouge*. His instincts told him his platoon would soon be out of shot. He was about to order a full retreat to the canoes when he saw the flash of a saber blade coming through the trail.

Herrera burst through brush, his arms latched to Gabrielle's body as she struggled to keep up with him. Juan Carlos rushed forward along the trail, a sword firm in his hands as he directed the fire of the three lines of pirates. He waved to Herrera, as if his hand could reach out and pull him behind the safety of his defensive line.

The pirate navigator was still ten paces from the pirates when two Indians dove from the trees, slamming against Herrera and forcing Gabrielle from his grip. The melee disappeared into a thicket of brush, the tussle of trees and branches indicating the fight had become a free-for-all. A pistol fired. Herrera stumbled back onto the path, falling backward as he lost his balance. He turned just enough for Juan Carlos to see the blackened cloth remains of his shirt.

Flashes of Calusa warriors flicked through spaces between leaves, drawing the fire of pirate muskets. Whether the lead balls found their mark was impossible to tell, except the Indians did not seem to be advancing on the pirate positions.

Another warrior dropped next to Juan Carlos, raising a conch hammer as a battle club. The army captain crouched as he swiveled, the point of the Calusa weapon missing his head as the edge of his blade cut through the waist of his attacker. The Indian collapsed, blood spewing from his wounds.

Juan Carlos turned back toward the path and saw Herrera defending himself from another Indian attacking him with a knife. He launched himself toward the fight but stopped as he saw a flash of movement that cut the Indian from behind. Herrera dove back into the brush, re-emerging with Gabrielle just as two more Indians appeared behind them on the trail. A diminutive man seemed to appear from the air, stepping between Herrera and Gabrielle to confront the warriors. Omena!

The Indians attacked, one swinging an ax while the other charged with a spear. Omena dodged the arc of the knife while appearing to roll over the shaft of the spear, landing on his feet. He then launched a powerful kick into the spear-wielding Indian's thigh, and the warrior collapsed, the angle of his leg definitive evidence that the Japanese had snapped his leg in two. Before the Indian could react, Omena pivoted to push the shaft of the spear into the second Indian. The warrior was in mid-swing, but the spear prevented a complete arc as it pinned the arm back. Omena seemed to work in one fluid motion as he brought a hand up to the warrior's head, grabbed his hair, and used his weight to pull the attack forward in a move that snapped the neck of the attacker.

Omena's fury gave Herrera just the moments he needed to transport Gabrielle to the pirates.

Juan Carlos relieved Herrera of Gabrielle's weight and began to walk her back toward the canoes.

"I have her," Jean-Michel said as he let her body fall onto his shoulders. "We'll prepare the boat! Organize the retreat!"

Jean-Michel brushed warm cinders from her clothing as he marched her toward the canal. Her entire body smelled like the burning embers of a forest fire.

"Isabella," Gabrielle wheezed.

"We have to get out of this village," Jean-Michel said.

"We can't leave her."

Jean-Michel stayed silent as he rushed her to the edge of a canoe and lifted her into the bottom. "We'll come back for her."

"She's in the temple lodge."

Jean-Michel looked above the woods, saw the billowing smoke, and fought to hold back a river of tears. He had to stay in the fight. He had to focus on saving the men of *La Marée Rouge*. He could not afford to let his love for Isabella sacrifice the men he could save now. "We'll come back for her," he said in a soft voice.

A stream of pirates began to emerge from the woods, each line firing a shot and then jumping into canoes. They reloaded their muskets as one pirate prepared the paddles, and the others provided cover for the retreating lines. Arrows started to pepper the water around them; a few lodged themselves in the wooden sides and planks of the boats.

"No, no, no," Gabrielle sobbed. "Get her now! We can't leave her."

As another volley of musket shot met a hail of arrows, Jean-Michel's canoe shoved off from the shore and loyal deckhands began to paddle with a vigor that showed they knew the stakes of moving too slow.

26

Isabella focused on her breathing, inviting the air to recharge her lungs and body. As her body gained strength with each breath, the pain in her side became more intense. She tried to push herself up to her knees.

"Careful, Cap'n. We ain't out a danger yet. No need to make your head a target."

"How many men did we lose?"

"We got you out. That's our goal."

"Sarhaan?"

"Doc'll take look at em. Right after you."

Isabella rested her head on her knees. "Jean-Michel?"

"Ain't seen em, yet. Still some fightn' when we left."

She pulled herself up to the gunwale, letting her arm hook the side so she could see around her. They were in the canals, the ripples from the bow waves suggesting they were making significant headway. She saw one canoe ahead of hers, two men on each side poling their boat forward. She tried to turn and look behind her, but movement seemed to push a dagger into her side. "Can someone do something about that arrow?"

She heard someone make their way up the canoe from behind.

"One minute, captain. Let me take a look."

She recognized the voice but the face eluded her. "Fletcher?"

"Aye, ma'am. The arrow's in there pretty good."

She could feel the shaft move, the buried arrow head slicing more of her flesh with each nudge. "Argh!"

"Sorry, ma'am. I think Doc will be better at taking a look at it."

She heaved in a full breath of air. At least her lungs were free of fluid. "I can't go all the way back with an arrow sticking out of my back like a harpooned whale!"

"No ma'am."

"Hold it steady where the shaft goes into the flesh and break it off."

Fletcher hesitated, but then clasped a hand around the shaft, the flesh of his hand set against her blood-soaked blouse.

"Do it, Fletcher!"

"Aye, ma'am. Hold on."

The pain almost drove Isabella into unconsciousness but receded into a dull numbness. She felt the press of something against her wound. Then she heard the shuffle of boots and shifting of bodies as the boat pressed forward with a jolt.

Isabella lay her head against the gunwale, the sounds of life fading, as she hovered over and drifted into nothingness.

"Pull, pull, pull!"

The words registered outside Isabella's head, but failed to penetrate her brain. Her head jostled even as she felt the stillness of her body from her neck to her feet. A wisp of air tingled her toes with each command.

"Easy, mates."

A wave flooded across her head, forcing her eyes open as a thumping pain whacked at the back of her head. She caught her breath, her mind catching a rasping sound as she closed her eyes again.

"Easy!"

Was she dying? Why couldn't she feel? Why didn't she care…?

Isabella opened her eyes; the dark almost fooled her into thinking she was dead. But the press of the boat through the water told her she was very much on this earth. She turned her head to the sky. The black faded into a deep, dark blue background, and brilliant white flecks seemed to cast different patterns depending on which place her eyes landed.

"The moon is almost full," she whispered. "Is it time for me to let go?"

"Aaaahhh!"

Isabella's wail could not be stopped as much as she tried. She felt the pressure of the table top against her cheeks and breast, but her outstretched arms obscured any other objects or sight. Air stung her back as she tried to make sense of the pulsing glow around her.

"Damn, let's get it. Put some more on that…. There…, now get ready to slice. Then pull as soon as you see it."

A searing pain from her back proved that some nerves, some part of her flesh, still existed, rebelling against some attack.

"Now!"

More pain sheared her torso.

"Don't stop…. Get it… there…. Pull…. Pull it out!"

A groan burst from her lungs as something extracted something else deep inside. Another tug and she wondered if her skin would be stripped from her muscles and bones.

"Aaaahhhh," she sobbed, this time her voice weak and unsure. Her body felt nothing, her mind thick with thoughts she was unable to navigate. She needed to let go.

Binta. With God. She needed to let go. She needed to stop. But stop what? She felt the pain…, or at least she thought she felt the pain… but didn't care. She really didn't care. Her body was a suspended mass. She wasn't even sure she had a body. Just thoughts. No pain. Just thoughts. It could all go. Forever. She just had to let it go. Was this what God meant for her? Had she completed her mission? Was The Prophecy, foretold so many years ago around the slave cabin fire by her mother, true? Or fulfilled.

Yes, I can let go, she thought. I need to let go. The gibbous moon. It's almost full. It's time for me to let go.

27

The spray against his hands kept the salt from stinging his eyes, but his tears would have been enough of a defense without them. He pushed his hands further against his eye sockets, heaving with each crest of the ship over another wave.

"Doc thinks she has a fifty-fifty chance of making it through," said a familiar voice with a comforting French accent.

"*Sí, mi amigo*. But we have a long journey ahead of us."

"Doc's seen a lot of death."

Juan Carlos nodded, letting his hands wipe down his face as he turned to Jean-Michel. "Doc wants to see her live."

"We all do. Louis is holding a vigil by her bedside."

"*Mi amigo*—"

Jean-Michel put a hand on his shoulder. "We all want her to pull through."

Juan Carlos shook his head. "If you had told me two years ago, when I set sail from Cadiz for Puerto Rico, that I would fall in love with a slave woman—a pirate no less!—I would have…."

Jean-Michel laughed. "I think we have all asked ourselves that question at some point."

Juan Carlos brought a hand back to his eyes, squeezing the lids together. "An African. A pirate." He turned to look at Jean-Michel again. "I would give up my king and country?"

"I gave up my king and country long before I met Isabella." Jean-Michel looked into the late afternoon chops. The bow of the brig lifted and fell again as mist washed over a puffed blue-gray sky tumbling into the western horizon. The bundled clouds darkened as the sun stayed hidden. "We're lucky. This wind will keep us at thirteen knots or more."

"Will she last long enough?"

Jean-Michel's eyebrows turned up at the question and then shook his head. "If the fever breaks…. She's not awake yet. She needs to wake up. She needs food and water. Damn this weather. We've been fighting it for two days."

Jean-Michel put his arms on the railing. "She's fierce. Hardest woman I've ever known. Hardest man for that matter. Excepting Jacob."

"Jacob…."

"He saved her. She lost everything at fifteen. The burning of the plantation was brutal. But that was nothing compared to the dagos…." Jean-Michel cast a quick look to Juan Carlos before continuing. "… Spanish… did afterwards. Two dozen slaves, most not even connected to the revolt, lashed and burned, just to send a message. Isabella was on death's door by the time Jacob found her. He knew what she was. He knew what she could be."

"What happened to Jacob?"

Jean-Michel rubbed his chin as another mist washed over them. "Betrayed. We were ambushed at sea by a rogue." He smiled as he shook his head. "Honor among thieves, they say?"

"In Spain, we say, *piensa el ladrón que todos son de su condición;* the thief thinks that everyone is of his own condition."

Jean-Michel cast another look into the sea, watching the timing of the waves and checking the wind in the sails. "King Solomon was closer to the truth: Evil people desire evil; their neighbors get no mercy from them."

"I didn't take you for a religious man."

"I am not. But I am of noble birth, in France. I was instructed at an early age by the brothers."

"A nobleman becomes a pirate?"

Jean-Michel turned to face Juan Carlos. "We are not that much different, *mon ami*. You have an officer's commission, the privilege of the nobility with wealth. For the others, such as the third son of a poor nobleman out of favor with their king, our path is not so clear."

Juan-Carlos nodded. "But here we are, the second and third sons of nobility, on a pirate ship off the coast of La Florida in love with an African woman ship's captain.

The French pirate's laugh bellowed across the water. "*Oui!* King Solomon also said, if I recall correctly, God examines our heart, and He is more pleased when we do what is right. I follow her because it is right. She is on a path that is right."

"Do you think He is pleased with Isabella's path?"

Jean-Michel tipped his head. "According to the monks in our small monastery, God is always right. He always has a plan." He paused. "I would like to think they were right, and He is pleased with the path she has chosen."

"She seemed like a nice lady."

Louis looked up at the boy a year maybe two older than himself, using a few moments to think about his words. "Your French is much better than mine."

"Papa and Mama made me take lessons, even when he was away with his ships."

Louis turned back to Isabella and pulled his stool closer to the bed. He observed her breathing, counting the number of times her chest rose and fell on his fingers.

"Has she changed?"

"I don't think so," Louis said. "I don't have a watch or a clock. But Doc said to watch *capitaine* Isabella and let him know if her breathing changes."

Pierre ran the wool cloth of his shirt through his fingers. "This feels very strange. I liked not having to wear shirts or pants. Or boots."

Louis curled his eyebrows. "Everyone wears clothes."

"The Calusa do not."

"The Calusa tried to kill *capitaine* Isabella."

"They thought she was going to attack them."

"*Capitaine* Isabella saved my life."

Pierre hesitated. He took two more steps toward Louis and sat down next to him next to him, crossing his legs. "You were almost killed?"

Louis nodded. "Port-au-Prince was burning. Men were shooting guns and killing each other. Isabella saved me. And Gabrielle."

"I remember that night," Pierre said, tracing a circle in the deck under his legs. "The fires were burning all night. I could hear the guns going off. Mama said I should stay in our house, that they were far away. But I knew they were nearby. I remember the cannons going off in the harbor, too."

Louis counted again with his fingers. He stood up and looked over the outline of Isabella's body, using his eyes to check her from toes to head.

"Were you scared?" Pierre asked, still looking at the wood planks beneath him.

Louis sat back down at his stool. "Yes."

"Did someone shoot at you?"

Louis seemed to ignore Pierre's question.

The two boys sat for several minutes. Then Pierre said, "The Calusa shot at me."

Louis brought his hands to his thighs and rubbed them.

"I was scared."

Louis looked at Pierre. "I thought you said they were your friends."

"I did," Pierre said, still looking at the pine planks. "I guess they did not like me. Or my mother."

"Your mother is still here."

Pierre nodded. "And my little brother, Jean." He changed positions, lifting his knees to his chin. "Where is your mother?"

Pierre breathed in, letting the air out with a shudder. He lifted a hand to his face, wiping away a tear that crept from his eyes to the top of his cheek. "She's dead."

"I am sorry."

"You have your mother."

"Yes, I am very lucky."

The boys sat for a few more minutes.

Pierre looked up to Louis. "I think they were going to kill my mother."

Louis turned on his stool to look at Pierre. "Why do you think that?"

"Because they were going to kill the men that came with *capitaine* Isabella. They killed two white men before you arrived."

Louis's eyes widened, his cheeks becoming taut. "They were going to kill Jean-Michel? And *Señor* Santa Ana?"

Pierre nodded.

"*Je déteste le calusa.*"

"They were my friends."

Louis glared at Pierre.

Pierre looked down at the deck again. "For a little while. They taught me how to hunt and fish in the canals. They taught me how to catch fish with my bare hands. And to shoot a bow and arrow. And make a canoe."

"They taught you how to make a canoe?"

"*Oui.* It's very hard. And takes a long time. They chop a big tree down. They use these axes made from really hard shells and stones to crumble the wood inside. Then they burn it."

Louis considered what Pierre said, letting his head nod. "Maybe you can show me some time."

"*Bien sûr!* When we make port." Pierre stood up and walked to the edge of Isabella's bed. "Will she live?"

Louis shrugged his shoulders.

"Have you seen many people hurt like this?"

Another tear welled in Louis's eyes. He lifted another hand to wipe the tear away. He nodded.

"I am sorry."

"*Merci.*"

"Were they brave?"

"*Oui*, very brave."

"Were they your friends?"

Louis nodded, wiping another tear away. "They saved me from the streets of Port-au-Prince."

Pierre looked over Isabella. "She is very brave. She protected me, my mother, and my brother. She helped us escape while she fought the warriors."

Louis smiled. "*Elle est très courageuse*. She wanted to save my mother, but she couldn't. No one could."

"I think I want to sail with *capitaine* Isabella. And Jean-Michel. And monsieur Santa Ana. And mademoiselle Gabrielle. And monsieur Doc."

Louis laughed. "This is a good ship."

The boys laughed together.

Louis turned back to Pierre. "Your French is very good."

"Why isn't your French as good? We are the same age."

"I am slave."

"That's not fair."

"You are a slave on this ship?"

Louis shook his head. "No, everyone is free on this ship. I even saw them vote to keep Isabella as *capitaine*." He paused. "I want to learn better French. You sound like Governor General Bellecombe."

Pierre looked at Louis, his eyes widened by curiosity. "You know the Governor General?"

Louis nodded. "I was his driver."

Pierre put his arms around Louis. "I will teach you better French."

28

The two women huddled in the stern of the brig as it rode up onto the waves and the bow crashed into the trough of another one.

"When do you need to check on little Jean?"

"I should be able to hear him from here. He is below, outside Isabella's cabin. Pierre will get me if he wakes up."

"Pierre was very brave."

"We were very scared."

"But you kept moving. When the warriors attacked, many men would have frozen and allowed themselves to be overrun or killed. Pierre kept his head. He did not run off on his own."

Marguerite pulled the blanket over her shoulders closer, protecting herself from gulf winds that now reminded her of the approaching winters in Bordeaux, France. "I think he was very upset that his friends would try to hurt him. He thought the Calusa were his friends."

"You did not?"

"As a white, I was never brought into the tribe. I tried to make my time valuable, but I was never sure of my place. But Pierre…, he tried so hard, to learn their ways, to learn their language."

"Spain's history with the Calusa did not help us."

Marguerite turned toward the bow. "What do you think they are talking about?"

Gabrielle followed her look, spotting Jean-Michel and Juan Carlos near the bowsprit. "Juan Carlos is in love with Isabella."

"Jean-Michel is not?"

"Yes…, in a different way." Gabrielle laughed. "We all love Isabella."

Marguerite smiled and sighed.

Gabrielle leaned against the barrel of one of the cannon secured on the aft deck, its portal closed to protect it from the water.

"Your crew," Margeurite said, admiration in her tone. "They followed her... and you... into the swamps."

Gabrielle looked around the deck, noting Sarhaan at the tiller. Another pirate, Fletcher, she thought, was standing nearby, intent on watching the sails and waves, ready to throw his back into navigating the windswept seas at the signal of the helmsmen. Herrera, she knew, was below decks with Smoothy, checking the charts. St. Marks should be within a day's sail, Herrera said, if they could find it. A miracle would be needed in the best weather to decipher the outer banks, shoals, and barrier islands. How would Herrera and Sarhaan find the needle they needed to thread their way to the San Marcos trading post?

"*Capitaine* Santa Ana was about to be killed by a revolutionary in Port-au-Prince. A mad man. He was going to lead all the *gens de couleur*, and whatever slave he could find to join him, in a revolution." Gabrielle looked at her boots as she shook her head. "He ordered Isabella to kill him, to show the men, *les révolutionnaires*, that they could rise up to overthrow their French masters."

Gabrielle looked up at Marguerite.

The French woman, a former Calusa captive, seemed confused. "Why wouldn't you want to overthrow their masters? Slavery is terrible."

"Oh, *mon cher*, we do. All of us, *gens de couleur* and slave, want to end slavery. We were not ready." Gabrielle crossed her arms and looked more directly into Marguerite's eyes. "And you, Margeurite, and your boys, are here now, on *La Marée Rouge*, because that mad man did not play his cards right. If he had, you would be dead. He had no sympathy for anyone who opposed him."

"But I would not have opposed him. I am just a woman with two children."

"You were European, white, and French. That's all D'Poussant would have cared about. *Liberté, égalité, fraternité*—but only for those that are like him and believe in him."

203

"The fires were burning all night. I heard the guns, too. I told Pierre to stay in his room and try to sleep. I barred our door and stood by our travel chests with a musket and pistol."

"They would have burned you out before they would have shot you."

"Why did they fail?"

Gabrielle buried her cheek in her sleeve as a gust of wind swept the rear of the warship, forcing Sarhaan to lean into the wind and adjust the tiller.

"D'Poussant was a strong leader, but a poor general. Our Governor General, Guillaume Léonard de Bellecombe, was a decorated military officer and official. He hates slavery, he hates the British, but he loves and is loyal to France. D'Poussant made the mistake of thinking the departure of the West Indies fleet to help the Americans weakened Bellecombe's defense of Port-au-Prince and Saint Domingue. His so-called revolution did not last more than a day. But he left many dead—Louis's mother, maybe my father."

Marguerite slipped her blanket around Gabrielle's shoulders, and turned to watch the churn of the *La Marée Rouge*'s wake as it rolled the waves. "I am sorry."

Gabrielle folded her hand over Marguerite's. "I am sorry you and your sons had to go through captivity with the Calusa." Gabrielle let her head drop so her lips touched Marguerite's hand. *"Nous avons la chance d'être en vie.* We can make our next life, the one we live now, much richer."

29

"*¡El tiempo es terrible!*" Herrera grabbed the side of the table as the ship pitched without warning. "*¡Este barco mejor permanecer juntos!*"

The crusty faced pirate across the table from him slapped a hand on the map as *La Marée Rouge* rolled back to upright. "Speak English, damn it! Ya know I ain't got no understandin' of Spanish!"

"*Lo siento*.... I am sorry..., Smoothy." Herrera shook his head. "This weather is impossible."

Smoothy raised his eyebrows as he looked at Herrera. "How many years have you been at sea? This ain't nothin'. We got her storm rigged. Sarhaan's at the tiller. And he's got Fletcher up there if he needs 'm. This brig's small enough it won't take more than a shout down the hatch to muster a load of tars up in the yards if we need 'm to reef more sail."

The sound of a box spilling metal and wood objects cut across the small open area converting the officer's mess to a surgeon's table and now a map room.

"Sorry gents," Doc said in a voice that said they should have expected his tools to scatter across the deck. "You took my work table."

Smoothy shot a glance over Herrera's shoulder. "Apologies to the good doctor! We'll scare up another battle once the weather lets up. We'll give ya more business. Muñoz's probably right over the horizon."

"Much obliged Mr. Smoothy," said Doc as he found a place around the table. "But I don't think I will take you up on the offer. We lost three back in the swamps, and I had to stitch up another five hands once you got back to the ship." He ran his finger across the map, tracing a line from what the chart marked as the Caloosahatchee River to a point north of two named bays. "I know we are past these two. Any idea where we are Mr. Herrera?"

Herrera lifted a hand to his chin and started to rub it, then pulled his fingers through his hair. The deck began to tilt again, sending six hands to the side of the table, before the boat evened out.

"Doc," Smoothy said and hesitated. Doc looked at the gunner's mate who nodded toward Isabella's cabin.

Doc nodded his head. "I don't know. She's got an infection and lost a lot of blood. Two arrow wounds. The shoulder wound wasn't that bad. She didn't lose a lot of blood. The other wound, the one in her side, looked like an arrow head sliced her cleanly before burying itself. That's where most of the blood loss was from." He looked at Smoothy and then to Herrera, their eyes dull and faces drawn. "I just don't know. Two more days will give me a better understanding."

Doc looked at Smoothy and Herrera. "What about the boys?"

Smoothy shook his hid. "I can't figure kids out. Ain't been around kids… and don't care to be around 'm…, but a pirate ship is no place to raise a boy."

Herrara nodded. "I was fourteen when I went to sea. I had lost my mother to sickness. That's nothing like seeing your mother shot during a bloody revolt or being hunted by hundreds of rogue Indian warriors. They're too young for any of that."

Doc stepped around the table and peered into Isabella's cabin. Louis and Pierre were sitting vigil over Isabella who seemed to lay in a peaceful state. "Louis! How is our captain doing?"

Louis and Pierre both turned at the sound of Doc's voice. "*Bien! Bon!*" they said, almost in unison. They turned to each other, and Louis gave Pierre a playful punch in the shoulder.

"Good, let me know if you see any change."

Doc turned back to the captain's table and the chart. He raised his hand and let his finger fall about one-third of the way down the west coast of La Florida. "I think we are here."

"Ha! Not bad for a doc, a seafarin' one to boot!"

Herrera nodded again. "Si, not a bad guess. But the weather has taken us off course, and we are facing seven or eight-foot waves. We cannot make much time or distance under these conditions. I thought we could tack northwest against winds coming from the west. But we're fighting the waves even heading back to the coast. We could be facing a strong gulf current."

Doc shook his head. "What does that mean?"

"Usually the current just flows up in the gulf from the Caribbean over the north coast of Cuba and under La Florida. Sometimes, when the weather is right, the current pushes up to off the coast of Pensacola or New Orleans. When the current turns back, it's like we're fighting a stone wall. That's what this feels like."

Doc picked up a rag and began to wipe his hands as the boat took another roll. The tins and bowls rattled, and wood creaked under the strain all around them. "How long will it last?"

Herrera shook his head. He leaned back over the map. "As best I can tell, we're here." His finger landed on a spot about a hundred miles to the west of La Florida coast and fifty miles south of what looked like a big bend in the coast line where land started to connect points west toward New Orleans.

"Aye, less than a half day sail," Smoothy said.

Herrera cocked his head. "If I'm right. We were running from the Calusa. I didn't get a chance to get a good read on our position before we lost sight of land. I have a good idea, but not precise. We have been sailing under clouds since we sailed from the river."

"Dead reckoning."

"Si. I cannot say with complete certainty."

"So, we jus' sail 'round in circles in the gulf?"

"Maybe we should go straight to New Orleans," Doc said. "We have twenty men that desperately need food and fresh water. I think we will lose two of them. Their wounds are not healing from the ambush by Muñoz south of Cuba."

Herrera shook his head. "We're taking a bigger chance with their lives if we go straight to New Orleans. Even with this weather, there's no guarantee we can get to port in less than a month even with good fortune. The Mississippi River winds through the bayous. I've never made it from the bottom of the delta to the port in less than a week, and we're hundreds of miles from there."

Smoothy looked at Doc. "Can Isabella make it that long?"

Doc caught his breath as he grabbed the table to steady himself as another wave forced the pirate ship to heel over. "Not much we can do about Isabella. Whether she makes it is up to her body. Food and water will certainly help; she needs to be conscious to eat. We have to wait for the fever to break."

Doc leaned over the map again. "San Marcos is here, correct?" His finger landed on a spot on the map just as the land began to bend toward the west, about thirty miles south of what was an equal distance between Pensacola and St. Augustine in La Florida territory. "It's controlled by the British, right?"

Herrera nodded. "An Indian trading post, San Marcos de Apalache, is at the mouth of the San Marcos River."

Smoothy looked at the spot. "How sure are you a trading post is there? We thought a post existed at the Caloosahatchee River. All we found there was a load of hurt and trouble with the Calusa."

Herrera pulled another map, this one showing the bending coast line and the mouth of a river. He traced a river marked San Marcos north for several miles. He stopped when the river turned to the right and a second smaller river marked Guacara River turned left, creating a triangular point extending from the north bank of the San Marcos. He tapped the point where the rivers diverged. "Creek Indians now control an abandoned Spanish fort where these two rivers meet. The area is controlled by the British, but an American company now operates it as a trading post with the Creek Indians."

Smoothy nodded. "I guess a fort is more certain than a trading post. I guess the Creek Indians aren't supposed to be ghosts like our Calusa friends down south, either."

"The trading post has been there for more than fifteen years," Herrera said.

Doc nodded. "Nice of the British to kick the Spanish out of La Florida for us. I guess some wars have their benefits. They won't take it too kindly if Muñoz decides to follow us up the river. How extensive is this trading post?"

"When I was with the Spanish navy, my captain sent me on a provisioning mission. That was several years ago, but the trading post had most of what we need. Deer, bear, beaver, mink hides. Salted meat and fish. Rice. Cotton. Naval stores—tar, pitch, turpentine—to seal our ships from the weather or when we scrape the hulls."

Doc's nods increased. "Turpentine. Good. We can use it to clean the wounds, mix it with some other herbs or molasses. That may save a few lives. Is this the course Jean-Michel set?"

Herrera nodded.

Doc looked over toward Isabella's cabin. "We might have to make a decision if this weather doesn't break. I am not sure how many of our wounded will make it if we have to give up on St. Marks and go straight to New Orleans."

Herrera shook his head. "Isabella is in God's hands now."

30

The gust of wind smacked Herrera as he stepped onto the main deck, throwing him onto one leg as he grasped for something to steady himself. His fingers found a belaying pin, and his body wrapped around the pin rail as the deck heeled over. He looked forward as he waited for the boat to come back to a steadier angle and started toward Jean-Michel and Juan Carlos in the bow.

"She's taking a beating with these winds," Jean-Michel yelled, once Herrera made his way up the main deck.

Herrera looked out toward the horizon. A thunderous black cloud had mushroomed into the sky. White hot flashes and streaks lashed at the cone, the gray hanging below the clouds as a distant window into the carnage unloosed upon the seas and the hapless seamen caught in its convulsions.

He turned back to Jean-Michel, seeing that Juan Carlos had also leaned into the conversation. "The storm's only part of the problem."

Juan Carlos pulled a hand up to cup his ear.

"Looks like we're caught in a strange Loop Current," he yelled, daring to let one hand shield his mouth from the wind while the other clung to a rope.

Jean-Michel shook his head.

"The Florida Current," Herrera continued. "It's reaching far north and heading back south to go around La Florida and into the Atlantic Ocean. The current is supposed to be weak right now, but it's very strong. It's like the gulf is a river not an ocean, and we're trying to sail upriver!"

Jean-Michel looked out toward the western horizon and back toward the shore. "The current is like a river? If we get closer to the coast can we escape the current?"

"I don't know," Herrera said. "I think yes. But the coasts of La Florida are very shallow. The waves are running seven and eight feet. We need ten feet of draft in calm waters. We need at least twenty feet to make sure she doesn't break up on a sand bar, or shoals, or run aground. We can't do any reliable soundings under these conditions."

"We can't sail into that storm," Jean-Michel said pointing to the horizon. "We have to stay on course. We have to make St. Marks."

"Some of the crew are wondering about following the winds to New Orleans."

"What do you say?"

Herrera paused, looking at Jean-Michel. "Our choices are not good for our wounded. But there's no telling how long it will actually take us to navigate up the mouth of the Mississippi River."

Jean-Michel smiled. "You know what Isabella would do. Bring us closer into the coast. Bring more hands on deck to keep watch. Send two men into the tops. We'll stay the course. It's the best chance we have for our wounded."

Herrera nodded and started his way back to Sarhaan.

Jean-Michel looked back out to the storm in the west destroying whatever was in its path. The storm needed to break. His crew needed a break.

The storm broke one hour after the sun should have fallen below the horizon and nearly three hours after *La Marée Rouge* continued its flight in darkness. Jean-Michel ordered all sails taken in except for a storm jib to give Sarhaan enough forward movement to steer two-hundred-fifty tons of wood and metal. Two deckhands immediately started taking soundings.

"I've never seen anything this black," muttered Juan Carlos.

Jean-Michel and Herrera stood in the quiet, disturbed only by the soft thuds of bare feet.

"Thirty-four feet."

"Plenty of water," Juan Carlos said, his tone conveying relief.

"Thirty-four feet."

Jean-Michel and Herrera remained silent at the helm. Juan Carlos took the hint and listened to the gentle breeze as it coaxed the pirate brig further north.

Several minutes passed before Herrera said, "Still too shallow for me to sleep."

"If we keep on this northern course, we have to hit land," Jean-Michel said.

Herrera stepped to the railing and looked into the sea. "We must be following a shelf up the coast."

Juan Carlos yawned. "I am heading below deck. I trust you will not need my supervision."

Jean-Michel and Herrera laughed.

"Keep her steady on a northern course," Jean-Michel said. "Once we get to twenty feet, heave to. Set a watch of one man in the tops, two on the bow, and two at midships. Fully armed."

Daylight broke with brilliant oranges and yellows rising above tall, slender poles of pine trees that were much too close for Herrera's liking. "We should have hove to at thirty feet, not twenty."

Jean-Michel stroked his beard as he looked at the trees. They were slender and straight, without branches, except for the very top, which seemed to balance deep green canopies. The poles faded into the pine forest as their tops shielded the ground from the sun's rays. Smaller, scrubbier trees formed a barrier that hid the roots of the trees. The beaches fell away from the forest along clean lines, and, as the sun rose, the brilliant white color was exposed for full inspection by the water-born nomads. "You did not tell me these beaches were so beautiful, Señor Herrera."

"A well-aimed bow could strike all of us on this deck."

"And the trees," Jean-Michel marveled. "They are so tall and straight. *Magnifique!*"

"I don't see any obvious place where we may be attacked."

"Do you know where we are?"

Herrera shook his head. "The clouds finally broke up around five this morning. I was able to get a reading but could not finish my calculations."

"We'll have Smoothy inspect the guns to make sure the powder is dry and ready to fire. Finish your calculations. We'll prepare to get underway."

"The trees, the sand, it's beautiful."

Jean-Michel smiled and turned to see Gabrielle. "*Bon matin. As-tu bien dormi?*"

Gabrielle smiled. "*Oui,* I slept very well. *Merci.*" She turned to look into Jean-Michel's eyes. "Best of all, Isabella's fever broke one hour ago."

Jean-Michel let a smile crack his storm-weathered faced. He rested his elbows on the railing and let his face fall into his palms. Gabrielle put her hand on this back, letting it slip over his shoulder as she brought her head up against his. They watched the beach in silence as the sun climbed into the sky above the trees.

"La Florida is still warm," Jean-Michel said.

"Yes. After the past few days, the sun and the warmth it brings are very, very welcome."

Jean-Michel smiled. "A clear sky gives the day a bright start." He turned to Gabrielle. "You are a fighter."

Gabrielle's eyebrows creased as she turned to look at the pirate quartermaster. "Thank you?"

"I meant that as a compliment," he chuckled. "I have sailed with Isabella for five years."

"She is a fighter. And it looks like you will sail with her again, hopefully for many more years."

"You no longer have a home. Have you thought of sailing with us?"

Gabrielle laughed. "Me? A pirate?"

"*C'est vrai*. Women are bad luck on pirate ships. Many articles forbid women."

"That makes this a truly odd pirate ship."

Jean-Michel's nod became exaggerated. "That is one way to describe *La Marée Rouge*."

"A pirate ship commanded by a woman."

"Isabella earned her command. You earned a place on this ship. You are a fierce warrior."

"We have both seen what Isabella is capable of accomplishing! She is a worthy leader."

Jean-Michel nodded. "I have seen her face down rogue pirates. I have seen her lead men into battle to retake what was rightly hers. I have seen her reject corruption that destroys the soul."

"You talk about her like she is a God."

Jean-Michel turned to square his body toward Gabrielle, his elbow resting on the rail as his thumb rubbed his jaw. "She is not a God. She is human. But an extraordinary woman with a life force that I can't describe."

"She seems capable of great generosity."

"Generosity?" He turned his back to gunwale, pausing for a moment to think about Gabrielle's words. "I think I would call it grace. I have never seen her take a life for pleasure or practical purposes.

"For most pirates, killing is a tactic. We don't want to spend time negotiating. We threaten our prey with death. If they resist, we kill them. Our reputation spreads. When we raise our flag, the merchants, if they are wise, give in. We have to follow through on our threats to make sure they believe us. A tactic. Isabella has never used a person's life for bargaining. She honors their life, gives them dignity even in death."

Gabrielle looked at Jean-Michel and crossed her arms. "But she has killed people." She remembered Doc stripping the blood-soaked cloth from Isabella's back just a few days ago, and how she almost fell to her knees. The raised and hardened strips of flesh that scarred her back turned her stomach. "So many lashes," she said in a quiet voice. "She should be angry and hurt. I would have snapped. I fight out of anger and indignation. Isabella is different. When I lashed out at Muñoz and his ambush, she was steady and focused."

Jean-Michel edged closer to Gabrielle. "Isabella has only killed when she has had to. To save herself, or someone else."

Gabrielle's shoulder sagged as her chin dropped. "So many people have betrayed her. They have put targets on her back because she was a slave. Then because she was a pirate."

"Becoming a pirate was her choice. Loving Jacob was her choice. Loving Juan Carlos is her choice."

Gabrielle allowed a small smile as she turned her eyes back to Jean-Michel. "She follows her heart."

"Her heart tells her to lead. And I follow her."

Gabrielle's head lifted as she let out a resounding laugh. She brought her hands to her cheeks and buried her eyes in her sleeves as she laughed again. She turned to Jean-Michel and let her hands fall on his chest. "You love her!"

A sheepish smile crossed Jean-Michel faces. "I think I told you that."

Gabrielle's eyes sparkled as she looked into his eyes. "Yes, you did, but I now know how deeply you love her. But you don't love her as a lover!"

"*Mon Dieu! Bien sûr que non!*" Jean-Michel's expression turned to mild alarm. "I love her like my daughter... or my sister... or... I don't know. But not as a lover!"

"*Pardon moi,* Jean-Michel," Gabrielle said, her face light with the joy of revelation. She let her hands slide to his shoulders. "Binta. With God. She is not your lover. She is not God. But she has a peace, a resolve, a center that is good. You love her as I have learned to love her, for her spirit, her guidance, her drive to see the dignity in each of us, no matter what our past."

Jean-Michel smiled, and he found himself slipping into Gabrielle's arms. He lifted a hand to her face, letting it touch her cheek, and she smiled. He felt her press against him. He could not tell if her lips, or his, touched first, but he didn't care.

215

31

Juan Carlos sat on the stool vacated by Louis, watching the steady rise and fall of Isabella's chest. He returned a half-filled ladle of water back to a bucket. He picked up a cloth and wiped water around her lips and chin. He then gathered her hand between his, felt its warmth, and lowered his lips until they touched the back of her hands.

"Captain very strong. She okay."

Juan Carlos shook his head. "Omena, I appreciate your ability to turn up anywhere when the Calusa had us cornered in the swamp. But I think I would like to spend time with her."

"Understand, Captain Santa Ana-san. But Isabella-san good. She live. She strong."

Juan Carlos sighed, straightened his back, and looked over to the slightly built, but deadly, Japanese. "I have never seen anyone like you, Mr. Omena. I am glad you are on my side. But how can you be so sure Isabella will be okay?"

"She has strong heart. She has strong spirit. She fight."

"She is fierce. But sometimes that is not enough. She lost a lot of blood. The infection has taken her body."

The Japanese walked up to the cot where Isabella lay. He sat at the base of the bed, watching her. "Isabella-san breathing strong. She is awake now. She drink. She eat."

"Not enough."

"She fight many Calusa. Many Spanish. Her body tired, weak."

"What if she dies?"

"She will live. But if she die, you go on. Just like I go on. My family gone. My teachers gone. Killed by Shogun. I go on. Family live in me. My father live in me. My mother live in me."

"I never thought I could love a slave. Love an African. But here she lays, and I feel broken without her."

"Captain Santa Ana-san." Omena stopped to gather his words. He lifted his hands to his heart. "You empty because she you. You her. She always… with… you. My family always with me. My teachers… always with me."

"She sacrificed herself for me. I could not have escaped if she had not given us a pathway."

Omena let his head drop in a small bow. "And you sacrifice… for her."

"I would give everything for her."

"Yes…, and she ready to live… for you."

"I am not ready for her to go."

"You ready to be with Isabella-san."

Juan Carlos breathed in and pulled Isabella's hand to her lips. "I am ready to dedicate my life to her."

"You already dedicate life to Isabella-san. She need not die for you commit to her."

"I also almost had her killed. In Port-au-Prince."

Omena pushed himself closer to Juan Carlos so he could look into his eyes. "You dedicate life to Isabella-san in San Juan."

Juan Carlos's eyes shot toward Omena.

Omena nodded once. "El Morro."

Juan Carlos put Isabella's hand back on the cot. "What do you know about El Morro and Isabella?"

Omena nodded again. "I know she tortured. You saved her. You gave her life."

Juan Carlos felt the tears grow behind his eyes, as a lump in his throat seemed to stop his breathing. "How do you know about that?"

Omena lifted his finger to his head. "I listen. Spanish think Japanese do not understand. I listen."

"So, Rodriguez knows."

Omena nodded.

"Rodriguez knew all along."

Omena's steady stare confirmed his conclusion.

"He was not trying to test me. He wanted me to fail. So then he could remove me as he removes pirates and other criminals."

Omena closed his eyes, and let his head drop in a shallow bow.

"Her death—her execution—would have been unjust."

"Yes, Captain Santa Ana-san."

"She was a slave reclaiming her life, her value, her dignity."

"I see, now she part of you." Omena pulled his hand to his chest to cover his heart. "She never leave you."

"*Gracias, señor* Omena."

32

"Got it!"

Herrera's voice was triumphant as two fingers landed on the map at a space in Gulfo de México just forty-five miles from a dot he had labeled San Marcos de Apalache. "It's going to be tricky, but I think I can find it."

"*Bon*," Jean-Michel said. "We can't afford to stay here much longer. Isabella is out of the woods and getting stronger, but she needs food. We all need meat and fruit. We may lose half our hands within a week to sickness and more of the Fever if we don't."

Herrera turned to Sarhaan. "Keep our current course due west. The winds are not favorable, but we should be at the mouth of the San Marcos River by noon."

Herrera slapped Jean-Michel on the back. "Good call, Captain."

"*Trés brien*," Jean-Michel said as he lifted himself upright. "Well done, Señor Herrera."

Jean-Michel turned toward the older bearded sailor standing next to him. "Smoothy get the list of stores we drew up for the Calusa. My guess is the men in Saint Marks will want salt. Maybe gun powder and shot, too. We have a few guns we can trade if necessary. Make sure we keep a month's store of salt; we can trade the remainder."

"Aye, cap'n. Got the list in the quarters. I'll get Fletcher to fill in any holes."

Herrera scanned the trees as *La Marée Rouge* sailed northeast on its third tack in from the Gulf. His perch at the top of the mainmast gave him a clear view of the sand bars extending from the bayou like swirling tentacles from a giant squid. The shortened sail had slowed their speed, and he looked down to where Sarhaan watched him from the tiller. Sarhaan lifted his hand, acknowledging the navigator, and Herrera turned back to his watch.

The soundings began as five tars paced the drop of each weight to mark depth at each minute: Fourteen, sixteen, fifteen, fourteen, thirteen…. Ten was the magic number for keeping *La Marée Rouge* from running aground.

The shoals crisscrossing the mouth of the St. Marks—if they were indeed at the mouth of the San Marcos River—were dizzying. Stay focused on the shades of water, he told himself. Stay away from the green. Keep the vessel heading into the dark blue…, if he could find water that color.

Herrera waved left twice, prompting Sarhaan to give the tiller a hard push to the right and nudge the bow left. Herrera raised his arm straight above his head, and the tiller returned to a spot equidistant between the aft gunwales.

The swamps extended for miles on either side of the winding band of blue. Green reeds and swamp grass were thick enough to entice a drunken sailor into the belief he could walk all the way to San Marcos de Apalache. Clumps of smaller trees with tightly knit branches, clusters of leaves hiding whatever lay close to the trunks, dotted parts of the swamp. Few could challenge the height of the pirate brig's tallest mast. Spanish moss drooped over branches, a heavy cloak to conceal predators of all types. Memories of the Caloosahatchee prompted deckhands to check their muskets and blades.

The wind pushed the pirate ship up the river, zigzagging through the sand bars, crocodiles and alligators too lazy to follow a potential mid-day meal up the river. Once well past the mouth of the river, Herrera descended from the mainmast top.

He walked toward the bow, joining Smoothy and Jean-Michel looking up the river.

"How far up ya reckon the fort is?"

Herrera crossed an arm and lifted the other hand to his chin. "I cannot tell for sure. My chart says two or three miles."

"At least we are through the major shoals," Jean-Michel said.

"Si, the water depth seems to be steady at ten and eleven feet. When I sailed with the Spanish, we had to anchor about a mile south of the fort."

"We will see how far we get. If the water levels fall to ten feet, we will drop anchor and row our way into the Fort." Jean-Michel turned to look toward the stern. "We need to be far enough up river to make sure we are out of sight of the river's mouth. We do not need to announce our presence to anyone that follows."

Jean-Michel ordered *La Marée Rouge* to lower its anchor in the middle of the river, about a half mile from a modest wharf they hope marked the location of a trading post. His eye darted from place to place along the thick, brush-lined banks of the river. The Calusa had reminded him of how deadly the marsh can be, even when populated by clever and crafty groundling creatures such as humans.

The left side of the river widened as the water continued north. Bleached sawgrass and pockets of brush marked a vast marsh extending to the west but occasionally reaching its tentacles into the center of the river. The right side forked into what seemed to the main river based on the color of the water and a subtle shift in current. The mix of tree trunks and leaves laden with Spanish moss encroached on the river, creating a gauntlet for boats passing through. Sawgrass extended upwards from the brush, a telltale sign of unstable ground—swamp.

Jean-Michel looked up into the flying tops, checking the positions of sailors keeping watch on both masts and turned back to the dock. The length of the wharf could handle two cutters, but not a larger merchant ship the size of *La Marée Rouge* even without the armament.

"A trading post? That's a beautiful sight."

The sound of Isabella's voice triggered an immediate pivot. Jean-Michel rushed toward her, as if preparing to catch her as she fell. *"Trés bien! Te sens-tu mieux maintenant?"*

"Oui!" Isabella smiled, extending her hand, but retracting it quickly to seize a part of the rail to steady herself. "I am feeling much better, *mon ami*. Doc has taken good care of me. I have eaten too much of our remaining meat. I am much better on deck."

Jean-Michel nodded, his smile still broad. He glanced at Juan Carlos who confirmed Isabella's story with a rise from his eyebrows. "Where you belong. Looks like I will be handing the ship back over to you, if the crew obliges."

Isabella lifted her hand to Jean-Michel's arm. "Looks like you have done quite well on your own, my friend."

Juan Carlos followed Isabella close enough for his hand to steady her. "Doc says she needs the fresh air. She's strong enough to stay up on deck. The crew can decide soon enough based on the Articles."

Isabella breathed in and closed her eyes. "The air below feels so heavy and stale. I might as well have been in a tomb."

"Any sign of Muñoz?" Juan Carlos asked.

Jean-Michel shook his head. "British are supposed to control this part of La Florida now. I do not think he would chase us up the river even if he saw us."

Isabella stepped over to the railing, a wince gripping her face as her body revolted against the pain from her wounds. "What do we know of this war for independence the Americans are fighting?"

A cackling chuckle announced the arrival of Smoothy. "No one took'm seriously! Now, seven years in it, the Brits still ain't quashed it. My money's on the Americans."

"Merci, monsieur Smoothy," Jean-Michel said, his tone suggesting a rolling of the eyes even if they didn't stray from his chief gunner's gleeful face. "We know your politics. The French and the Spanish

222

support the Americans right now. Muñoz would have no difficulty explaining a raid on a British trading post on the San Marcos River."

Isabella kept her focus on a batch of trees just beyond the dock. "Have you seen any activity on the wharf?"

"Not yet," Jean-Michel said. "We just laid anchor a few minutes ago."

"Still, I think they would be curious."

"*Oui bien sûr*, but I am sure those trees hide a stone wall with cannon. They could open fire anytime they want. Our sails are furled and secure on the yards. They know we aren't going anywhere."

Isabella nodded. "Then let's go pay our new trader friends a visit."

33

Jean-Michel and Gabrielle stepped off the cutter first, pulling the boat in tight against the dock and lashing it securely. Juan Carlos steadied Isabella as she stepped off the railing and onto the dock.

"Isabella, stay in the boat," Jean-Michel said.

Isabella's steel-hard look at Jean-Michel told him the answer. "This is an established trading post. Herrera says it's more than twenty years old. What are they going to do? Shoot a woman?"

Juan Carlos shook his head. "It's no use, Jean-Michel. She is stubborn and pig-headed."

Isabella shot a playful look toward Juan Carlos. "I need to get off this ship! My body is slow and needs to be challenged for me to recover. I am sure Doc would agree."

Jean-Michel laughed. "Doc said you should stay on the ship! But you've never listened to him anyway."

"Sure you don't want me to join you?"

Jean-Michel's face turned serious as he turned to the sailor still sitting in the stern. He pulled a pistol from his sash and checked the hammer, flint, powder pan, and frizzen. Another deck hand was stowing oars and checking the position of several muskets in the bottom of the boat. "Both of you stay here. If this post is not what it seems, we will need to get out quickly. Smoothy and Herrera's got the cannon loaded and ready on *La Marée Rouge*. But, Jack, you will need to start getting us back to the ship with those oars as fast as you can." He looked over toward Isabella, Juan Carlos, and Gabrielle as they were making their way to land. "We will do our best with Isabella."

Jack pursed his lips. "Well at least bring me back some salt pork or beef. I ain't had that in a long time."

Jean-Michel smiled, giving him a small salute as he turned back to the path leading up to what they hoped was a trading post more interested in gold than blood.

The path was well worn, leading into a natural tunnel of foliage just high enough for a good-sized man to walk through. Juan Carlos dodged branches and Spanish moss as he kept a pace ahead of Isabella. Jean-Michel forged forward, unaware of the leafy whiplash he created by bending branches.

"Halt!"

The command brought the entire party to a stop. Juan Carlos tried to peer through the brush but all he could see was a pair of boots attached to two legs and the barrel of a musket pointed right at Jean-Michel.

"Who are yeu?"

"Sounds like we've run into a Scotsman."

"Aye, Mr. Forbes likes to keep business among the kin. State your business. Yeu sound like a Frenchman. We can't be too careful these days, with a war and revolution goin' on."

"*Oui,* I am Jean-Michel. I am the quartermaster of *La Marée Rouge,* the brig you see anchored at the fork of these two rivers."

"Aye, Mr. Frenchman, I can see that. But yeu've got some lassies thar w'yeu."

"Yes, sir, we do, but since one of these women is the captain of the brig, and the other knows how to handle a gun and a blade, you might want to think before you pull that trigger."

"My, yeu come prepared, don't ya?" The man laughed. "Looks like that thar brig has an awful lot of cannon for a merchantman. Since I don't see the flag of King George, I can only assume yeu are with the French, or the Spanish, both of whom are at war with my homeland."

Isabella grabbed Gabrielle's arm and pulled past her, extended another hand to grab Jean-Michel's arm, and pulled herself to the front. "Sir, we are none of those. We are on our way to New Orleans and are in desperate need of provisions."

The man let his musket barrel drop a few inches as Isabella spoke. He was tall, too tall to walk easily through the bulwarks of a brig. A full beard hid most of his face, but his features resembled those of a man used to the frontier and long months, perhaps years, on the trap lines. His breeches and coat showed he had practical knowledge of how to use deer and beaver skins and pelts. A wide brimmed hat, also crafted from animal skins, shaded his face even though the trees were already doing their job.

"My name is Isabella. This is Jean-Michel, my quarter master. This is Gabrielle, and the Spaniard is Juan Carlos. We would be appreciative of your help. We have provisions to trade."

The man lowered his musket and walked up to Isabella. "Pretty thing, yeu are. African no doubt. But you're a bit lighter in skin." The man turned his eyebrow up. "Creole?"

Isabella steadied her gaze into the trapper's eyes. "I am Isabella. *La Marée Rouge* is my ship. We are in need of provisions, and we have means of payment."

The trapper closed an eye, as if trying to focus on Isabella's face. "I think ye be pirate."

A rustling of feet preceded Juan Carlos's body next to Isabella's. "*Señor*, we are not asking for anything but trade."

"Not sure about pirates." The Scotsman lifted his chin as he peered over Isabella's shoulder. "Another African. Looks to be pure blood by my reckon'n."

"*Gens de couleur*." Gabrielle's response was firm and sure.

The trapper smiled and nodded. "Saint Domingue."

Isabella took a half step toward the trader, just enough to catch his eye and begin to bring the musket barrel up again. "And your name, Sir?"

The trapper cocked his head and took account of the party. He looked at Isabella directly. "Yeu know I can get a pretty penny by capturing a pirate." He glanced over to Gabrielle. "And an escaped slave."

"I am sure you know," Gabrielle said, her voice cold, "*gens de couleur* are not slaves. We are free blacks in Saint Domingue."

The trapper rocked his head back and forth. "Just sold an Indian from the southern swamps up in Charles Town for seventy-five pounds."

He looked at Gabrielle. "Yeu be strong and fit. I bet my Creek Indian partners could fetch more than one hundred pounds for yeu." The Scotsman looked down at Gabrielle's feet, inspecting her deck boots and then moving up, his eye raking every inch of her body. "That's goin' rate, yeu know."

Isabella shifted her weight, moving enough to break the Scotsman's line of site.

He shifted his eyes to Isabella. "But a pirate, one with a handsome ship like the one anchored in the San Marcos, I bet yeu have more than a hundred pounds on yur young lassie head. I can get one-hundred-fifty pounds for a strong male about yur age. A bet yeu've got a price of two-hundred-fifty pounds on yours."

Isabella's breathing deepened as her fingers tapped the hilt of her sword.

"Monsieur Trader." Jean-Michel's voice was steady and purposeful. "You have one shot in that musket. If we are pirates, as you conclude, you know that shooting one of us will not save you or anyone in this post. If you shoot my captain, you will not be so lucky to die now."

The trapper eyed Jean-Michel, one hand on the barrel and the other on the trigger. "A pirate crew loyal to their captain?" A smile broke across his face as a laugh roared through the trees and down the pathway. He let his hand fall from the trigger and cradled the musket in the crook of his arm. "Yeu can call me Alastair! I am Mr. Thomas Forbes' representative in this godforsaken part of the swamp. Mr. Forbes, Mr. William Panton and Mr. John Leslie control the fur trade all along the coast and in La Florida."

The Scotsman swung around and started to walk up the pathway.

"What do you call this post?" Juan Carlos said.

"San Marcos de Apalache is what the dagos call it. I call it *paraíso para los ángeles alados de la muerte*."

Gabrielle tapped Juan Carlos on the shoulder.

Juan Carlos turned to look at her, his expression confused and troubled. "Paradise for the winged angels of death. Mosquitos."

"If yeu plan to stay, I'd trade out that wool for leathers. We've got some nice beaver and deer. If yeu've got the gold or silver, bear will keep the winged killers out."

Jean-Michel slowed as he followed Alastair through the wooden gates that opened into the fort's interior. Indians, some dressed in patterned breechcloths and others in leather leggings and matchcoat draped across their torso, searched stacks of tanned skins and furs. Some seemed to be searching through various iron skillets, fire pokers, pots, and ceramic bowls. As the pirates walked in the center of what looked like a courtyard, stockpiles of tools appeared in selected areas.

The quarter master looked up to find more Indians standing on ramparts on top of the stone walls, their muskets resting in their arms as they watched the Indians below.

"You appear to have an army posted in San Marcos."

"We are thirty miles from the nearest village. The dagos had a mission up the road, but the British and their Red Stick allies ran them out decades ago."

"Red Stick?"

Alastair propped his musket up against a stone pile. "Creek Indians allied with the British." He turned and pointed to a group of three other Indians, including a woman clad in a long leather dress. "Those Indians are Muskogean. Farmers. Work the fields up in a village called Tallahassee, just a few miles from the abandoned mission."

Gabrielle picked up a hide and ran her hands across the smooth leather. "The tanners are skilled."

Alastair nodded. "Indians are eager to trade for powder and shot. I get to pick the best."

Isabella found a small barrel and sat down, bringing her hand up to wipe her brow.

"Yeu look like you could use a drink, Lassie."

Isabella shot a stern look toward Alastair.

Alastair leaned up against the wall of what looked like a block house. He pulled out a small knife and begin to clean part of the metal around the frizzen of his musket. "I mean, captain."

Jean-Michel found a hatchet and picked it up to inspect the blade. "How can you tell the difference between the ones that are on your side and the ones that would like to see you dead?"

Alastair chuckled. "I hire Indians I trust to watch the wagons and fort. The British were kind enough to build the stone walls, then give it to the Spanish, who abandoned it to the Indians about twelve years ago."

Isabella slid a scowl over to the Scotsman. "And how did you acquire such a fine piece of property from the Indians?"

"I'm a Scotsman. I'll trade with anyone. I don't care if they're white, brown, or black. I treat them all the same."

"Not all," Gabrielle said. "You would have easily sold me into slavery even though you knew I was free."

Alastair shook his head. "I didn't know you were free. Still don't. You said you were free, but just about any slave would say that if he didn't have papers." The trader pulled out a pipe and tamped tobacco into the bowl. "Slavery is legal, yeu know."

Alastair struck a match and puffed the pipe to life, a spark sending a plume of smoke swirling around his head.

Gabrielle looked up at the Indians walking the ramparts above them. "You would have taken me and sold me."

Alastair rocked his head as if he were engaged in an invisible debate inside. "Hard to say. I saw yur ship. You came ashore armed. Yur pirates, for sure. I want yur gold more than yur body for someone else's work."

Gabrielle whirled to look at the Scottish trader. "You have no right to my body or my gold."

Alastair chuckled. "Depends on what country yur in."

Juan Carlos picked up a mallet. "No, *señor*, it doesn't. You do not have a right to Gabrielle's body, or anyone else's for that matter. The law may give you a legal entitlement, but that is a corruption of a higher law."

Alastair puffed on his pipe, sending more smoke twirling into the late afternoon sky. "That thar piece is great for tanning hides."

"Mallets have many uses, *señor.*"

"Aye, they do. Just remember if yeu destroy anything, yeu pay for it."

Juan Carlos looked at Alastair and then toward Isabella. "We should conduct our business and leave."

"Ah, yeu won't be dining with me, then?"

Isabella had walked the perimeter of the outdoor market, returning to a spot in front of Alastair. "These Indians seem to be quite concerned. They are buying a lot from a trader near the water."

"Yeu be sharp one, Captain Isabella. Most of them Indians are Red Sticks. Events in the American colonies don't appear to be going their way."

Isabella looked back at the men and women collecting leather goods, salted beef, and tools for working the land. "They are farmers but buying as if they are nomads."

Alastair nodded. "Creek Indians came in to Tallahassee yesterday and told them some very unfortunate news. The British were defeated at the mouth of the York River in Virginia. Captured a big British general, a man named Cornwallis, if I recall. Looks like the colonies will be independent after all."

Isabella caught her breath, locking eyes with Jean-Michel.

"Looks like the Red Sticks can't count on the British protecting them anymore," Alastair continued.

Gabrielle leveled a cold stare at the Scotsman. "You don't seem too worried."

"Ahh, *mademoiselle* Gabrielle, I am a trader. I have no loyalties to country or King."

"You are loyal to your patrons."

"Aye, I am. Mr. Forbes and I have a bond, in trade."

"And to the Creeks?"

Alastair stood and pointed to the Indians watching over the men and women looking for goods for their journeys. "I am loyal to the men... and women... that stay by my side and help me in my trade."

Juan Carlos looked over to Alastair. "So you do have loyalties."

Alastair nodded. "I am realistic about my loyalties. I know that the loyalties of these men and women last only as long as the trade is good. Once they have journeyed beyond the bend, their loyalties lay elsewhere. The men guarding these goods? They are loyal to me… and Mr. Forbes… as long as they are paid what they believe they deserve. No one has a right to these goods, *señor*, unless they have paid for them in an honest trade."

"But you would sell me into slavery," Gabrielle repeated.

"I am a practical man," Alastair conceded.

Isabella turned on the heel of her boot. "We have a list of our needs, Alastair. We have gold, and a good bit of silver. Most of our bulk is in salt."

The word "salt" piqued the Scotsman's ears. "Salt? I have a real need for salt. We have to bring salt in by merchant ship since we have no salt mines nearby. Could use some powder as well."

Isabella nodded, and then turned to Jean-Michel as if asking if she missed anything.

"Stores," Jean-Michel said. "We have a fast vessel, but she's been slowed by the barnacles. We have a pirate hunter on our tail."

The mention of a pirate hunter caused Alastair to pause. He looked as Isabella, and then inventoried the weapons on the pirate shore party. "How far back is yur pirate hunter?"

"No easy way to know," Jean-Michel said.

"We last engaged him off the west coast of Cuba," Isabella said. "We are sure he followed us into Golfo de Mexico, up the west coast of La Florida."

Jean-Michel looked over to Isabella. "But we haven't seen him since."

"Is that where yur captain's injuries came from?"

"These wounds are from Indians."

Alastair brought a hand up to pinch the bottom of his beard. "Not in North Florida. I would have heard of it."

Juan Carlos rose from a stool he had found to rest while he inspected several other tools next to the mallet. "You must have quite the reconnaissance."

"Aye, I take care of the Indians around here, and they know I can help them with the white men. Word can reach me almost as fast by land as by sea. I haven't heard of Indians fighting pirates, let alone women."

"We were further south. The Caloosahatchee River."

Alastair shook his head. "Impossible!"

Isabella touched the spot where her shirt covered her wound. "My body challenges you, Scotsman."

Juan Carlos stepped closer. "Isabella was under a fever for several days."

"What kind of fever," Alastair asked.

"A fever…, how many kinds are there?"

The Scotsman seemed to roll something in his mouth and gums. "What did the wound look like."

Juan Carlos looked at the trader with disbelief. "Why does that matter?"

Alastair smiled. He pointed the end of his pipe at Isabella and drew a straight line to Juan Carlos. "I see." He looked at Juan Carlos. "Was the pain around the entry wound, or did it extend like fingers to other parts of her body?"

"The fever started several hours after we had been on ship and she was attended by our ship's surgeon."

"What were her symptoms?"

"Like anyone with a fever from an infection," Jean-Michel said, his frustrated tone evident. "She's kicked the infection. She's healthy."

Juan Carlos hesitated. "The skin changed colors around the wound entry. Doc said some of her tissue around the wound had died. Her breathing was difficult. At times she tried to speak but we could not understand her. Doc said her tongue swelled, and he worried she would not be able to swallow food or water."

Each symptom seemed to send Alastair deeper into thought.

"You were below Charlotte Harbor?"

"Si, we were looking for a trading post, but it was gone."

"Isabella was wounded on shore?"

Juan Carlos nodded.

Now all four pirates stood listening to Alastair.

"Did you fight Indians?"

Isabella nodded.

Alastair shook his head. "I never would have believed if I didn't see yeu with me own eyes." He looked at Isabella, then Jean-Michel. "The Calusa were supposed to be out of La Florida twenty years ago. Taken to Cuba by the Spanish as slaves."

Isabella touched her side. "I can attest to the fact they are still very much in the swamps of South Florida."

"The Creeks sent raiding parties into those swamps for decades, taking the men and women and bringing them north to sell them as slaves. We still send parties south to hunt panther and bear. I sent a hunting party of four—two Creeks and two white men—down about eight weeks ago. They didn't come back."

Isabella remembered the heads outside of the *maśuhoma*. "I think they were captured by the Calusa tribe we found."

Alastair nodded and looked back at Isabella. "The Calusa were known for dippin' their arrows in the venom of coral snakes. Nasty beast, those snakes. Yeu will know a rattlesnake bit ya the minute they sink their fangs in yeu—ungodly pain, fever, bloating of your limbs. Yeu can see the poison work up through yur body. Coral snakes? Venom doesn't hit yeu for hours later. Nasty business the poison is. It's a miracle yur alive."

Gabrielle smiled at Isabella. "Binta."

Alastair sent Gabrielle a quizzical look.

"God has not chosen for her to leave this world."

"God, or something else. Yur lucky to be alive. Yur a strong person, that's for shur."

Alastair stood up and looked at Jean-Michel. "Let's get that list together. We've got plenty of naval stores. Pine trees all along the north coast are yellow pine—best trees we've found for making the tar, pitch, and turpentine. We ship this out all the time, can hardly keep it in stock."

Isabella walked over to a cluster of barrels under one of the ramparts. "This is a profitable business?"

"I suppose," Alastair said as he began assembling the items Jean-Michel had identified. "Pine trees are everywhere. Land is plentiful. And

233

cheap. Plantations are everywhere. Still can't keep tar, pitch or turpentine, none of the naval stores, in stock."

Isabella nodded. She looked up at Juan Carlos. "I think I know the solution to our problem, *mi amor*."

34

The treacherous shoals of La Florida coast lay before the pirates, as their navigator drew a line from the San Marcos River west, below a bump in the shoreline extending into the gulf. Louis and Peter leaned over the table, their toes just touching the tops of two tackle blocks they had towed from the bow of *La Marée Rouge*.

Herrera straightened his back. "Getting to Nueva Orleans is not that difficult if we could sail into her harbor. About four-hundred miles by my reckoning. Three days with good winds, six if we're cursed."

Juan Carlos pointed to two marked spots about halfway down the coast. "What about these ports?"

"Dauphin Island," Herrera said, resting his index finger on a barrier island appearing to block off a large body of water marked Mobile Bay. "Legend has it Fort Louis de la Mobile was located there. Floods forced them to move further north to these narrows at the head of the bay. Nothing but swamp north of there."

He moved his finger to the east. "This is the port we want to stay clear of. Pensacola. Spanish retook the port and Mobile. Once we're at sea, we won't be able to make a friendly port."

"We can make it," Jean-Michel said, although his voice lacked the confidence he projected when making important decisions. "We have to sail deep into The Gulf of Mexico, and the chances of us running into a Spanish warship is very small."

Herrera shook his head. He leaned over the map and pulled another chart from below, spreading it out on the table. "The problem is we will not be able to sail right into the harbor of Nueva Orleans." He pointed to a marking for a fort along a river marked "Mississippi" a long distance north of a river delta that emptied into the gulf. The fort looked like the head on top of the long thin body of a squid, with tributaries spreading out at the base like tentacles. "The port is eighty miles north of the mouth of the Mississippi River. I think it is more than one-hundred miles since the river twists and turns so much."

Gabrielle leaned against a chair. "Why would they put the city so far up the river?"

Herrera smiled. "Where would you put it? There is no real land from the city to the Gulfo de Mexico. It's all swamp. It floods."

Pierre's lips twisted. "Just build canals, like the Calusa."

Herrera laughed. "Very good idea. Perhaps, one day, they will be smart enough to do that."

Louis sighed. "I am ready to get off this boat."

Gabrielle reached over and wrapped an arm around his shoulders. "*Oui mon jeune garçon.* You are not the only one."

Jean-Michel looked at Herrera. "I have not sailed these waters before. Neaveau Orleans is still a legend for me. How long will it take us to sail up the river? One hundred miles. Another day?"

Herrera laughed again. "Oh, we should be so lucky if the stars are aligned, God has blessed us, and our gold buys us a happy life! I have heard sailors say the journey can take thirty days, depending on winds, tides, and current."

"We'll starve before then!" Louis's high-pitched whine was shrill enough to capture the mood of an entire sea and battle-weary crew.

Isabella had started a silent pace while the others talked. "We have food and water, thanks to Alastair and the White Creeks." Her response seemed to take Louis's complaint as a serious criticism of their plans.

Herrera leaned over the chart again. "There is another possibility. Lake Pontchartrain. This body of water is north of the Gulfo de Mexico. Entering the lake is very dangerous, and the water is never more than twelve or fourteen feet deep. Rivers feed the lake, and the tides are very low. We should be able to sail across the lake if the water levels are normal and we are careful."

Jean-Michel nodded. "*Certainement,* our crew is very experienced with depth soundings!"

Isabella turned to face Herrera. "Do we have to worry about the Spanish?"

Herrera paused, looking at the dot marked Nueva Orleans on the paper. "Not like Pensacola or Mobile. Spain has tried to colonize this place for hundreds of years. It's a colonial backwater. Most of the citizens are French, and Havana sees little value in trying to control the city. A few more pirates will not be noticed."

Isabella dipped her head, raising her hand to her lips. She walked into her cabin, and sat down on her cot, resting her head in both hands as the others watched in silence.

"Isabella, what's wrong?"

Juan Carlos sank into the mattress, its bounce restored by new layers of Spanish moss and canvas. He raised his hand to touch her shoulder. "I thought Neuva Orleans was our destination."

Isabella lifted her head so that her fingers covered her mouth as she stared at the wall in her cabin. The jagged mirror had been replaced over the washbasin, a small tank of water nearby. She stood, and walked over to the basin, dipping her hands in the water and lifting it to her face. Was the woman in the mirror, lines curving under her eyes, really her? Her red bandana held her hair in place although waves from her curls struggled against its restraint.

She breathed in. "Binta," she said is a low voice.

Juan Carlos's eyes and face appeared in the mirror behind her. "With God," he said. He placed his arms around her, and let his lips fall to the bend of her neck. "You have journeyed a long way."

Isabella turned her head so her cheek rested on his hand. "As have you *mi amor.*"

"*¿En qué piensas?*"

"What am I thinking about? My journey. Your journey. Pierre's journey. My crew. *La Marée Rouge.* Everything and all things."

"That is a lot to think about all at once."

237

She let her hands fall to the rim of the basin and looked into the water. Juan Carlos let his hands run up her back, over the raised skin that reminded her of the years she and her family lived under the cat-o-nine tails of the overseer in Santo Domingo. "Five and half years on this ship as a pirate."

Juan Carlos let his hand fall on hers, slipping his fingers through hers. "And you have done well."

She turned her eyes to look into his in the mirror. "Have I? Have we? Jean-Michel was already a pirate. What have I done to end the wretched practice of enslaving men and women for the enrichment of the landed class?"

"You and Jean-Michel have done more than any other person, more than an army. Rodriguez has dedicated hundreds of men and tons of resources to capture you. You have sunk more ships than he has in his current fleet to keep the West Indies safe! No one else can claim so much."

"How many slaves have I freed? How many plantations have I vanquished?"

Juan Carlos turned Isabella around so he could look into her eyes, bringing his hands up to cradle her cheeks. "You have done more than almost anyone I can think of. This pirate ship alone keeps scores of men out of bondage. It allows them to chart their own legacy. You have achieved what the arrogant D'Poussant could not—kept men and women alive as free persons, giving them the gift of hope as a substitute for the darkness of slavery."

"They deserve more."

Juan Carlos leaned in and let his lips touch hers with a gentleness that proved the intimacy of the moment. "We all deserve more."

Isabella looked at Juan Carlos, her lover, a man so far removed from the royal court of King Charles III she barely remembered what he looked like that first time she interrogated him as a prisoner. She lifted her arms and let them snake around his neck as she let her head rest on his shoulder. "You were so arrogant that first time we met."

Juan Carlos smiled and kissed the top her head. "You were not very humble, either."

"I was empowered by my indignity."

"And I was empowered by my self-righteousness. But I knew you were different. You were nothing I was trained to expect. Your heart, your soul…, I loved watching you."

Isabella let the palm of her hand run up his chest, to his neck and to his check. She pulled away, looked into his eyes, and raised her lips to his.

Their kiss carried them as one into another realm, far away from the cannon and powder and shot, and into the soft, steady breeze of the ocean as the boat rolled with the waves under a brilliant afternoon sun. Their bodies pressed together, each feeling the curve of the other, the press of their fingers, and the taste of their will and desire for each other.

"I want more," Isabella said. "I want to be with you, forever. I am not yet finished…. The Prophecy still holds my heart and soul, but I can no longer commit to the violence of this life. I saw what it could do in Port-au-Prince—so much more suffering, and death. Louis's mother, and I almost lost you."

"I have made my choice, and I am with you."

Isabella dipped her head back to his shoulder. "And now we have children to consider!"

Juan Carlos laughed. "*Si, mi amor*. We have children, and families to consider. But I believe Jean-Michel and Gabrielle have taken quite well to our brave young man from Port-au-Prince. And Marguerite is a strong, fine mother to Pierre and Petit Jean.'

"Jean-Michel is no longer a pirate, even though he does not know it. Gabrielle never will be a pirate, although she is a fighter. Marguerite was a victim of accident."

"And Pierre and Petit Jean?"

Isabella chuckled. "They have very strong imaginations, and they watch everything. If we are not careful, the brothers Lafitte might become pirates!"

"If they choose to go to sea, let's hope they are smart enough to be merchantmen or privateers."

Isabella breathed in, pulling Juan Carlos close. "I am ready to leave this life, but I still feel the pull of the prophecy. I still feel a call to attack the brutal indignity of slavery."

"Binta," Juan Carlos said, resting his lips on Isabella's forehead. "Accept the call. I will be with you."

She sighed. "Naval stores."

"What?"

"Naval stores. Tar. Resin. Turpentine."

Juan Carlos pulled away from Isabella and looked into her eyes. "Naval stores?"

"The entire coast is lined with long-needle pine trees. The forests go deep onto land."

"Yes, but—"

Isabella lifted her finger to his lips and looked into his eyes. "The American war for independence is over. You heard Alastair. The colonies are going to be trading and growing in peace for the first time in eight years. Trade will explode. Ships will be coming into these ports."

"Si, but I don't see how... I don't...."

Isabella smiled, letting her hand fall back to his chest. "Money. All these ships need naval stores to stay afloat. These forests are a gold mine. We can buy land and start producing naval stores. Jean-Michel and Gabrielle can provide the warehouses and put our tar and resin on the market. They will become rich."

"So, you want to become rich?"

"Si, very rich."

Juan Carlos looked at Isabella and pulled his head back, a slight shake showing his confusion. "You want to start a pine-tree plantation to harvest the sap to make naval stores and sell it to the traders and merchantmen?"

"Si, and we will be very rich."

Juan Carlos sighed.

Isabella smiled. "And we will use the money to buy slaves."

Juan Carlos's eyes widened, as if he was seeing evil for the first time.

She lifted a finger back up to his lips before he could object. "We will give our slaves a choice. Before they can make that choice, they have to be free. We will free them. We will give them papers to prove their freedom if they choose to leave us. Or they can choose to stay as free men and women and work for us. We will pay them a fair wage, and, if they work hard and prove their worth, we will help them start their own businesses in Nueva Orleans."

Juan Carlos laughed and pulled Isabella into a close, tight hug. "You will give them the means to secure their freedom for their lifetime, and their legacies! Isabella, your mother was right. The prophecy was right. You are With God."

Isabella and Juan Carlos brought their lips and bodies together in an embrace so close, so tight, they moved and felt as they were finally, truly one.

Glossary of Calusa words used in *Calusa Spirits*

cacique – chief
ka – the, this
ño – war
ñoka – warrior
ri – house
ra – fierce
kuči – destroy
kuhpe – assemble
lete – run
maśu – build
maśuhoma – house of prayer
mayai – on the other side
ño – stop, rest, lie down
śahka – tree
śeha – to examine
śera – watch over/guard
śihpi – harpoon
tepe – join
wíši – water

Vocabulary interpreted by the author from Julian Granberry, *The Calusa: Linguistic and Cultural Origins and Relationships* (Tuscaloosa, AL: University of Alabama Press, 2011)

Acknowledgements

Calusa Spirits, as the third book in a trilogy, represents a significant step in the evolution of the Pirate of Panther Bay series (although certainly note the end). Isabella, Jean-Michel, and Juan Carlos have endured torture, betrayal, high-pitched battles on land and sea, voodoo, and brutal revolutions. But nothing has prepared them for what they have to face in the wilds of Florida in the year closing out the American Revolutionary War. Nor did past exploits prepare their creator! Historical fiction is not easy to write, and Volume III wouldn't have been possible without a boatload of people supporting me, assisting me, and reading the series.

The quality of the story owes a lot to the candid and sometimes hard (but necessary) to hear feedback from beta readers. First and foremost, the comments, observations, insights, and criticisms I've received from my intrepid critique group continues to be incredible and of very high quality. Pat Murphy, Terri Lewis, Liz Jameson, Lisa Blackwell, and Jane Minard refused to let even the smallest error or missed opportunity go by unnoticed. The care and attention to the story and characters given by Colette Willins as she fit precious time between family and professional duties also played a key part in the preparation of the manuscript. Colette has read and commented on every one of the books in the series (and more), and her commitment to my writing, fiction and nonfiction, has been unwavering.

Information about Florida during this particular period of its history (1780s) is surprisingly scarce and inaccessible. Very little of a historical record exists prior to the U.S. acquisition of the territory in the early 1800s. Michael Kinnett, curator for the Orman House State Park Museum in Apalachicola, Florida, has been an incredible resource for deep knowledge of early Florida history, North Florida, and understanding how the state's economy and culture evolved. His observations and knowledge are evident in the places and events that unfold in these pages as Isabella and her crew sail north along the Florida coast. I also benefited greatly in my effort to understand the natural environment during this time from the writings and insights provided by outdoor expert Doug Alderson, particularly the river systems, and how they may (or may not) have evolved over the years. Rick Rhodes' *Cruising Guide to Florida's Big Bend: Apalachicola, Chattahoochee,*

Flint, and Suwannee Rivers provided a visual and narrative tour through some of the rivers navigated by the pirates.

A hopeful side benefit of *Calusa Spirits* will be to revive interest in the Calusa Native American culture and its legacy in Florida, including the language. A number of resources are available to readers and those interested in going into more depth. I relied heavily on Darcie A. MacMahon and William Marquardt's *The Calusa and Their Legacy: South Florida People and Their Environments* as well as *Missions to the Calusa* edited and translated by John H. Hann. Much of the language and its structure was reconstructed with the aid of Julian Granberry's *The Calusa: Linguistic and Cultural Origins and Relationships*, although I remain fully responsible for any errors in syntax, grammar, or interpretation. Randolph J. Widmer's *The Evolution of the Calusa: A Nonagricultural Chiefdom on the Southwest Florida Coast* is also a rich source of information and insight, although this text is much more academic.

"Book learning" however, can only get you so far. The possible world of the Calusa really came alive to me after a visit to the Florida Bureau of Archaeological Research in Tallahassee. This is an incredible resource for historians and authors. Jeremy Vause, Collections Technician for the Bureau, was incredibly helpful and gracious with his time, providing me with a tour of Calusa Indian (and many other maritime) artifacts stored in their facility. The pictures were indeed worth several thousand words! Jeremy's enthusiasm for his work also allowed me to tap into the best information available to help understand the culture, their use of tools, and their way of life. Many of my observations looking at these ancient tools and implements made it into the narrative.

The future pirate Jean Laffite and his family figure prominently in *Calusa Spirits* as well as the next installment in Isabella, Jean-Michel, and Juan Carlos's story. Unfortunately, little is known about the early years of Jean Laffite, his older step-brother Pierre, or their mother Marguerite. I have taken creative license to build some mythology around their journey to America! The family histories that exist are contradictory and the available data is still more a puzzle than a coherent tapestry. Nevertheless, I found nuggets to inspire elements of the story embedded in William C. Davis's *The Pirates Laffite: The Treacherous World of the Corsairs of the Gulf* and, although directly contradictory in several areas, in Jack Ramsay, Jr.'s *Jean Laffite, Prince of Pirates*. I also consulted *The Journal of Jean Laffite*, but the origin of this book's content is now suspect. Fortunately, I am writing historical fiction!

Of course, the ongoing support for The Pirate of Panther Bay series by Terri Gerrell, owner of Southern Yellow Pine Publishing, can't be over emphasized. Her commitment to my writing and the series is very much appreciated. I also would be remiss in not mentioning Claire and Evan Staley, my ongoing inspirations for continuing the Panther Bay saga. And finally, and by no means least, thank you to my readers. They are the ones that keep the series and story alive!

SR Staley
Tallahassee, Florida
July 4, 2018

About the Author

SR Staley's (www.srstaley.com) fiction and nonfiction books have won more than 10 literary awards in categories as wide ranging as Literary Fiction, Young Adult Fiction, Historical Fiction, New Adult Fiction, Political/Current Events, and Information/Educational. *Calusa Spirits* is the third book in a planned six-book series from Southern Yellow Pine Publishing. Sam speaks regularly on the craft of writing and has been on the faculty of the Florida Writers Conference sponsored by the Florida Writers Association. He is also active in the Florida Authors and Publishers Association and the Tallahassee Writers Association.

In addition to his books, Sam's articles have appeared in a wide range of publications, including the *New York Times*, the *Washington Post*, the *Los Angeles Times*, the *Chicago Tribune*, the *Miami Herald*, and others. Sam has traveled extensively for work and pleasure, visiting China more than 30 times, more than 100 U.S. cities, and four continents. A self-defense coach, he holds a black belt in the To-Shin Do, a revisioned approach to ninjutsu pioneered by Stephen K. Hayes to focus on contemporary threats and concerns.

Sam is currently on the full-time faculty of the College of Social Sciences and Public Policy at Florida State University where he teaches social entrepreneurship, research methods, and urban planning. He is also a movie reviewer and film critic for the Independent Institute in Oakland, California. Follow Sam at:

(www.srstaley.com)
blog (http://blog.srstaley.com)
Facebook (https://www.facebook.com/srstaleyfiction)
Twitter (@SamRStaley)
Instagram (samuelrstaley)